Reaching into the darkness, he produced the can, clanking it softly against the door as he lifted it out with the hammer and screwdriver, then he moved quietly round the vehicle until he found the petrol tank.

Placing the point of the screwdriver against the tank, he gave the handle a sharp whack with the hammer. The chattering of the Italians, the rattling of the palm fronds and the moving bundles of brushwood drowned the sound. Unscrewing the petrol cap, Rafferty threw it away and they stood for a while in the dark, listening to the petrol running into the can from the hole they'd made.

'That ought to surprise them when they come to drive it away,' Dampier murmured delightedly as Rafferty screwed the cap on the full can. 'Think we could hole another, Mr Rafferty? So they can't chase us.'

Also in Arrow by John Harris

Cotton's War
The Fox from His Lair
A Funny Place to Hold a War
Live Free or Die!
North Strike
Ride Out the Storm
The Sea Shall Not Have Them
Swordpoint
Take or Destroy!

UP
FOR GRABS

John Harris

ARROW BOOKS

Arrow Books Limited
62 – 65 Chandos Place, London WC2N 4NW

An imprint of Century Hutchinson Ltd

London Melbourne Sydney Auckland
Johannesburg and agencies throughout
the world

First published by Hutchinson 1985
Arrow edition 1986

Printed and bound in Great Britain
by Anchor Brendon Ltd, Tiptree, Essex

ISBN 0 09 945090 9

AUTHOR'S NOTE

For a short time during the war of 1939–45 I found myself a member of a service concert party in Africa. I'd originally been recruited to write material for the comedian who'd been sweating blood trying to write it himself but, unfortunately, when one of his group disappeared into hospital, I found myself raked in to play a more active part and, in a nightshirt and fez, ended up onstage auctioning 'slave girls' in a mini-play which served as an introduction for the tunes of *The Desert Song*. I was dragged in deeper and deeper but, my heart not being in it, could never manage to learn my lines so that I always had to be given parts where I could hold a magazine with them secreted inside for easy reference. By the time I finally escaped, I had learned not only quite a few of the tricks but also more than one of the disasters that can occur in showbiz.

The tricks, as anyone knows who served during the war, were not confined to showbiz. In North Africa especially, the war was an extraordinary affair in more ways than one. Since the natives were always short of everything, stealing, swindle and fraud were indulged in on an enormous scale. The British were not alone in this. The Italian army also suffered from it and, according to the Rommel Papers, so did the Afrika Korps, and despite the efforts of specialized groups designed to stop it, it was never put down. Confusion was added to by both sides using each other's captured weapons, vehicles, even clothes. As each ran short, they refitted themselves on their next move forward in the yo-

yo war that was being conducted. And men of both sides managed from time to time to live for considerable periods behind each other's lines – deliberately to gather information or for sabotage, or accidentally as they found themselves cut off by the fighting. One escaped German prisoner was reported to have worked for a time as a waiter in a British senior officers' mess where plans were discussed over food.

It couldn't have been too difficult to merge into the crowd. I myself once saw a group of Italian prisoners passing through a station entrance under guard when several of them were cut off by the hurrying people heading for trains. For several wild minutes they were free men and, had they not obviously considered it safer to remain prisoners than to be free, could easily have escaped and vanished because, despite their Italian uniforms, no one took the slightest notice of them.

All this is mentioned merely to show that the events described in this story *could* have happened, even if they didn't.

I am indebted for concert party details to *Fighting for a Laugh*, by Richard Fawkes, and for information concerning the misappropriation of equipment to *Tail of an Army*, by J. K. Stanford.

Part One

1

Edward Kitchener Clegg had been enjoying Cairo, even if he didn't enjoy being in the army.

He'd been in a show at Golders Green when his call-up papers had arrived and, though he'd managed to put off his appearance in khaki until they'd found a replacement for him, in the end he'd had to go. Because of an old injury caused by falling into the orchestra pit during a comic ballet at the Hippodrome in Wallasey in 1938 when he'd had a couple of drinks, he'd been made a Pay Corps babu. But, working at accounts during the day and following his old profession at night as part of a concert party that entertained the troops of Northern Command, he'd just decided that the war was bearable after all when he was posted to Cairo.

He wasn't over-excited at the prospect, but when he arrived in Egypt he found that even for a corporal pay clerk Cairo wasn't bad. There was plenty to eat and drink and everybody worked peacetime hours, staff officers lunching, sleeping and playing games at the Cairo clubs, while men in on urgent business from the desert with scorched skins, burned-out eyes and sand in their hair, had to kick their heels until five o'clock when they strolled back to their desks. Even the fitters in the workshops of the Delta avoided doing too much so they could keep up their strength to go out dancing in the evening.

Morale, however, was said to be low – not at the front, of course, where nobody seemed very worried about the war, but at the back where there was no danger of being shot at – and every now and again there was a blitz with orders from the High Altar that everybody had to buckle down, work harder, get their hair cut, wear sun helmets, avoid exposing themselves to the sun, and be smart and alert at all times. Such orders never had a chance, of course, because the men out in the desert had worn nothing but side hats for some time and staff officers regularly fried themselves to crisps round the Gezira swimming pools without coming to any harm; while the technicians in the base workshops considered that smartness indicated a lack of professionalism and preferred to be scruffy. Come to that, they also liked to sleep off their lunch and when, because of the lost man-hours that resulted, an attempt was made to give them their main meal at night, they complained they were weak from hunger during the afternoon. It was important enough to occupy the minds of the staff for some time.

The panics never lasted long, of course, and they all got back to their personal comfort as quickly as possible. Everybody had vehicle seat cushions as pillows for their beds and if you were in need of cash you could, if you were that way inclined, sell socks and shirts by the hundredweight in the Cairo black market. Food was wasted abominably and Egyptians by the dozen lived from the swill bins. And while the men trying to organize camouflage in the desert were desperately in need of paint and timber, no base unit was complete without flagpoles and barriers all glittering with white paint, and a forest of huge notices adjuring you to 'Save timber' and that 'Salvage wins wars'. Since the conflict was being run by professionals, Clegg had to assume it was the only way.

He couldn't do much about it, anyway, but, because he was a cheerful, gregarious, uncomplaining type, he determined to make the best of it until it was over.

Because he'd been performing in front of people since leaving school, he could play the trombone, the trumpet, the piano and the piano accordion and, bored with the routine, he started a small dance band to amuse his friends. In no time at all, he found himself amusing not only his friends but the sergeants' mess and eventually became part of a small group which played for the officers as they ate their evening meal. There was, he felt, something vaguely immoral about this but, since the band were excused guard and supplied with free beer, he raised no objections.

Eventually, weary of the repetitious music when his inclination lay in other directions, one evening, without saying anything to anyone, he launched into a comic monologue he'd adapted from one he'd done on the halls before his call-up. It was about an Italian officer talking to an Egyptian ice-cream merchant and it went down very well. Even the Egyptian mess servants laughed at it. To his surprise, the following week he was ordered to report to the general's office.

Wondering what had gone wrong, because no riot or civil commotion had resulted from anything he'd done, Clegg appeared at the appointed hour and was shunted through a variety of senior NCOs and officers to the general's door. He wasn't a fighting general, of course, because he was getting on a bit; he was just the general in command of the Cairo depots whose job was to organize everything that went up to the troops in the desert. Nevertheless, he was quite a popular old boy, without any side and a lot of gongs from the previous bunfight. He was tall and beefy with a marked sense of humour and a great feeling for the good things in life. On his desk were two books – *King's Regulations* and *No Orchids for Miss Blandish*.

'Clegg,' he said. 'Eddie Clegg.'

He sounded like one of the boys meeting an old mate and Clegg half expected him to offer him a gin and tonic.

'Comedian chap.'

'That's right, sir.'

'Saw you at the Theatre Royal, Sheffield, in 1938. That right?'

'Yes, sir.' Clegg was amazed. 'I was there.'

'Did a monologue. Saw you do a sketch about a fire and a bucket chain where you did a bit of sleight of hand so that the full buckets went back to the tap and the empty ones back to the fire. Reminded me of Harry Tate at his best.' It appeared that the general was an enthusiastic visitor to West End shows.

'Not much of a one for culture,' he admitted. 'Prefer to laugh. Makes you feel better, laughing. Pity we haven't got the Crazy Gang out here. They'd fit in nicely.' He leaned forward. 'Got an idea that might interest you. Concert parties.'

'Sir?'

'Concert parties to entertain the troops. You've heard of ENSA – Entertainment National Service Association.'

Clegg was beginning to feel almost like an old buddy by this time and he replied almost automatically. 'We call it "Every Night Something Awful", sir.'

The general laughed. 'That's about it,' he agreed. 'Well, they seem to have made a pills of things at the moment out here and it's been decided at rather a high level that we've got to provide our own. You'd better get on with it.'

'Me, sir?'

'In the mess when you did that monologue. Remembered it from the Theatre Royal and when I enquired around I discovered you were just about the only professional in the area. Think you could organize something?'

It was a startling order but Clegg had no doubt.

'Know anybody else who was a professional?'

Clegg didn't. But he knew a few keen amateurs who were willing to get up in the Naafi and sing or tell jokes.

'Talk to them,' the general urged. 'Might be able to make something of 'em. Something to amuse the troops out in the blue. They're bored, it seems, and we've got to produce entertainment for them. Toot sweet, too. The tooter the sweeter. We'll make you up to sergeant to give you some thump and you can have anybody you want so long as you don't ask for too many. And you can take them from anywhere. One exception: you can't have the adjutant of 58 Maintenance Unit.'

Clegg immediately assumed the adjutant of 58 MU was essential to the war effort, but when he started interviewing among the first to offer himself was the adjutant of 58 MU. He was overweight, toothbrush-moustached and had a voice like a penny whistle. When he announced that he occasionally sang ballads in the mess, Clegg saw at once what lay behind the general's veto.

Some of the men he spoke to were genuinely keen, some had done semi-professional turns before the war, some saw a concert party as a soft number. Several of the acts were appalling. There was a conjuror who was one degree better than the magic sets you gave the kids at Christmas, a tenor so shrill he sounded like a castrato, a man who called himself the International Entertainer and would have been dreadful in any language, and a large man with a tremendous belly who did a comic apache dance with another smaller man dressed as a girl and ended up whirling his partner round his head so much he staggered dizzily offstage to throw up his lunch in a corner. There were also dozens who imitated bird calls, dozens more who imitated Churchill and couldn't imitate anyone else, tap dancers who couldn't tap dance, jugglers who couldn't juggle, and a balancing act that fell apart at the crucial moment so that one of the participants had to be carted off to hospital with a strained back. Clegg began to see he was going to have problems.

Since the troops out in the blue would need to laugh as much as anything else, he decided on comedy and a few tuneful songs and in the end settled on a group of no more than four. That way, he felt, they could travel light with one lorry for themselves and all their props. Nobody in the desert, he decided, was going to welcome a bloody great crowd all needing to be fed and watered.

The men he chose were a mixed bag. Second-in-command was Lancelot Hugh Morton who, born of wealthy parents who disliked English weather, had had the good fortune to

13

grow up in southern Switzerland and could speak Italian, French and German without an accent. He had a Cambridge degree in European languages and should have had a commission, but a sardonic manner had put the interviewing board off and instead he had ended up as a corporal in Intelligence, examining captured Italian stores NCOs and investigating the inventories of equipment seized in Wavell's dash to Bardia the year before. Since it was hardly the most exciting job there was, he had decided to seek a change and, though he was an oddity, he had appeared in shows at university and Clegg thought that between them they might produce some good material.

For the songs he found Private Ivor Elwyn Jones, of the Gordons, who, of course, turned out to be Welsh and, like all Welshmen, knew everything there was to know about singing. Trained on hymns, he loved applause, sang well enough to deserve it and could reach notes so high Morton insisted he must have had a nasty accident at some point in his career. 'High Cs, man, see,' he liked to boast. 'Not always, o' course, but mostly.' Unfortunately, his appearance didn't match his talent; he was a small highly strung man with a worn gnome-like face who was unkempt and vaguely unhygienic in a uniform that fitted where it touched. His badges were unpolished, his buttons hanging off and his boots unshined. Happily, he sang most of the time in prop clothes.

Finally, there was Arthur Caccia, whose father ran a grocery shop in Soho. As he was in the catering trade in Civvy Street, the army had naturally made him a mechanic and he was more than eager for a change. He had a good voice, a nice line in Cockney humour and a swift mind that could produce ideas. Being on the small side, he could also do female impersonations and, coming from the RASC, could drive and service the lorry they'd been given.

Careful about what they were to put on, Clegg decided jokes about Egyptians were all right because even the song 'Up your pipe, King Farouk, Hang your bollocks on a hook' had never offended the Egyptian labourers who crowded the doorways to watch rehearsals. They could also mock the soldiers' plight and could be vulgar, but they couldn't be really obscene because up in the desert the men lived a puritanical life, while jokes about unfaithful wives would only cause worry. They decided to play on nostalgia a lot, however, and dug out the sort of songs that made men think of home, and from Clegg's monologue worked up a sketch about a German officer and an Italian soldier he was trying to send forward towards the fighting. It was an immediate success because everybody laughed at the Italians, who *would* persist in surrendering, and there was a lot of comic arguing in mock Italian, German and English, and a lot of talk about ice cream and spaghetti, the leaning Tower of Pisa and Mussolini's underpants.

'Variety, comedy and somebody who looks like a girl,' Clegg decided at their first programme conference. 'And we never perform on Saturday night anywhere near Cairo because Saturday night's the troops' traditional booze-up night and nobody's going to stay in to watch a half-arsed show like ours when he's got money to spend on beer.'

They collected planks and curtains and a few props and moved about the Nile Delta brushing up their performance on base details until they were ready to go into the desert. Whatever the disasters, they were always welcomed as a change from Shafto's Shambles, the Arab cinema where you saw old films featuring Gloria Swanson and Mary Pickford at three and a half ackers a go – when it did go, because usually it didn't. It had Egyptian operators and the films usually began upside-down, invariably appeared with the reels in the wrong order and were so overprinted at the sides and bottom with French, Greek and Arabic subtitles the actors were barely visible.

They weren't the best concert party in the world and their material probably wouldn't have raised a laugh back in England but the men they tried it out on loved it. With Jones's soaring tenor always on hand in case things went wrong, they decided they were in business and Clegg reported to the general, who announced he would see their next performance.

They put it on in a Naafi marquee and Jones was in splendid voice so that, his success going to his head, he announced that as an encore he would sing the *'Ave Maria'*. 'In the original Italian,' he said.

It was a lot of gibberish because he couldn't speak Italian but the audience didn't know and the rest of the show couldn't have gone better, though Caccia's female turn when he donned a wig and sang 'Olga Paulovski, The Beautiful Spy' looked a little odd because they'd had trouble with the lorry so that his hands, which were never on the small side, still bore traces of oil and his fingernails were heavily in mourning.

The general was delighted. 'Just one or two tips,' he pointed out to Clegg. 'And I hope as a professional you won't take them amiss. I always thought the original of the *"Ave Maria"* was in Latin, and you should tell your female impersonator not to raise his arms at the end of his act when he's acknowledging the applause. Either that or he should shave under his arms. Otherwise, no complaints. Just what the troops want. Tits and tinsel. Pity we haven't a few spare ATS girls.'

Calling themselves the Desert Ratbags, they put on a show wherever anyone would erect a stage from ammunition boxes. Once the curtains fell on them as they were being opened and stopped the show before it had even started; once Caccia fell through a gap in the ammunition-box stage and sprained his ankle; and once, when a German aeroplane came over and dropped bombs nearby, the whole audience and cast bolted, leaving an amateur escapologist they'd recruited from Base Workshops still tied up onstage. But they improved all the time as they thought of new material. Clegg worked up a comic strong-man act, then, because there were two of them who could rattle off Italian at full speed – Morton who had grown up with it and Caccia who

16

had spoken it constantly at home – they worked up the German-officer-and-Italian-soldier sketch into a finale with three 'Italians' on stage so they could finish with a song the South Africans had sung about them after Wavell had kicked them out of Libya – 'Where do we go from here, Now that we've lost Bardia?' To make it look better, they obtained captured Italian uniforms and a German jacket and cap.

For a month they moved about the desert between Sidi Barrani and Mersa Matruh. The Italians had been the first to push forward in 1940, making a hesitant thrust into Egypt, which had been wiped away before the year was ended as Wavell's army flung them back all the way to Beda Fomm on the bulge of Cyrenaica. Unfortunately, while they'd still been crowing at their success, there'd been a shout for help from Greece and, with half the crack units of the Desert Army crossing to the mainland of Europe, while nobody was looking a lot of uncomfortably aggressive Germans had appeared in Africa and in no time at all had slammed the British back again so that, after a little to-ing and fro-ing, the line had finally settled down just west of the Egyptian border. It was now considered to be the British turn again.

At the end of May Clegg was asked to put on a few performances at Zuq, which was just beyond the Egyptian frontier. They'd all been to Zuq at one time or another. It was a picturesque coastal settlement that had been part of Mussolini's scheme for the colonization of Libya, one of those strange bastard towns on the coast which was neither Arab nor Italian, but a mixture of both. To create jobs, under the Ente Colonizazzione Libia, put in force by the Italian government after they had acquired the territory from the Turks after the war of 1911, there were smallholdings providing vegetables and fruit for the Italian mainland, and a furniture factory where Arab craftsmen created excellent North African furniture to grace the homes of party officials in Rome, and a cheaper range that was not so excellent to fill the small box-like houses the government had provided for the colonists.

There was a mosque among the palms and spreading bougainvillaea, a bombed-out white church and a few shops, a governor's residence, a hospital and, in the centre of the town, an amphitheatre dating back to the empire of Hadrian. It was only small and at some time in the past it had been partly destroyed by an earthquake, but there were still tiers of stone terraces and a lot of chambers filled with drifted sand. Finally, just outside the town there was a fort looking like something out of *Beau Geste*, built years before by the Italians as an observation post but now out of date and used only as a transport base, and, near the harbour, a few corrugated-iron huts and warehouses erected by whichever army happened to have possession of the place in the backwards and forwards sway of the war, or by the few Libyan or Italian civilians who had businesses there.

Clegg agreed at once. Zuq, he felt, was far enough forward for them to be performing to genuine front-line troops but just far enough back for them to be safe from anything but a prowling Messerschmitt.

'Okay,' he said. 'We'll give it a go.'

As it happened, it didn't work out quite as they expected because before long other people became involved. Among them Colonel Horace Thomas Dampier, MC and Bar, Inspector of Equipment to the Army in the Middle East.

2

Colonel Dampier wasn't naturally an even-tempered man. He was tall, good-looking, inclined to plumpness as age caught up with him, but upright in bearing in the best military fashion, complete with greying temples and brisk clipped moustache.

For months now, he had been struggling to stop the theft of army stores. In other wars, plundering hadn't started until you'd beaten the enemy, and it had never been easy anyway, because in those days everyone moved about on foot and you had to carry your loot on your back. Nowadays, nobody bothered to wait until the enemy was in retreat and, since everyone now used lorries, the loot had grown larger and things were a great deal easier. With half Egypt waiting with open arms for anything that was going, people simply stole everything that wasn't screwed down and flogged it in the Cairo black market.

To Dampier, a magistrate in peacetime and so honest it hurt, people who stole military equipment in wartime were like maggots in cheese. A landowner in his home county of Devon, he had done all the right things, hunting, shooting, fishing and the rest, and to his blunt mind there were only two shades – black and white. He had won his MC in the holocaust that was the first day of the Somme in 1916 and the bar to it in the same area in 1918. By 1939, he had in the very nature of things grown a little pompous, but he was patriotic and brave and, confident the army would welcome him back with open arms, had left his adoring wife and family and offered himself once more, fully expecting to face the enemy at once with teeth bared and eyes ablaze. At fifty-one, however, Dampier was a touch too old for front-line stuff and, to his fury, he was given the humdrum job of running a training camp in the north of England until he finally exploded and demanded to be sent where there was some risk to life and limb. The army obliged by sending him to Cairo, where, if anything, he was safer than in England and you had to look very hard about you to find the war. There was certainly no sign of it in the Gezira Sporting Club or the Continental Roof Garden, though it *was* occasionally mentioned at the Turf Club.

To his disgust he found himself laying on concerts and film shows for back-area troops, to say nothing of boxing and cricket tournaments and football matches against Egyptian teams. A second furious explosion translated him once more, this time into the head of a team investigating the disappearance of army equipment. In his no-nonsense way, Winston Churchill in London had noticed a vast discrepancy between the stores shown in the manifests of merchant ships aimed at the Middle East and those which the army claimed to have available for use, and had demanded that someone should do something about it. Because everybody else was comfortably established and Dampier was a newcomer – and a nuisance to boot – he found himself with a lorry and a brief to investigate.

At the permanent camps round Tel el Kebir he found the pilfering was amazing. A two-ton charging plant had been removed miraculously on donkeys between dusk and dawn; and a consignment of fifty thousand razor blades destined for the troops had dwindled to twenty-five thousand by the time it reached the army canteens. It didn't take him long to decide that the Sudanese watchmen recruited for their honesty were in reality the eyes and ears of the gangs.

Without realizing it, the army had picked the right man for the job. Cairo had always been noted for its thieves, prostitutes, pimps and swindlers, and the arrival of a vast army had merely worsened the situation. Caught up in the vast net of conscription, it was inevitable that a few shysters had arrived in the Egyptian capital and it hadn't taken them long to realize that the army, preoccupied with fighting the war in the desert, had little time to look after its rear end, and almost at once a traffic in spare parts, tyres, food, even arms, had sprung up. Soldiers who fell for Egyptian girls in the cabarets in Emad-el-Din Street overstayed their leave and, provided the girl they followed home hadn't a large boyfriend waiting round the corner with a knife, became the target for Egyptian wide boys eager to get them into their clutches.

In addition, the War Department employed four hundred thousand Egyptian civilians who had no compunction about robbing it blind. Even the payroll system for hired help invited frauds. And when the vehicles of the Société des Autobus du Nord came to a standstill for lack of tyres, supplies with the War Department mark removed quickly arrived from the army dumps, with steel, chemicals, textiles, cigarettes and food, all of which were up for grabs and leaking in a steady stream from military warehouses into civilian channels.

Since all Egyptian labourers wore flowing robes it was impossible to search them unless you hung them upside down by their ankles, and women employed in the married quarters went home mountainous with the sheets and pillowcases they stuffed under their clothing. Even the men wore cache-sexes beneath their galabiyahs in which they secreted spanners, torch batteries, spark plugs, cap comforters, knives, watches, compasses and anything else that was small enough to fit in easily. Once when Dampier instituted a search at the gate of a maintenance unit the home-going crowd of fellahin collected in a scared gibbering group, and the ground where they had waited was found later to be littered with unexpected jetsam. Trains, whistling to waiting gangs, slowed down to allow bales and boxes to be tossed to the side of the track. Sleeping soldiers woke to find their tents gone. One bright spark arrested for setting up a totally non-existent scheme for which he drew labourers' wages had actually received a mention in despatches for his work on it the day before he was picked up. You could buy counterfeit rubber stamps in the back streets of Cairo and in twenty-four hours have a set of forged papers that made everything easy and, because the Egyptian police were slack enough never to check lorries at the gates of the dumps, every crime imaginable involving bribes, stolen property and trafficking in currency was taking place. In many cases even the police were involved.

Dampier managed to get a few people jailed – a corporal caught driving a lorry containing a million cigarettes which no one would admit losing, a man running a mobile laundry that was the cover for the fact that he was pimping, a warrant officer running a repair shop who was equipping private cars, a welfare officer smuggling radio sets to Syria, Naafi managers flogging spirits from their stores. While Dampier regarded looting as stealing, for the most part his anger was only laughed at. Captured Mercedes cars, horses, large consignments of wine, were reputed to be finding their way home for the use of fortuitously placed high-ranking officers, and there was an apocryphal story about a brigadier who, insisting that loot was not something he was interested in, had been hit by the grand piano which had been blown out of the back of his bombed lorry.

Dampier found a major at a base ordnance depot who was selling rifles to Palestinians for use against British troops in Tel Aviv, and even turned up a group of Italian prisoners of war who, unknown to anybody, had set themselves up as a base repair depot on the outskirts of Alexandria. Wearing Arab galabiyahs, they had infiltrated themselves among the local workers who went every day to labour in one of the base stores depots and, with the tools and equipment they managed to steal, had gone into business on their own. Having all at one time worked in England or America, they could speak English, and they finally went so far as to change their galabiyahs for British uniforms, pose as Maltese and employ their own Arab labour. There was, Dampier noted, far less stealing from *their* base than from others.

Finally, incredible as it seemed, he had discovered that a contractor whom he'd been watching for weeks over missing consignments of steel was a German. Small, dark-haired and swarthy, he had been clerk to a German liaison officer with the Italians and had been captured in Wavell's advance in 1941. Having escaped, as a means of earning money he had set himself up as a shoe-shine boy and fly-whisk seller. Becoming a waiter, the German had decided it would be more profitable to own a restaurant himself and, when he resolved to enlarge his premises and had met the contractors, had finally realized that, if he wanted to be really in the money, he ought to be a contractor himself. He was running half a dozen rackets when he was picked up by the Military Police for no other reason than that he had one night parked his car outside the flat where he lived with his Egyptian mistress, and it happened to be passed by a Special Investigation Branch officer with a keen sense of smell who had detected the scent of musty hay which meant smuggled hashish.

While the fighting units roosted austerely on sand, and in winter wore drill despite having begged for greatcoats and leather jerkins, the base units helped themselves to the rubber cushions of ambulances to make mattresses, to driving mirrors to hold photographs of their girlfriends, and to batteries to power bedside lights; and cut up tents, tarpaulins and signal cable to make bed springs on stolen rifle racks. As many as thirteen blankets were found to be possessed by some men, while others used them as curtains and tablecloths or, nailed to walls, as makeshift wardrobes to keep best uniforms clean. Despite the shortage of timber, enormous bedsteads had been erected for the comfort of both officers and men, some even with a tier beneath for books and boots and clothing. It was a wonder, Dampier thought, that they didn't paint the bloody things to match their pyjamas.

'This war,' he growled, 'will not be won on soft beds, tea and buns and moaning for cigarettes. And I intend to see that it isn't lost.'

He had finally found his niche. He had been successful enough to draw attention to himself and, with Churchill now complaining indignantly that the number of vehicles the Eighth Army claimed to have in the field was nowhere near the number which had been sent out from England and asking what the Eighth Army intended to do about it, Dampier was upped a step in rank, designated Inspector of Equipment to the Eighth Army, and told to find out which units were holding stores and vehicles they were not supposed to have.

By this time the gleam had reappeared in his eye and he was beginning to enjoy himself. He smelled with the eagerness of an old warhorse, if not the enemy, at least his own kind of battle; his unit now consisted of a warrant to hold inspections without warning, a group of clerks and storemen in Cairo, and a couple of expert assistants.

Warrant Officer Patrick Rafferty was an ex-quartermaster and a first-class fitter who could unravel enormous and complicated lists of spares and tools without blinking an eye. Utterly confident in his own ability, he was reputed once to have visited a desert-based cavalry regiment which, as soon as he'd been sighted, had driven all the vehicles they weren't supposed to have out into the blue. Rafferty had made no comment, done his inspection and gone away, only to return at full speed half an hour later just as the vehicles all returned.

He was a short nutty-faced Irishman, a regular soldier who looked a little like a leprechaun with his thin blue-jowled face, black hair and pale blue eyes. He had a marked Irish accent, a mischievous sense of humour, and, for a man who had reached warrant rank, took an odd delight in seeing senior officers make asses of themselves.

He had a briefcase full of documents, both British and foreign, to which he constantly referred and there was little he didn't know about the supplies and supply methods of any army – British, French, Italian or German. He knew backwards the G1098, the booklet which set out in detail what arms, equipment, vehicles and stores each unit should hold, reckoned about forty thousand items could be scrapped from it without being noticed, and could spot at once what a quartermaster's store was holding that it shouldn't be holding. 'I was once bet a fiver by an RASC adjutant,' he said with a smile, 'that I'd find nothing irregular. At half-time he retired to his room, saying he felt ill.'

In addition, because radio spares – even whole radios – were being flogged to the Egyptians to listen in to Radio Cairo, perhaps even to Radio Rome or Grossdeütsche Rundfunk, Dampier had been allotted a corporal wireless operator from Signals called Clinch who not only checked radio equipment but also drove their Bedford three-tonner. He was a young man with a face as blank as a cowpat but, despite his blond hair, blue eyes and an expression as innocent as a choirboy's, had a reputation for knowing his way about.

In no time they had recovered a complete consignment of radio valves, turned up a deserter who had acquired thirty thousand gallons of petrol by the simple process of appearing at an army filling station and filling his lorry with fuel which he then promptly sold in the Cairo black market before going back for more, and discovered that, at a time when army tyres were fetching ninety pounds apiece, civilians could get new ones merely by leaving their cars in a certain square in Cairo with a sum of money hidden under the dashboard.

'Given a chance,' Dampier pointed out, 'they'd steal an anvil.'

Rafferty smiled. 'One did,' he said. 'I caught him staggering home bow-legged with it strapped round his waist and hanging between his knees.'

When they were ordered into the desert, where the forward troops were complaining that when they sent a vehicle back for repair it never returned, it was a challenge that pleased Dampier. In his own small way, he felt that at last he was contributing to the winning of the war, if only by putting behind bars a few of the people who seemed intent on losing it. But he wasn't deluded.

'I suppose,' he said cynically, 'the truth is that somebody decided we were getting too close to his own pet little racket and were best out of the way.'

3

Because they were going to be away from the bright lights for a while, the Desert Ratbags each in his own way made a point of having a good night-out before setting off for Zuq. Jones the Song, his heart aching for the Land of his Fathers, looked up another Welshman from Swansea, his home town, and got drunk singing Welsh songs. Caccia, who was a great one for the girls, especially in such a randy-making climate, headed for a dance hall he knew. Clegg and Morton ate at an Egyptian night club, where Clegg tried to set fire to the muslin drapes of the belly dancer. He was always inclined to be aggressively mischievous when he'd had one or two.

The following morning they drove out of the city past the single-decker trams hooked together like trains, the gharries, the crowding fellahin, the businessmen in tarbooshes, the beggars asleep in the gutters, the befezzed policemen with whips, and the inane Arab music from the cafés where the customers crouched over their hookahs and dominoes. At the level crossing outside the city the usual hold-up was taking place. Clad in stolen army boots, a discarded British topee worn backwards, several days' growth of beard, and two frilly women's dresses circa 1905 draped over plus-fours, the gatekeeper seemed to be enjoying the uproar.

The queue was a quarter of a mile long. Among the camels and donkeys blinking at the flies, small boys were darting about offering their sisters to anybody who would listen. Egyptian labourers were asleep in the shade, their heads on the rails, knowing that the vibration when the train came, or Allah, or both, would warn them in good time. A tatty-looking fruit cart, its wheels sagging at weird angles to the frame, stood nearby, its driver asleep underneath. Just astern, a donkey, its backside tattooed with its owner's name, dozed in the shafts of a cart as big as a wheelbarrow. There were also a flock of fat-tailed sheep that seemed to draw their sustenance from discarded cigarette ends; a field gun on a truck; a funeral coach pulled by two sway-backed horses; a youth on a bicycle with a small trussed pig lashed to the handlebars; carts laden with sand apparently on their way to top up the desert; an Arab stallion which kept trying to mount a donkey mare; and a camel with a load of straw, a bell on its neck, a red lamp slung to its behind for after dark, and wearing an expression of considerable unease because it was closely backed up by a tank whose driver kept revving the engine to show his impatience.

Despite the non-arrival of a train, the level-crossing keeper, having obviously decided he had collected enough customers, opened the gate at last and they all went away like the field heading for the first fence at a point-to-point. The donkey's legs seemed to twang like harp strings as it took the strain; it was followed by the wobbling cyclists impeded by their robes and the addition of a pillion passenger – sometimes even two. And the whole tribe of them trailed away to the west.

After their night-out, none of the Desert Ratbags, all dressed in shirts and shorts like everybody else in the desert – even the Germans and Italians – was feeling at his best, but they found the sign to Zuq and headed west, careful to keep plenty of distance between them and other units because, to a man, they had no wish to get too involved with the army in case someone thought of making them soldiers again. They spent the night at a camp run by the Military Police, who weren't expecting them and weren't interested, taking the view that they were an unnecessary appendage to the war and even begrudging them food and drink.

'Where do we sleep?' Clegg demanded.

The policeman he asked gestured at the empty desert. 'Anywhere you like,' he said. 'There's plenty of room.'

They woke to a violet-streaked dawn with a smudge in the south that grew rapidly, spreading outwards at either end. It rushed towards them, an enormous crimson cloud tearing in from the horizon, and arrived in a red whirlwind of dust, raw, burning, covering everything, hissing and beating at the ground, the sun a vague purple sphere above. Clegg started to sing 'Sand in My Shoes'.

Unknown to the Ratbags, Dampier's group was just ahead, moving along roughly the same route.

On the way up, they stopped at a café where a bored Egyptian in a greasy evening suit served them with coffee. On the wall was a picture of King Farouk and his bride, taken when both had been a lot younger and slimmer, and, nearby, RAF lorries were dumping stores to make a new airfield. It was here they bumped into Albert Micklethwaite, a war correspondent from Nottingham who was anxious to get a lift forward so he could do a few interviews with men from his home town.

Micklethwaite was plump and pink, his uniform didn't fit him, and he hadn't been long in the Middle East, where for most of the time he hadn't had the faintest idea what was going on. But, with everybody else called up, he had been the only reporter available when his editor had been accredited a war correspondent, and he had been sent out to see 'what the local lads were doing'.

Micklethwaite had long since decided he didn't like Egypt. Within two days of arriving he had acquired a rash of prickly heat and been stung by a fly which, judging by the effect it had on him, had a poison sac as big as a cow's udder. He had no sooner recovered when he'd had his wallet

29

lifted and, before he could report it, had been asked for his documents by a military policeman. Unable to prove he was what he claimed to be, he had been whipped into the Bab-el-Hadid barracks, where the Special Investigation Department of the Military Police had their headquarters, and it had landed him in endless difficulties, which he had only just managed to sort out. He had found a few men from Nottingham around the base camps but they were hardly suffering for their country, and an indignant telegram from home had insisted that he get among the fighting troops. In desperation he had scrounged a lift west with the B echelon of a lancer regiment who, having just informed him they were about to swing south, had advised him he had better scrounge a lift from someone else.

Dampier looked at him in astonishment. 'A war correspondent?' he said. 'One of those fellers who write all that tripe in the newspapers? All that about lean, hard warriors in Cairo? "Bronze, suntanned and muscular." "Uniforms showing the wear and tear of their hard living." My good chap, most of the people in Cairo are fat and flabby, with uniforms starched and pressed ready for the next session at Groppi's.' He snorted. 'Too many damn women in Cairo. There weren't women about in the last war.'

Rafferty lifted his eyes heavenwards. It was a complaint he had already heard many times.

'Wives were supposed to have been banished to South Africa,' Dampier went on. 'But a lot got jobs as secretaries and stayed on, and when you tick somebody off for her bad work you find she's the bloody brigadier's better half.' He lifted an angry face to stare at the newspaperman. 'The Gezira Club's full of women and you can play polo and tennis and swim and be watched by crowds as leisurely as at a Test match at Lord's on a hot day. No wonder the chaps in the desert call them Groppi's Hussars, the Gaberdine Swine and the Short Range Desert Group. The bloody place's full of drones of both sexes. Cairo, my good chap, is in perpetual conference. On welfare, passive air defence, morale, sport, entertainment, improvements to hostels, but never, it seems, on fighting the war. Very well' – he dismissed Micklethwaite with a careless gesture – 'jump in. We'll take you forward.'

Grudgingly fitting the chastened Micklethwaite into his little caravan, the Inspector of Equipment moved on at first light, driving fast before news of what he was up to arrived ahead of him. Most of the stores they had unearthed so far had turned out to be honestly held against emergencies by frustrated men who had grown used to having their requests ignored by Cairo. Because so many orders came down the pipeline, no one really knew what they *should* hold, anyway, so they held as much as they could for safety.

'When you can't get the stuff, sir,' one dogged stores warrant officer caught with three hundred extra suits of battledress admitted, 'you hang on to it against the time when it's needed.'

Another unit was found to have seven surplus shirts per man for the same reason, and yet another, a field battery, held a hundred new tyres, none of which fitted any of the vehicles they ran. 'It's because when you get new vehicles, sir,' the quartermaster argued, 'you can't get the bloody tyres for them, so we hold 'em just in case.'

The attitude of the men who had stood with bared teeth against the enemy was different again. They carried loot and weren't ashamed of it. They'd won it from the Italians in a fair fight and, despite orders to the contrary, were not going to hand it in. Every old hand rode a motorbike or in a motor car or lorry, fitters had tools they'd previously only dreamed of, medical officers had equipment they'd never seen since their training; every wrist sported a watch, every officer and sergeant wore Zeiss binoculars, and everybody had dainty Biretta automatics and cameras, all obligingly supplied by the Italians during Wavell's 1940–1 campaign.

'After all,' one cavalry unit's engineer officer, weary of fighting a running battle with the sand and the engines it was wearing out, said, 'if *we* don't keep them, the bastards in Cairo will, and they haven't even fought for them. We once captured a crate of Zeiss X12 binoculars and, because we were new to the game in those days, we sent them back to base. They never arrived but, while our chaps were still using X6 glasses, when I was on leave I saw staff bods going to the races with X12s that could well have come from the lot we captured.'

Far from being unsympathetic, Dampier agreed to say nothing provided a few pairs of the X12s were turned over to him. They weren't new and one or two were even damaged, but honour was satisfied.

'Even if we haven't caught many thieves,' he observed to Rafferty as they headed for their vehicles, 'we've surely frightened back a lot of stores.'

They had made a respectable start but dozens of vehicles were still missing. Hundreds had been torn apart to provide the spares the forward troops couldn't get in any other way, but many more had crept into repair units which refused to admit having them because they were being used to convey sergeants to and from the mess.

'They come under the heading of BLR, sir,' Rafferty pointed out. '*Beyond local repair*. It's a very useful label, especially when they're not.'

Dampier sighed. 'I suppose,' he said, 'that we have to expect that, like laxative pills, we're probably doing more good than we realize.'

At midday, they came to a group of tents and two fifteen-hundredweight trucks. Outside stood a painted sign: *38 Light Aid Duties, RASC*. As the lorry stopped, a corporal appeared. Seeing Dampier's rank, he saluted smartly and announced that the two men who worked with him were at that moment away.

They got down to business quickly and almost at once it occurred to Dampier that something fishy was going on. On the benches were two engines and the shiny surface of the metal of the casings indicated that the serial numbers had been filed off. To Dampier that meant only one thing – that they were there illicitly.

He had noticed that the corporal and the two missing men each had a tent to himself and that their beds were made from inner tubes stretched across the welded frames of old cars. Ammunition boxes stood alongside them for toilet sundries, mess tins were used for soap dishes, car-inspection lamps for reading in bed, and each man had a War Department padlock for securing his kitbag and a Tannoy for listening to the communal radio – kept in another tent nearby which looked as though it had been fitted out as a dining-cum-living room. There was a remarkable absence of oil, petrol, drills, lathes and tools.

'You're not very big,' Dampier said.

'No, sir.' The corporal, a smooth-looking man with a Ronald Colman moustache, was all attention and military alertness. 'At the moment there's just the three of us. There was a sergeant and two privates but they was told to report back to base.'

'Who're you attached to for rations and so on?'

'Base Depot, RASC.'

'And the other two men?'

The corporal answered briskly. 'At the parent unit, sir. Returnin' a vehicle what belongs to the Royals. They're also picking up petrol. We're a bit low at the moment. I expect 'em back tomorrow.'

'I'd better have your names.'

'025, Corporal Clutterbuck, R., sir.'

'Full number.'

Clutterbuck looked wary but he gave his full number, and those of the missing two men, whose names turned out to be Dow and Raye.

'Dow, Raye an' me,' Clutterbuck said with a large smile that was designed to show willingness, open-heartedness and honesty. Dampier wasn't deluded.

'Where are your tools?' he demanded.

''Ere, sir.' Clutterbuck indicated an array of personal

tools set out on a folding table which appeared to be doing duty as a workbench.

'These are Italian tools,' Dampier pointed out.

Clutterbuck was not put off. 'Everybody's got Italian tools, sir. They're good. Italian screwcutters is the best there is.'

When Dampier asked to see the inventory, it appeared to have disappeared in the last move forward.

'You know 'ow it is, sir,' Corporal Clutterbuck said earnestly. 'Things get lost.'

It didn't satisfy Dampier but he continued to display the polite expression that was the stock-in-trade of all trained investigators when they sensed problems. 'What about other stores?' he asked.

Clutterbuck waved vaguely at a tent that turned out to be full of clothing, blankets, tyres and jerrycans of petrol, all of which, as Dampier well knew, were the currency of deserters.

He spoke quietly to Warrant Officer Rafferty. 'What do you think?'

'Sure, I'm thinkin' they're adrift, sorr,' Rafferty said cheerfully. 'Deserters. I bet they've been at this for months, movin' about in the blue, pretendin' to be a workshop and gettin' petrol where they could.'

'That's what I think, too.' Dampier turned to Clutterbuck. 'What do you use to repair vehicles?' he asked. 'I see no drill, no lathe, no spare batteries, no oxyacetylene gear, no electric equipment.'

'We don't do electrics, sir.'

'I'll bet you don't. You're not a repair outfit at all. You're deserters, aren't you?'

Clutterbuck looked a little sick. 'Well, we *was* attached to 71 Vehicle Repair Depot but they moved off and left us behind to check the stores. I think they forgot us and there we was.'

Dampier could well believe it. The desert was full of men

who seemed to be attached to nothing and were responsible for nothing.

It didn't take long to get the story clear. Dow and Raye, both corporals like Clutterbuck, had been deserters for a year now and had roped in Clutterbuck because he had picked up Arabic through working with mechanics at the Base Repair Depot. Following the usual practice, he had been given money by an Egyptian with the smiling assurance that it was to help the brave British soldier enjoy himself, and he had overstayed his leave until he had become classed as a deserter. Not fancying what might be coming to him, he had found himself being introduced to Dow and Raye, who said they could use him in their organization.

Finally disappearing with them into the Cairo underground, Clutterbuck had been away from the army now for four months, even accepting twenty pounds to drive a stolen lorry loaded with contraband between Egypt and Palestine. Despite wives in England, Dow and Raye had even married Egyptian girls, and turned Mohammedan to justify it.

'Didn't anyone ask questions when you turned up here?' Dampier asked.

'No, sir.' Clutterbuck was looking distinctly uneasy now. 'When we went to 97 MU, we told 'em we was attached to 86 Repair Unit but 'ad lost touch, so they supplied us. When we'd tapped them a bit, we went to 86 Repair Unit and told *them* we belonged to 97 MU. We drew rations and petrol, and people brought vehicles in for repair. We even actually did a few. I worked on Lancias afore the war and, as a lot of vehicles comin' in was captured Lancias, people thought 'ighly of me.' 'e seemed proud of his work. 'I once did one for a brigadier and 'e slipped me a few bottles of wine to show 'is appreciation.'

Dampier was all for collaring the brass to set an example to the lower orders and he pounced at once. 'What was his name?'

Clutterbuck backed away. 'Oh, I couldn't tell you that, sir,' he said. 'What you might call business ethics.'

'Honour among thieves, I'd call it,' Dampier growled. 'Go on.'

'We wasn't never involved in drugs, sir.'

'How about stolen weapons?'

'I think Dow and Raye 'ad a go at it. They took 'em back to Cairo and the Egyptians ran 'em southwards aboard feluccas. They carry fifty foot of sail and can outrun any of the launches of the Gyppos' Inland Water Transport Board. I never got in on that, though. They wouldn't let me.' It seemed it was only pure chance and the greed of his companions that had prevented Clutterbuck becoming even more deeply involved.

'They wasn't the only ones,' he went on. 'After every advance every bloody Arab in the desert was in the arms game. If there was minefields they used their wives to walk ahead of 'em. I once saw three of 'em outside Zuq, every one of 'em with a stolen Lee Enfield, all pointed up with metal and studded wi' jewels like they do wi' their guns. Gold bands round the barrels an' stocks an' the butt plates replaced wi' silverwork. They even 'ad 'and-carved bullets. Special for killin' important people, they said. After all, the police was at it as well, wasn't they? Not just the Gyppo police neither. One of 'em was an orficer in the Special Investigation Branch.'

'And what about those spare engines in there with their serial numbers filed off?'

Clutterbuck sighed. 'There was six originally. But Dow an' Raye loaded four of 'em up and set off for Cairo with a pile o' spare parts an' tools. Dow's got two taxis an' 'e needs to keep 'em runnin'. An' it's 'eavens 'ard for civvie outfits to get spares.'

'It's also heavens hard for the chaps at the front to get them.'

'Yeh – well.' Clutterbuck gestured heavily. 'After all, there's more than one REME major in Cairo and Alex what does up civvie cars cheap. You can buy 'em cheap, too, when they can't get spares, then all you 'ave to do is refit 'em an' sell 'em at a good profit. There's fellers back in the Delta makin' thousands. Raye changed 'is cash into gold an' 'ad it made into bangles for his girlfriend. She's a walkin' bloody bank account.'

It finally emerged that Clutterbuck's involvement in the garage business had not been entirely honest even *before* the war because in those days he had been engaged in changing the colours and removing the serial numbers of stolen cars.

As he grew more and more convinced that he'd been left to hold the baby, Clutterbuck came up with still more evidence. 38 Light Aid Duties was only a small part of a larger organization which encompassed British soldiers – NCOs and officers included – Egyptians, Maltese, Greeks, Jews and Syrians, with a headquarters in the Sharia Marika Nazli, near Cairo Main Station.

'They said they was comin' back to load everythin' up,' Clutterbuck said gloomily.

Dampier gave him an icy look. 'I don't think they'll make it,' he said. 'So, for the moment, we'll have you in the car. And don't try to bolt because we're armed. We'll load the lorries with the stores and the tents, Mr Rafferty. Micklethwaite can drive my car, you and I will drive the fifteen-hundredweights and Corporal Clinch the Bedford.'

Micklethwaite looked surprised but he realized he was seeing a bit of real army life which would stand him in good stead when he came to write the book he'd been planning ever since his arrival in the Middle East. 'Right,' he said briskly.

Clutterbuck was looking alarmed. ''Ow about Dow an' Raye?'

'When they return,' Dampier said, ' – if they return – they'll find their little nest deserted and bolt straight back east where, by that time, thanks to the miracle of radio, the Military Police will be looking for them. I don't see any alternative, do you? They certainly won't wander far. It's a big desert and it's very hot and thirsty.'

4

Continuing west into a blaze of orange, Dampier's party were guided by white tapes through a large minefield to the east of Sofi. As they moved on, they left the cinder-coloured plains behind them and struck red sand which sent up coils like angry flames round the wheels, and they began to notice that the wind had risen. Within an hour the desert was blotted out by rolling clouds of crimson dust fine as flour that got into their eyes and ears and ground between their teeth. Everything was covered with it and it seemed as if the lorry was being lashed by purple streamers under a livid sky. The visibility was only a few yards now, with the sun blotted out, the oppressive murk deepening to a dull orange then paling to a dusky yellow as the wind slackened.

Muffling their faces against the wind, they got their heads down and, as it grew worse, Dampier decided to head north for Zuq itself, where they might be able to shelter for the night and hand Clutterbuck over to the Provost people.

By the time they drove in, however, the wind had increased and most of the town was obscured by whirling clouds of sand which was already building up in drifts against the walls, and it was almost impossible to see what lay ahead. Not that it mattered because they already knew. The place had been bombed and shelled by both sides so often there wasn't a great deal left. The houses still stood, though some had sagging roofs and walls, and the harbour was filled with wrecks, their funnels and masts showing above the water, rusty relics constantly pitted and twisted by fresh high-explosive until they were almost unrecognizable as ships. But there was still a passage between them so that lighters could move at slow speed from the freighters, which were obliged to anchor outside the harbour, to a pontoon wharf newly constructed from planks and oil drums against the ruins of the old one. The war had swept three times across Zuq and few of the buildings near the harbour had escaped the scars of battle.

By this time the sky had turned a dirty grey and they wore their respirators as they groped about for their belongings. The heat in the flying sand was appalling and they could hear the monotonous beat of the wind drumming the canvas of the vehicle covers. Strangely empty, the town was like a new kind of suburbia with the houses all standardized. Even the furnishings came in three natty shades approved of in Rome.

Reaching a stretch of parched grass beneath a group of wind-whipped palms on the outskirts, they decided not to struggle any further and bedded down inside the three-tonner, taking it in turns to stay awake to make sure Clutter-buck didn't bolt. With the sandstorm still raging, they became aware during the night of aircraft overhead, and then the whango-whango-whango of guns and the clatter of machine-gun fire. Assuming it was just another air raid on Zuq, they turned over and went to sleep again. The noise was all at the other side of the town and most of the bombs seemed to be falling on the wrecked ships in the harbour.

In his corner of the truck, Micklethwaite was looking miserable. He had developed a nasty case of the trots and kept having to disappear into the darkness with the spade. Fortunately, Clinch had a bottle of tablets which he carried around for just such an emergency.

'What are they?' Micklethwaite asked.

'I dunno,' Clinch said. 'And I don't want to. That way, if they kill you, I'm not responsible.'

Eventually they became aware of vehicles passing and the noise of engines and the excited chatter of men, but they were all tired and weren't sufficiently involved in army movements to care much. When they woke the following morning, the town seemed more empty than the previous evening and during a lull in the storm Rafferty saw a flight of Messerschmitts heading towards Cairo. He eyed them with a grave face and said nothing, but soon afterwards, seeing rolling clouds of dust to the east, he watched them for a long time before turning to Dampier.

'With respect, sir,' he said, 'I think the Italians are on the move.'

Dampier, who had been leaning on the side of the lorry drinking the first mug of tea of the day, came bolt upright at once.

'I've seen it before, sir,' Rafferty went on. 'Something's up. Where is everybody?'

True enough, the town appeared to be deserted by troops, though a few Arabs were still in residence. The white houses stood in pairs on the yellow cliffs above the harbour, like shoeboxes set at mathematical intervals, all alike and nearly all empty. Once there had been gardens and sheep and cows, but the sheep and cows had long since been eaten and the white houses were beginning to have a shabby look. On the edge of the town, where the road that ran along the coast entered, there was one of the triumphal arches that Mussolini liked to erect in his own honour. On one side of it was his virile slogan: *The Italian people and the Fascist people deserve to have the victory. Benito Mussolini*. On the other, in case the passers-by had failed to notice the first, there was another slogan: *A people that abandons the land deserves to be condemned to decadence. Benito Mussolini*. In paint some British soldier had written his reply: *And any nation that puts up with a pompous pill like Mussolini deserves all it gets. Arthur Farnall, RASC*.

Rafferty and Dampier stared around at the white buildings and the parched lawns. Something very odd had happened. The town was there all right but where were the British troops who were supposed to be garrisoning it?

Moving cautiously round the outskirts, they came across an empty British gun position. Nearby a group of vehicles kneeled forlornly on smashed front axles, one of them still sending up wisps of smoke from burning tyres. Around it were scattered scraps of uniform, and a pile of silver British petrol cans caught the sun. Because they were running short of fuel, it seemed a good idea to fill up from them. As usual, most of them were punctured and only half full.

Rafferty looked grim. 'I think we're in trouble, sir,' he announced. 'I think that somehow the front's moved further east in the night and we're behind it.'

Dampier looked alarmed. 'You mean our people have pulled back?'

Rafferty looked worried. 'I mean, sir, that I think Zuq's been evacuated.'

Even as he spoke, a line of lorries came roaring towards them from the desert through the thinning clouds of sand. The signs and numbers they carried looked unfamiliar and the leading vehicle had a flag flapping from its cabin roof, something the British army didn't usually go in for. Then, as the vehicles drew nearer, Rafferty recognized the red, white and green of the fluttering material.

'Howly Mother of God!' He snatched his cap off and, tossing it into the back of the lorry, knocked Dampier's off his head to the ground and stood on it. In his excitement his accent slipped back to his native Galway. ''Tis Italians they are, sorr!'

Dampier was just about to bolt when Rafferty grasped his arm. 'Stand still, sir,' he said. 'Put on your sunglasses and wave.'

Bareheaded, the badges on their shirts blurred by the coating of dust, they stood by their lorry, grinning like death's heads and waving as the Italians roared past. Their waves were answered but nobody took the trouble to stop and they could only assume the Italians were in too big a hurry.

'They think we're prisoners,' Dampier gasped as the last lorry passed.

'No, sir.' Rafferty shook his head. 'They're thinkin' we're Italians, and I reckon it might be a good idea if we hopped it. I don't fancy ending up in the bag.'

Climbing hurriedly into the vehicles, they swung them round and started heading eastwards again. Half an hour later they were obliged to stop once more. Ahead of them in the desert to the south through the rolling clouds of dust they could see a column of vehicles stretching right across their front.

'Italians, Mr Rafferty?' Dampier asked.

'That they are, sir. And a lot of 'em too. And their direction's east. Which, from our point of view, is the wrong one.'

At roughly the same time as Dampier's party was trying to get out of Zuq, the Desert Ratbags were hurtling along the coast road, trying to get in. Their audience was supposed to be waiting, and, directed through a narrow gap at the north end of the minefield east of Sofi, like Dampier's group, they had been stopped in their tracks by the storm. Bedding down in the lorry among their property baskets and flats and folded curtains, they had passed a disturbed night. There had been a lot of noise in the darkness and the sound of grinding gears but with the dawn they had got going again. By this time, however, though the visibility had improved, the sun was totally blotted out. Their lips were dry but, muffled against the flying sand and aware how late they were, they were in a hurry.

They were passing now through an area of pinky-red gravel with areas of stony ground where the going altered and the land grew uneven, with large plate-like stones jutting from the earth and flat pebbles rattling away from under the wheels. Here and there were patches of shrubs, dried out by the sun, uprooted clumps of it clattering away before the wind which blew with a parching dryness to leave

42

sand in the folds of their clothes and in the sweaty wrinkles of their faces.

'We can't let them down,' Clegg said with showbiz indestructibility. 'They said they'd fix up a stage for us. They'll play hell if we don't turn up.'

The lorry's engine had been giving trouble after the storm and they had had to stop for a while for the cursing Caccia to stick his head inside the bonnet to put it right. He was now trying hard to catch up on time.

'We can't be late either,' Morton said. 'We'd start with the audience hostile. The show'd die on us.'

'Name any theatre you like,' Clegg replied. 'I died there at some time in my career.'

Deciding to dress as they drove so they could go into the opening sketch as soon as they arrived, they fought to keep their scarves over their faces against the flying sand.

'It'll be a hell of a performance in this lot,' Clegg observed, scratching at the grit that had got under his shirt. 'Even Jones can't sing with his mouth full of sand.'

'They'll have rigged something up indoors,' Morton said. 'They'll have found a warehouse or something. There are a lot of old sheds near the harbour.'

After a while, they passed a couple of guns and a few groups of men. They were in khaki shorts and shirts like everyone else in the desert, and like the Ratbags were well coated with dust so that nobody in the lorry took any notice of them because they were busy getting everything ready to go straight into their first number.

'I think I'm going to have a headache.' Jones's nerves always seemed to take over when things went wrong, and his small, ugly, dirty face was gloomy. 'And I've forgotten me lines. What do we open with?'

'The song. Then the Eyetie sketch and "I've broken me bootlace". Caccia comes back with "Use spaghetti". Remember?'

Surrounded by dust, the lorry rolled past another group of soldiers. As Caccia slowed down, everybody stuck their heads out, Italian caps and all, to see where they were. The soldiers, their faces muffled against the sand, waved them past. A few minutes later, Jones looked at Clegg. He'd gone pale, Clegg noticed, and his headache seemed to have started because he was staring with such intensity he seemed paralysed.

He gestured nervously. 'That lot back there, man,' he muttered, looking at the uniform Clegg was wearing. 'They thought we were Italians.'

'Well,' Clegg said, 'that's what we're supposed to be, isn't it?'

'Why, aye, boy,' Jones agreed. 'But that lot weren't *English*, see?' His voice cracked as he expressed the opinion that had already occurred to Warrant Officer Rafferty. 'They were Italians! *Real* Italians!'

Part Two

1

The thought that had occurred to Jones the Song and Warrant Officer Rafferty had crossed Caccia's mind, too, because instead of slackening speed when the lorry reached the spot where they were supposed to put on their performance he simply kept going.

Nobody argued. Suddenly they were all too scared. The stage was there all right, in the open against the blank wall of a warehouse, built of ammunition boxes and facing rows of sandbags laid out to make tiers of seats. It might have been a good show, Clegg thought, because the wind was dying and somebody had actually taken the trouble to advertise it. A large handwritten notice had been attached to a door: *Desert Ratbags Concert Party*. The wind had torn the paper and it was flapping about in the fading gusts, strangely forlorn.

There were a lot of vehicles standing about and the divisional signs on them were none anybody had ever seen before. On one of them was painted an Italian fasces and on the side someone had scrawled *Egitto, Veniamo Qui*. The vehicles looked dusty and battered and, round them, in corners out of the wind, tired-looking men were eating from dixies and drinking from straw-covered bottles. They were dressed in a haphazard mixture of khaki and grey-green, as if shortages had forced them to wear whatever they could lay their hands on. On their heads were round stubby helmets adorned by a spherical insignia and on their collars a variety of coloured flashes. A few wore narrow-brimmed felt hats or sun helmets with feathers, and they all seemed to be armed to the teeth.

As the men in the back of the lorry stared at them one of the Italians waved and pointed towards the east. Clegg waved back automatically.

'*Quella via,*' the Italian shouted.

Speechlessly, Clegg nodded and forced a grin. 'What's he say?' he asked.

'He says,' Morton translated, as if he were gagging for need of a drink, 'that we're going the wrong way.'

'I wish to Christ we were.'

As they reached the other side of the town, Caccia swung the vehicle off the road into a grove of trees. Through the drifting clouds of dust they could see the sea and a few corrugated-iron sheds in the distance, but the Italians seemed to be sticking to the built-up areas of the town and there was no one near them. Still shocked, Clegg heard the driver's door slam, and Caccia's face appeared at the tailgate of the lorry.

'Am I off my onion?' he asked in a shocked voice. 'Or were those buggers Italian?'

'That's what I said, boyo,' Jones insisted shrilly. 'They *were* Italians!'

'Well, if they are, where the bloody hell are we?'

'I'll tell you where we are, bach,' Jones said. 'We're behind the Italian lines. Our lot have moved back, see, and left us here on our own. That's what all that noise was last night.'

They had all scrambled out by this time and were standing in the lee of the lorry out of the flying grit.

'Zuq was full of our fellers a week ago,' Clegg pointed out.

'Well, it isn't now,' Caccia said. 'I reckon we're proper in the dripping.'

'Something's gone wrong,' Jones wailed, his whole shabby shape expressing woe.

Caccia turned on him angrily. 'Give over, you miserable

48

Welsh gnome,' he snarled. 'Can't you think of anything else to say?'

Jones backed away, his Italian forage cap low over his eyes, his greasy hair sticking out beneath it in spikes. Caccia, spruce, clean and polished as any good lady's man should be, was always bullying him for his complaints and his general grubbiness. 'My headache's getting worse,' he said.

'The best thing we can do,' Morton decided, 'is get straight back in the lorry, turn her round and push off.'

'And probably get shot for our trouble,' Clegg pointed out. '*I* reckon, comrades and boon companions, that the best thing is to stay where we are until dark, *then* head back. It'll be a damn sight safer. If they can't see you, they can't shoot you.'

There was a lot of arguing about whose fault it was but they all knew it was really only the back and forth, the to and fro of the desert war, that was the reason for their plight. It was like fighting a sea war on sand, with lorries instead of ships. You could go in any direction you wanted except up or down and, because the front line wasn't a set of trenches running from the sea down into Central Africa but just a series of fortified outposts where soldiers sat by their lorries and tanks and watched and waited and bit their nails, it wasn't difficult for any aggressive group to circle another and come up behind. That, it seemed, was what had happened to the outfit they were supposed to be playing to. The Italians had put them in the bag.

'All the same' – the thought seemed to worry Morton – 'it's funny we didn't hear about it before we set off.'

'These Eyeties are treacherous bastards,' Caccia said.

'Look who's talking.' Jones was itching to get his own back and he gave a mock fascist salute. 'Up the *inglesi* and fuck Winston-a Churchill.'

'That bloody Italian uniform's gone to your head,' Caccia snarled.

'I'm glad I was wearing mine all the same,' Morton

pointed out. 'Otherwise, they'd probably have turned a machine-gun on us.'

Caccia gave a sudden grin. 'Well, you can't have it all ways,' he said. 'If they catch you like that, all done up like rabbit stew, they'll stick you in front of a firing squad instead and shoot you as a spy.'

Morton's jaw dropped and he wrenched off the German jacket and cap he was wearing and tossed them into the back of the lorry. As he turned, visibly shaken, the others also started wrenching at their headgear until they all stood bareheaded in shirts and shorts, staring at each other and wondering what to do.

'Why don't we,' Morton said after a moment or two, 'stick the lorry among those ruined sheds and wait until dark?'

'We'll never get away with it,' Jones wailed. 'They'll spot us at once, boy.'

'I wonder if they would,' Clegg said slowly. 'Once when we gave a show at a camp near Richmond, we were doing a sketch about two German officers and, just before it started, two of us strolled out, German uniforms and all, to buy some fags. The guard saluted us.'

Through the thinning clouds of dust, they headed the lorry back on to the road and round to the corrugated-iron sheds near the harbour. Nobody stopped them. Nobody even looked twice at them. Most of the soldiers they saw, wearing only shorts and shirts as they were, were keeping their heads down against the flying sand, while the Arabs were muffled to the eyebrows in their robes. Near the sea the bombing had reduced the area to heaps of shattered walls, splintered wood and twisted iron, and Caccia drove the lorry into a half-collapsed shed. It effectively hid them from sight and they clambered down and stood in a group again, wondering what the hell to do next.

'I think we should sit on our bums here until we can take off,' Morton suggested. 'But not *too* long.' He indicated the cigarette ends that lay under the surrounding trees, the bare patches of oily ground, the marks of tyres and the discarded British petrol cans. 'By the look of it, this is a favourite camping ground for motorized troops and when the Eyeties take over properly there'll probably be a lot of 'em round here. We'll make a dash for it after dark.'

'Oh, will we?' Caccia snorted. 'We'd catch a right old cold if we ran on to mines. Especially me in the driver's cab. We'll do it in daylight. Dusk perhaps. We might make it at dusk.'

'Suppose we run into a patrol?' Clegg asked.

'We could wear the Italian hats and things,' Morton said. 'I speak good Italian.'

'Oh, do you?' Jones was clearly going through one of his periods of nervous tension. 'Perfect, is it, then?'

'Yes, you stupid little man!' Morton snapped. 'I've spoken it all my life.'

'So how does that bloody help us?'

Morton stared at Jones as if he had crawled out from under a stone. Sometimes he looked as if he had. 'We have Caccia, he pointed out. 'He speaks Italian because his family speak Italian. Cleggy has a few words. Even you, you little Welsh twit, can speak the few phrases we use in the sketches.' Morton gestured, suddenly in control of the situation. 'That makes two who speak it well and two who can get by with a few words they've picked up. *Che bel tempo*. What lovely weather. *Fa freddo*. *Fa caldo*. It's cold. It's hot. We ought to be able to bluff our way past with that. Jonesy could always have a go at "*Santa Lucia*". Surely that would convince them.'

'In a Bedford lorry?'

'The war's been going on long enough out here for there to be a lot of each on either side.'

'We've got British div. numbers,' Caccia pointed out. 'They stick out like the Rock of Ages in a fog.'

'Then let's get an *Italian* div. sign and you can screw it on over the one we've got.'

51

For the first time they began to discern a glimmer of hope. 'Think we can do it?' Clegg asked.

'You saw the lorries back there,' Morton said. 'What's to stop us going out after dark and helping ourselves?'

'And then?'

'Then we set off east. A bunch of Italians led by a German officer.'

'You?'

'My German's as good as my Italian.'

'They told you so in Berlin, I suppose?'

'No. Innsbruck and Munich.'

Clegg managed a grin. 'Well, that makes everything all right, doesn't it? Lancelot Hugh Morton's going to save us and win himself a Victoria Cross.'

'Boy,' Caccia said. 'What it is to have courage on our side!'

Morton looked at them stonily but they knew it was an idea and they accepted that at least they'd be doing something. They'd been running simply because nobody had thought of shouting 'Stop'. Now that Morton had offered them a plan – even if, as they suspected, it was a bloody awful plan – it was better than nothing. The desert was big and easy to hide in and, until they were forced to give up, nobody fancied ending up behind barbed wire.

Hatless and with his uniform devoid of British insignia, Warrant Officer Rafferty stood in the doorway of the wrecked warehouse where they'd hidden their vehicles, and peered out into the growing darkness.

Even as they had discovered their dilemma and decided to disappear southwards into the desert, another column of trucks and light tanks had appeared up the hill and an Italian military policeman on a motorbike had waved them to get out of the way into the town.

'I'm thinkin', sir,' Rafferty had murmured under his breath to Dampier, 'that we'd better do as he says.'

Dampier had looked startled. 'Go into the town?'

'We don't seem to have much option, sir. If we go the other way someone will want to know why. There are plenty of ruins in Zuq, so we'll collar one of the old waehouses and use it to do somethin' to disguise ourselves so we can slip out again after dark.'

It hadn't been difficult to find a shed near the harbour that had been wrecked by a bomb. It was built of corrugated iron, had a distinctly drunken look about it and was minus one end. To hide their nationality they had parked the vehicles stern-outwards and carefully draped blankets across the tailgates to hide the British army signs until they could do something to remove them. There was room for no other vehicle and nobody could get past.

Nobody came near them, although throughout the evening Italian vehicles in columns roared into the town towards the vehicle park at the old fort, and in the darkness they heard the squeak of brakes, the sound of excited laughter and the clank of chains as tailgates were dropped and men climbed out. By this time the wind was fading.

'Got any ideas, Mr Rafferty?' Dampier asked.

'We can try going south, sir. That's what we did when we were cut off in 1940. Tomorrow night, perhaps. Unfortunately, we don't have much food or water. Come to that, not much petrol either.'

Inevitably Clutterbuck set up a wail. 'What about me?' he said. 'If I'd stayed with 38 Light Aid Duties, I'd 'ave been all right. Dow and Raye'll be waitin' for me, I bet.'

'I bet they won't,' Dampier snapped. 'They'll have heard by now that the Italians are on the move and, if they're anything like you, they'll stay where it's safe.'

As they became silent again, they grew aware of movement all round them in the dark. They heard engines and brakes again, the murmur of voices and once a sharp tenor laugh that didn't sound like a British laugh. Then they heard the clatter of dixies, and the clink of bottles, and someone shouted.

'*Guido, i freni sono guasti!*'

53

There was a laugh. '*Che fortuna. C'è un garage qui vicino.*'

'Italians,' Dampier murmured. 'What are they saying?'

'Something about his brakes not working,' Rafferty said. 'The other feller suggested he should take it to a garage. My Italian's not very good.'

'It must be a whole column, Mr Rafferty. What should we do? Pity we can't do them some damage.'

'Much better to clear off,' Clutterbuck whined.

Rafferty was silent, listening, then he stared into the darkness again, his whole body alert. He looked like a terrier at a rathole.

'What's on your mind, Mr Rafferty?' Dampier demanded. 'Something obviously is.'

'Thought I might just scout round to see what's goin' on, sir. Might pick up some information we could take back.'

Dampier stared at him. The urge actually to see the enemy, something which had been plaguing him since the war had started, got the better of him.

'Two heads are better than one,' he said. 'I'll come with you. I'm an old man and nobody will miss me if anything goes wrong.'

Leaving Clinch and Micklethwaite to make sure Clutterbuck didn't bolt, they moved off into the darkness, bent double more out of instinct than necessity because it was quite dark. The last of the wind was lifting the sand in little whorls and dragging trails of it across the surface of the road. The hissing of the grit was surprisingly loud now that they were silent, and every now and then they heard the clatter of a parched bush, uprooted by the wind, the creak of branches and the rattling of the dried fronds of the palms. Almost before they realized it, they were blundering into the back of a lorry. The Italian crew, eating their evening meal with the others in some shelter they'd found nearby out of the wind, were nowhere in sight.

'The buggers sound cheerful,' Dampier said resentfully.

'So they should be, sorr. They've kicked us out of Zuq.'

Dampier studied the lorry. 'Can we steal it, Mr Rafferty?'

54

Rafferty shook his head. 'No keys, sir.'

'We could short-circuit the ignition.'

'Make too much noise, sir. They'd hear us start up.' Rafferty's teeth gleamed in the darkness as he smiled. 'Much better to do a bit of damage and syphon the petrol out. There's an empty can in here with a tool kit, complete with hammer and screwdriver.'

Reaching into the darkness, he produced the can, clanking it softly against the door as he lifted it out with the hammer and screwdriver, then he moved quietly round the vehicle until he found the petrol tank.

Placing the point of the screwdriver against the tank, he gave the handle a sharp whack with the hammer. The chattering of the Italians, the rattling of the palm fronds and the moving bundles of brushwood drowned the sound. Unscrewing the petrol cap, Rafferty threw it away and they stood for a while in the dark, listening to the petrol running into the can from the hole they'd made.

'That ought to surprise them when they come to drive it away,' Dampier murmured delightedly as Rafferty screwed the cap on the full can. 'Think we could hole another, Mr Rafferty? So they can't chase us.'

'Perhaps more than one, sir. The more the merrier, because the Eyeties make a point of never chasing anyone unless they outnumber 'em five hundred to one.'

Synchronizing their activity with the outbursts of laughter from where the Italians were eating in a group just out of sight among the trees, they managed to puncture three more tanks, lift a couple of rifles and remove the valves from several tyres. The wind and the rattling of dried shrubs drowned the small sounds they made.

'Terrible careless, thim Eyetalians, sorr,' Rafferty observed.

Moving towards the tail of the stationary column, Dampier was just beginning to enjoy himself when Rafferty laid a hand on his arm and the two of them sank to the sand. Just ahead they became aware of someone moving and the faint clink of tools. There was no sign of a light.

'Repairs?' Dampier said. 'In the dark?'

Then they heard a quiet voice in the shadows. 'You've dropped the spanner, you silly sod!'

There was no mistaking the Englishness of it and Rafferty lifted his head. Glancing at Dampier, he looked again and raised himself slightly.

'Who's there?' he called softly.

There was an abrupt silence, then the voice spoke again, awed, scared and shaken. 'Jesus Christ!' it said.

Rafferty's teeth showed in the darkness as he grinned. 'I dare bet it's not,' he said. 'He trained as a carpenter not a motor mechanic, and it wasn't in *this* desert He did His forty days and forty nights.'

2

There were three men wearing Italian caps and carrying screwdrivers and spanners, and all looking scared.

'Who in God's name are you?' Dampier whispered.

'Sergeant Clegg,' one of the shadowy figures said. 'Corporal Morton. Driver Caccia.'

'What the hell are you doing here?'

'Come to that,' Clegg said. 'What are you?'

'Just answer the bloody question!'

There was a clipped authoritative note in the words and Clegg decided it might be as well to concede the initiative.

'We were helping ourselves to one of the Eyeties' number plates. We were going to stick it on our own lorry. We were cut off and thought it would help us get away. Are you cut off, too?'

'What do you think, man?' Dampier snapped.

Clegg ignored the rebuke. 'We've seen the Italians using captured British lorries,' he said. 'And Morton here – that is, Corporal Morton – speaks the lingo, and he stuck some Italian words on ours to make it look Italian. You know, that thing they paint on walls.'

'*Combattere, obbedire, vincere*,' Morton said. 'We thought an Italian sign might help a bit.'

'Have you still got the paint?' Dampier asked.

'Which paint?'

'The paint you used to write the words on your lorry. Perhaps we could use it on ours.'

Clegg glanced at the other two. 'It wasn't paint. Well, not that sort of paint. It was greasepaint. Black. No. 12.'

'Greasepaint?' Dampier looked at Rafferty. 'Who in God's name are you?'

'We're a concert party.'

'A what, for God's sake?'

'A concert party. Who're you?'

Rafferty decided it was time to identify themselves. 'This is Colonel Dampier,' he said. 'Inspector of Equipment to the Eighth Army. I'm Warrant Officer Rafferty.'

Dampier still seemed startled to be meeting anything so bizarre as a concert party behind the Italian lines. 'Not fighting troops then?' he said. Hearing the quality of contempt in his voice, it crossed Clegg's mind that an Inspector of Equipment and his unit were hardly the Brigade of Guards either. 'They're not going to be a lot of help, Mr Rafferty.'

'You might be surprised,' Morton said coolly. 'We've got some Italian uniforms.'

Dampier cranked his head round slowly. 'You've got *what*?'

'Italian uniforms,' Clegg said. 'Well – bits of uniforms. We used them in a sketch about this German officer and these Eyetie soldiers who – '

Dampier interrupted sharply. 'Where are the rest of your people?'

'There's only one more.'

'Only one?' It had been in Dampier's mind that if the concert party were big enough and had had any training at all they might be encouraged to attempt to overwhelm any opposition they met.

'We're not the cast from Covent Garden Opera House,' Morton said stiffly. 'There are four of us.'

'Songs and sketches,' Clegg added. 'To amuse the troops. Keep it simple, the general said. Jones the Song – that is, Private Jones – he's our tenor. He's the only other one.

He's back there with the lorry under the trees. Biting his nails, I expect, and having a headache.'

Dampier wasn't sure whether to accept the Ratbags as a welcome addition to his party or, because they were likely to be more hindrance than help, simply abandon them to their fate; it was Rafferty who made the decision.

'I think we'd better join forces, don't you, sir?'

Dampier ummed and aahed a bit, knowing full well it was his duty to collect any odds and sods that had been left lying around, but none too willing to jeopardize the chances of his own group.

'Go and collect this chap of yours,' he conceded in the end. 'We'll wait here. Think you can find your way back?'

Clegg soon returned with the lorry and Jones, who was scared out of his wits by his stay alone. They were just on the point of returning to where Dampier's vehicles were waiting when Rafferty lifted his head.

'Hold on, sir,' he said.

Over the whisperings of the wind and the clattering of the dry bushes, they heard the murmur of engines.

'Aeroplanes, sir.'

'Ours?'

'They don't sound like theirs, sir. It's the RAF. They're after the harbour.'

The sound grew louder and there were shouts from behind them as the Italians were also alerted to the approaching aircraft; then, seconds after an air-raid siren went, they heard the first of the bombs coming down.

'Jesus, this is a proper old game, played slow!' Caccia complained as they bolted for a nearby drainage ditch. 'Bombed by our own bloody side!'

Fortunately, none of the bombs came near, but the flashes lit up the sky and they could feel the thump of the explosives, as if through the veins and bones of the earth. There was a great deal of shouting from among the parked lorries nearby and the sound of engines starting, then there was a tremendous flare of flame, a huge blossoming flower of red edged with black smoke that spoke of petrol going up. Rafferty's teeth showed in a grin.

'Somebody t'rew a cigarette down where we punctured their petrol tanks, sir,' he said cheerfully.

Almost immediately, there were two more flares of red, as if sparks from the first explosive rush of flame had ignited a second and a third pool of petrol. In the glare they could see the square silhouetted shapes of lorries and the figures of running men. A few of the vehicles were moving off now but the flames had attracted the aircraft overhead and the second and third waves were aiming at them as they came in. Bombs whistled down among the vehicles and they saw more of them explode.

The shouts grew more alarmed and the lorries that were on the move began to lurch away more quickly. Shouting men – obviously the crews of the lost vehicles – were running after them. One of them was carrying a heavy bundle on his shoulder which they saw him toss aside to run faster. Eventually the whole lot of them had disappeared, leaving only the burning vehicles and a few scattered items of dropped equipment.

The noise of aeroplane engines died and there was nothing left except the flickering flames. As they watched, a fire engine, complete with a mixed Arab and civilian Italian crew, arrived. They stood watching the flames, shouting at each other and wondering what to do, then an army lorry appeared and the crew started to douse the flames with sand and a foam appliance. Eventually it was dark again.

'It's time we were away from here,' Dampier whispered.

'Perhaps 'twould be a good idea first, sir,' Rafferty suggested gently, 'to see what we could pick up.'

'Pick up? Why?'

'Sure, sir, we'll not get away in daylight. We've got nearly twenty-four hours to kill. So we might as well make ourselves look like part of the scenery.'

Dampier gave him a quick look, then he swung round on Clegg, his mind working quickly.

'Those Italian uniforms you said you had,' he said.

'Yes, sir. We used them in a sketch.' Clegg was still a little nervous of Dampier, who seemed bad-tempered and more than a little hostile. 'There was this German officer and these Italian soldiers – '

'We'll discuss that later,' Dampier snapped. 'In the meantime, let's have the uniforms.'

Clegg looked startled. 'Yes, sir. I'll dig 'em out.'

'And let's have this Corporal Morton, who speaks Italian, over here.'

Morton, cool, sardonic and indifferent to rank, appeared in front of Dampier.

'You speak Italian?' Dampier asked.

'Yes.' Morton was never one to waste 'sirs' on officers. His degree was inclined to make him think he was one up on them and they, like schoolboys, ought to address *him* as 'sir'. 'Also German.'

'Good at it?'

'Perfect.'

Dampier was conscious of Morton's indifference but he didn't push the matter at that moment.

'How perfect?' he asked.

'Perfect type of perfect. I was brought up in Switzerland near the Italian border and spent two post-graduate years at the University of Florence. I lived with Italian students and worked for three years in Naples. I shared rooms with a Count Barda and often visited his home. His favourite trick was to introduce me to fascist officials and, when I said something unpleasant about Mussolini and they were on the point of arresting me, to point out that I was British so they couldn't do much about it.'

Dampier was impressed. He looked at Rafferty. 'Could you go with Mr Rafferty here and scout round those wrecked lorries to see if there's anything we can use to help us escape?'

Morton looked startled. 'I'm not a fighting soldier, sir.'

Dampier glared. 'In 1918 when the Germans broke through on the Somme front,' he pointed out testily, 'cooks, butchers, clerks and mechanics found themselves in the line. Doubtless, if they were there, also actors. As they did at Dunkirk. This time, it seems the *Italians* have broken through.'

Morton considered. 'Oh,' he said. 'Very well. I'll have a go.'

'Sir,' Rafferty prompted.

Morton studied the warrant officer coolly. 'Sir,' he agreed reluctantly.

'Thank you,' Dampier said

Morton hadn't moved. 'For what it's worth – sir – ' he continued, 'we also have Driver Caccia who speaks Italian.'

In the end it was decided that Morton, Clegg and Caccia should accompany Rafferty and pick up anything the warrant officer thought worthwhile, and that they should go immediately while the Italians were still shaken by the air raid.

While the others disappeared into the trees, where Dampier's vehicles were hidden by the ruined warehouse, the salvage party headed for the burned-out lorries. The owners had withdrawn with their column to the safety of the desert but it was obvious they would more than likely very soon be back. Thin columns of smoke were still rising into the sky and, scattered around, showing the haste with which the Italians had disappeared, were abandoned dixies, a rifle, a pouch containing half a dozen of the light percussion grenades of Japanese manufacture that the Italians used, items of equipment such as belts and side packs, even a few scraps of clothing – two or three jackets, one an Italian sublieutenant's and one a sergeant's, an overcoat, two caps, three steel helmets – a few straw-covered chianti bottles and several undamaged cans of petrol and water.

There was also a sheaf of letters, which they found fluttering in the breeze among the bushes, a folder of orders and an inventory of supplies, signed, sealed and delivered, with the name of the man who appeared to be the quarter-master general at Derna, one Commandante de Brigata Ruggiero Olivaro, as well as a supply of empty requisition and inventory forms which were clearly about to be filled in. Obviously the commander of the Italian column had just received new equipment or supplies and was about to receive more and had not yet done his paperwork. Outwardly none of them seemed to be of much value and Clegg was about to toss them aside when Morton snatched them from him and handed them to Rafferty.

'Italian army forms D3801 and C2947, sir,' he pointed out. 'Inventories and requisition forms. Very convincing if anybody asks to see our papers.'

Rafferty grinned. Having been in the army all his adult life and for a great deal of it concerned with stores, he always felt that official forms – especially signed ones – were worth their weight in gold. If you possessed something you weren't supposed to possess, sneaked on the end of a signed list it at once became official, and he immediately appreci-ated what Morton was getting at.

'Good bhoy,' he said. 'How did you know what they were?'

'Used to be in Intelligence, sir. It was one of my jobs to go through these things.'

In addition there was an Italian flag and a picture of the Italian king, Victor Emmanuel.

'Looks like a startled ferret,' Clegg observed critically. 'We only want one of Mussolini and we're Italian patriots.'

They had just thrown the last of what they'd found into a heap and were unscrewing insignia from the remains of the shattered lorries when a small scout car drew up. An Italian sergeant climbed out.

'*Da dove viene?*' he asked.

Morton jabbered back at him. He seemed satisfied and gestured at the burning remains of the lorries before jabb-ering again at Morton.

Morton shrugged. '*È la guerra!*'

The sergeant stared round him, his large dark eyes sad, then he spoke again. Rafferty listened quietly. The only word he could pick out was 'Mussolini'.

Morton and the sergeant talked a little more, then the sergeant climbed back into the scout car, swung round and drove away.

'What did he want?' Rafferty asked.

'He wanted to know where we'd come from and who we were. I told him we were a recovery group sent to salvage what we could.'

'Good, good.' Rafferty nodded approvingly. 'What else?'

'He said in effect that it was a bloody mess and I said, "*C'est la guerre.*" It's an opinion most soldiers seem to hold. Then he went on a bit about Mussolini sitting on his fat backside in Rome and leaving people like him to fight the war he'd started. I agreed, he seemed very satisfied, and we parted the best of friends.'

'Good bhoy. Good bhoy.'

Even Morton seemed pleased at Rafferty's approval.

'Did he say what was going on?'

Morton's mouth moved in his cold smile. 'I got the impression that the Italian generals have been growing a bit fed up with the way the Germans have been pushing them around and wanted to have an advance of their own. The Germans didn't think they were capable so the Italians decided to show what they could do and the Germans agreed to back them up if they managed to break through. I gathered the troops themselves weren't quite as keen as the generals but that they pushed our lot out of Zuq, nevertheless.'

'Did he say when the column was coming back?'

'They aren't. He said they were on the move eastwards after our lot.'

'Right, boy, let's get as many of these signs as we can, then we'll bring up the three-tonner and mebbe have a sniff around to see what we can find.'

With daylight, the storm had gone and the air was sweet and the sky serene in a mass of gold and vermilion clouds. The inhabitants of the town, slipping back in with the Italian lorries from the desert, had been badly shaken by the air raid and near the little harbour a tremendous argument was going on. An ammunition ship was on fire and the ammunition was smouldering while everybody discussed whether they should move it out or not. Those who lived and worked nearby were eager to see the back of it while those who didn't couldn't have cared less.

By this time scattered lorries, in ones and twos and in groups, were moving eastwards from the lorry park near the fort on to the road that ran through the town. None of the occupants looked twice at the four men in Italian jackets and caps standing by the Bedford lorry bearing a scorched red and green palm tree insignia and the words *Combattere, Obbedire, Vincere* on the side.

The officer's jacket they had picked up had had a bundle of Italian banknotes in the pocket and, while they hadn't the courage to use the money to buy anything, they were able to fill up the watercans they had found at a standpipe in the street before heading back to the warehouse where the others waited.

In the courtyard of a wrecked building the Italians had erected a cookhouse. Fires were burning and several large iron cooking pots were simmering, and men with dixies were waiting in a queue. The smell of cooking meat and tomatoes reminded them how hungry they were. A few of the Italians waved and shouted and vehicles passed, towing guns, but nobody stopped them.

When they reached the ruined warehouse Dampier had been busy. He had taken one of the flats from the Ratbags' equipment and erected it. On it were scratched some of the few Italian words Dampier knew – *64 Unito di Riparazione*.

'Thought I might as well make us look as if we belonged here,' he said proudly.

Stuffing the documents they had salvaged into his already

bulging briefcase, Rafferty smiled approvingly but Morton gave it a cold look.

'It's *Unità*,' he said. 'Not *Unito*.'

With the tools and equipment that Clutterbuck and his cronies had been pretending to use, Dampier had set up a repair unit of sorts to go with the sign. A sullen Clutterbuck had lifted the bonnet of Dampier's car and had his head in the engine space.

Dampier explained. 'I thought some show of activity might put off anybody who came our way. After all, if the British army has vehicle depots in the desert, surely the Italians do, too. It seems to me, Mr Rafferty, that we have certain advantages that other units might lack. Such as two men who speak excellent Italian, a set of Italian tools, which, though it might not pass muster at an inspection, will do for the time being, two mechanics, one of them one of the Italian speakers; and one – Clutterbuck – who's skilled with Italian Lancias and, I might add, possesses certain other skills, such as deluding the authorities. In addition, we possess three Italian uniforms.'

'More now,' Rafferty smiled. 'We picked up two more jackets and several caps.'

Dampier nodded, looking like Napoleon outlining the plan for Waterloo to his marshals. 'Disadvantages: we seem to be totally surrounded by enemy troops. But I've done my best to make us look like a functioning Italian unit so no one will bother us and we can make plans to disappear as soon as we get the chance.' He looked round at the others in his pompous military fashion. 'When we move, the staff car will lead, the heavy vehicles following. I'd better wear the Italian officer's jacket and cap, I suppose.'

'No, sir.' Morton's voice jerked their heads round. 'Not you. *Me!*'

Dampier stared for a moment. 'What do you mean, you?'

'Can you speak Italian – sir?' Morton's look had become sardonic.

'Dammit – !'

'I may be only a corporal in the British army – sir' – Morton was obviously enjoying himself – 'but in the Italian army, I would *have* to be the officer. Because *I* speak the language. If we're addressed by an Italian officer it wouldn't be a corporal who would answer him. It would be the officer.'

'Good God!' This was something that hadn't occurred to Dampier.

'We can fit us all out now either with an Italian cap or a helmet. That ought to be enough to have us accepted at first glance as Italians. If anyone comes, those of us who can't speak Italian would be wise to remain in the background and leave the talking to those who can: Me. And Caccia.'

'Who gives the orders then?' Dampier asked.

'Oh, I do, sir.' Morton was smiling and self-confident. 'However, it would be necessary to consult with you and Mr Rafferty, naturally. It might be wise, in that case, if Caccia wore a sergeant's stripes and you wore a private's uniform because, as I've discovered from experience, private soldiers are seen and not heard.'

Dampier went red but Rafferty was smiling. 'The boy's got a point, sir,' he said. 'Mebbe, sir' – Rafferty's eyes were twinkling – 'we could arrange for you to be the general dogsbody. Just for the twenty-four hours till we leave, of course. Fillin' in the forms and bringin' in the refreshments an' runnin' the errands.'

'Filling in the – bringing in – Good God!'

'That way, sir, you'd always be handy for a little whispered consultation.' Rafferty seemed to be enjoying the joke enormously and he turned to Morton. 'Would that be what you had in mind, boy?'

'That's it exactly, sir.' Morton seemed to have taken a liking to the Irishman.

'For the rest of the uniform, sir,' he went on, 'well, everybody wears little else but shorts and shirts – even the other side's shorts and shirts occasionally, and sometimes

67

not even as much as that. The only thing that's different is headgear and we have plenty of that. We've got a German officer's cap and jacket in the props basket so, if the Italians come, we can be Germans. As I discovered in Intelligence, the Italians are afraid of the Germans and never ask them too many questions. But if the Germans come, we can be Italians who don't understand the German language. It should cover a lot of mistakes.'

Rafferty clearly approved but Dampier looked startled.

'Good God,' he said again as Morton stalked away. It was clear he regarded with some alarm the fact that his whole world, the whole military set-up, was being inverted, with the lowest form of animal life suddenly promoted to the top and the top levels demoted to the bottom. It was worse than a mutiny.

3

Within minutes they had been transformed into Italians in Italian caps or helmets, with Morton in the officer's jacket looking like the juvenile lead in a musical comedy. The *mostrine* – the coloured flashes on the collars of the jackets which indicated which regiment the owners belonged to – were all different but that provided no problem; they'd noticed that as often as not these were lacking anyway, because the supply situation from Italy was so bad they couldn't be obtained, and half the Italians did without them.

Caccia jerked his jacket straight, pleased, like any good ladies' man, with the fit. 'How do I look?'

'Like Pinocchio,' Clegg said.

Caccia stared down at the three red stripes on the arm of the grey-green jacket. '*I* reckon I look like two of cheese,' he said. 'Why do I have to be the sergeant?'

Morton looked at him coldly. 'Because you're a sergeant type,' he said.

'And you're not, I suppose?'

'The Italians are particular whom they commission in their army. They like them to look the part. You look like an Italian grocery assistant.'

Caccia looked up. 'That's what I was.'

'Exactly. And that's why you don't look like an Italian officer. They give stripes to grocery-shop managers but never commissions. They're more particular than our lot.'

There was one overcoat – the Italians always seemed to wear overcoats even when the sun was at its hottest – so they gave it to Jones. He was small and looked swamped in it but his scruffy appearance bore a fair resemblance to some of the Italian soldiers they'd seen and the oversize coat completed the picture.

'You could turn round in that without it moving,' Clegg said.

They were a strange-looking lot. Only Morton seemed at all smart. Because he was tall and slim, the officer's jacket fitted him as if it had been made for him, but the rest of the jackets and hats were mostly on the small side.

Their boots were dusty but somehow it added to the disguise because the Italian soldiers on the whole were a pretty careless lot and mostly wore their cheaply-made uniforms and board-hard overcoats as if they were tramps. In the desert everybody looked much the same, anyway, and for everyone – Germans, Italians, British, Free French, Australians, New Zealanders, Indians, South Africans, Poles – in summer the dress was normally never more than shirts and shorts, the shorts worn according to the military fashion of the country which issued them; the British ones were as wide as and almost as long as Oxford bags, to let what breeze there was blow where it would be most useful, the South Africans short enough to be almost indecent. The only thing that varied were hats, badges and boots, though the Italian officers enjoyed their plethora of badges and buttons rather more than most. At the other end of the scale, Australian officers were quite content to have their badges of rank drawn with a blue pencil on their naked shoulders.

'It might,' Morton suggested to Rafferty, 'be a good idea if we don't shave too often. The Italians don't go in for it much.'

Rafferty smiled. 'I hope you can convince the colonel,' he said.

To Dampier it was a strange feeling to wear a jacket with no insignia on his shoulder. When he'd joined the army in

1914, he'd been granted a commission at once because of the school he'd attended, so that there had never been a day in uniform when he hadn't had the advantages and privileges of an officer, and it seemed odd suddenly to be shorn of them.

'It's like being retired,' he admitted to Rafferty.

'Arrah, sir, yourself'll soon get used to it,' Rafferty smiled.

'It's my duty, if possible,' Dampier reminded him tartly, 'to get these chaps back to the British lines.'

'Then I'm thinkin', sir, 'twould be best to do as the officer says.'

Dampier gave him a suspicious look.

Later in the day, he drew Morton to one side and suggested he might give him a few tips on how to conduct himself.

Morton was casual. 'Oh, I don't think that will be necessary, thank you,' he said. 'It's really just a question of behaviour, isn't it? A gentleman's a gentleman whether he's wearing brass on his shoulder or not.'

Dampier glared. 'I was thinking of *military* behaviour.'

'Oh, that's all right, too. I've been in the army long enough now to know how officers behave. Some of them, I've often thought, might have profited by a lesson or two in good manners.'

As he stalked away, Dampier stared after him with his jaw hanging open. He turned to see Rafferty watching him.

'That damned man's getting ideas too big for his head, Mr Rafferty,' he said.

There were now two Bedford three-tonners, two fifteen-hundredweight trucks and Dampier's Humber. They were all dusty and, with the exception of the Humber which, being a staff car, was deemed to need a measure of dignity, were all plastered with the enthusiastic slogans the Italians enjoyed seeing – the usual *Combattere, Obbedire, Vincere*, and a few others that Morton had thought up: *Evviva*

Mussolini; *Avanti*; *In Viaggio per Londra*; and *Attenti, Inglesi! Veniamo Qui!*

They had attached the Italian flag to the front of the Humber so that it fluttered red, white and green in the wind, and they started off cheerfully enough in the late evening. Rafferty, his sleeves devoid of badges, led in Dampier's car, with Morton alongside him and Dampier, to his disgust, sitting in the back among the equipment. Caccia brought up the rear in the Ratbags' Bedford in case anybody came up from behind, while the rest were stuffed in between. Their progress south-east from Zuq went quite unhindered until at dusk they ran into units of German field police strung across their route. As they stopped, Morton climbed out, marched forward and spoke quickly in German. The German officer who answered him gestured towards the east. *'Etwas gehts los im Osten,'* he said.

Morton responded in the same language and there was a brief discussion before he returned to the car to inform Dampier and Rafferty what had been said. 'We'll not get past here,' he pointed out quietly. 'Things are happening towards the east and they're here to mark the junction of the Italian and German divisions. I think we should swop one or two of our vehicles at the first opportunity because he was a bit suspicious at seeing them all British. I told him we were a recovery unit and had picked them all up after they'd been abandoned.'

He climbed into his seat, still talking quietly. 'He also said we should be heading north and seemed at first to suspect we were trying to desert because we were too far forward. I told him our compass was kaput and he seemed satisfied.'

Gesturing with his arm for the benefit of the German, he led the little convoy north until they had swung over a ridge of dunes, when they promptly turned south once more. Almost immediately they ran into the German field police again. A carbide lamp appeared in front of them, swinging to indicate they should stop.

There was a long exchange between Morton and a German sergeant before they were turned back again. Rafferty decided it *might* be safer to head north for a while, after all, if only to get away from the suspicious Germans and back within the sphere of influence of the more easy-going Italians, who were always short of transport and less likely to question the origin of their vehicles. It was as well they did, because five minutes later a German *kübelwagen* came tearing up behind them, the German sergeant waving them further westwards.

'This is a bloody well-organized battle,' Clegg observed.

To the east the sky was filled with smoke from burning lorries to show where the fighting was going on and hundreds of vehicles had ploughed deep ruts in the soft sand. When they stopped and the engines were silent, they could hear the thump and rumble of gunfire.

Eventually they tried to edge southwards again but once more they ran into the German field police and were forced to head north again. They were all tired and dusty now, all on edge and nervy, and wondering just when some German field police sergeant would examine them closely enough to discover their identity. It was beginning to grow light again by this time and the Italians they met were elated by their unexpected success. But they were forward troops and no one claiming to be a repair unit had any right to be so far forward; so, as the sun came up like a gigantic gun flash on the horizon, they were forced to head westwards again and finally found themselves approaching Sofi, a shabby little village alongside the sea east of Zuq. Half the place seemed to be on fire and there were explosions and clouds of smoke. From a burning hut, Italians were carrying crates of British beer.

'I bet there wasn't a lot left, comrades and boon companions,' Clegg said, eyeing it enviously. 'I bet our lot got in there when the retreat started. Free beer's free beer even if the Empire falls apart, and bottled Bass's a bloody sight better than that horse piss and onion water that goes by the name of beer in Egypt.'

There were also cartons of chocolate, cigarettes that made their nostrils twitch, and Italian soldiers grinning under piles of British shirts, trousers, overcoats, shoes, tinned ham, fish and cheese, and bottles of liqueur.

Near the beach, the Italians had marked out an area as big as a football pitch and one group of them was busy knocking posts into the ground while second, third and fourth groups followed behind stringing barbed wire between them in rows. It was hot work and, since the Italians were stripped to the waist, it wasn't difficult to help themselves to more scraps of uniform when no one was looking.

The town itself started just beyond the cage, a huddle of flat-roofed, mud-built whitewashed houses with a mosque, a few palm trees and an apology for an inn that went by the name of the Sofi Hotel. There was a heavy traffic congestion with a column of British prisoners standing at the side of the road waiting for it to clear. Italian vehicles were parked at all angles and triumphant Italian officers were sitting on shabby chairs in the shade of a cane-roofed terrace outside the hotel, drinking wine, watched with envy and resentment by the prisoners, whose throats were working with thirst at the sight of the bottles on the tables.

Their faces were grey with dust and blank of expression like the faces of all prisoners – as if being a prisoner stopped the emotions. Soldiers were ill fitted by their training to defeat and there was something embarrassing about seeing them. They looked exhausted and distressed and were watched in their turn by Arabs and heavily veiled women in black robes. A donkey in the last stages of debilitation, its ribs like the strings of a harp, and with running sores on its rump, strained in the shafts of a cart whose load almost lifted it from the ground. The Arab owner was whacking at it with a heavy stick, raising a cloud of dust as he pounded the wretched animal's flank as if he were beating a carpet.

'Let the poor bastard alone, you wog shit!' one of the prisoners yelled and the Italian guards made menacing movements with their rifles as the shabby men showed signs of breaking their ranks to go to the aid of the donkey.

'I know those faces,' Clegg said quietly. 'They're that lot of Australians we gave a show to near Fayoum a week ago. They were due to move forward. They obviously did.' He frowned and looked the other way. 'The tall lance-jack with the chops there gave me a cigarette.'

The lorry, moving forward an inch at a time, was now alongside the column of prisoners. There were a few jeers at the supposed Italians, which they tried to ignore, then the tall lance-corporal with the lantern jaw stared.

'I've seen that sod before,' he said, looking up at Clegg. 'He looks like that big Pommy bastard who came up with that concert party and did a soft shoe shuffle in an Arab nightshirt.'

Clegg said nothing but when the lance-corporal repeated his comment he could contain himself no longer. 'I *am* that big Pommy bastard who came up with the concert party and did a soft shoe shuffle in an Arab nightshirt,' he said out of the corner of his mouth.

The Australian's jaw dropped. 'What in Christ's name are you doing in that get-up?' he asked softly.

'I'm escaping,' Clegg said. 'We all are.'

As he spoke the wretched donkey collapsed with a crash and the slowly inching traffic came to a stop. The Italian guards gestured with their rifles and the column of prisoners began to thread their way between the stalled vehicles. The tall lance-corporal winked slowly at Clegg as he passed.

'You lucky lot of Poms,' he said loudly to the empty air.

4

Morton, whose success seemed to be going to his head, stopped to talk to the Italian *sottotenente* in charge of the prisoners.

'*Che cosa c'è di nuovo oggi?*'

The Italian gestured and pointed, screwing his eyes up against the low sun.

'He says our lot have pulled back sixty kilometres,' Morton explained to Dampier. 'That's a long way. He also said the fighting's slowing down now but that there's to be a follow-up attack. But they need supplies and they've come up against our minefields on the other side of Sofi, so they've been ordered to regroup and re-equip. They're expecting more prisoners and they'll eventually be going to Zuq for shipment to Italy.'

'Pity we can't organize them and take the place,' Dampier growled.

He was itching to go to war in some way or other but he was well aware that moving east now that the line had stabilized and the area was packed with men was going to be harder than they had expected, and they had to have a base until the time was opportune for another shot.

'What about Zuq?' Morton suggested. 'So far, nobody's looked twice at us and we could go back there and try our luck.'

There was something in what he said, because by this time they were all growing hungry and none of them wanted to stay in Sofi, which was small enough for them to stick out like sore thumbs.

'We might be able to buy food in Zuq.'

Clegg's throat worked. 'Think they'll have beer?'

'Perhaps we could steal a boat,' Dampier offered. 'Anybody know anything about boats?'

It appeared that every man-jack of them had come from districts that were as far from the sea as it was possible to get, and nobody did.

A few Bedou traders huddled in their galabiyahs in a group of palms near the mosque, their heads down, unmoved by the war that racketed backwards and forwards along the northern coast of Africa. Their rope-haltered camels knelt beside them in the shade, gurgling, belching and farting in the manner of all camels, and they parked in the shade alongside, hoping the Arabs might have food to sell. But, since the Arabs promptly approached *them* for food, it was obvious they weren't going to get much; weak with hunger, they realized by the middle of the morning that before they could make another foray eastwards they would need to replenish their supplies, water and petrol. Finally, reluctantly, it was decided there was nothing for it but to do as Morton suggested and head back to Zuq.

They arrived at noon. The town lay reflected in the still dark water of the harbour, its square white buildings sharp against the shadows. The civilian population had returned now that the fighting was over, and the place had come to life. Shops had taken down their shutters and among the Arabs were a few Italians too old to be called up into the army. Someone, it seemed, had finally towed out the smouldering ammunition ship and had just got it clear when it had blown up, so that a pall of smoke hung over the town. Along the water's edge a crowd of people were still staring out to sea where it was possible to see the bow of the ship sticking out of the water, its name clear in the sunshine through the masts and rusty upperworks of the sunken vessels. A large freighter had appeared during the night and was anchored offshore, its cargo being transferred by motor lighters to the battered mole where a crowd of Italian soldiers and Arab labourers were carrying, pulling or pushing it towards a large supply dump on the edge of the town.

In the midday glare the walls of the houses were dazzling and the heat was enough to strike them speechless. The few Germans they saw – and there weren't many because under an agreement between the German and Italian commanders-in-chief Zuq was Italian territory – looked keen and well equipped in their grey jackets and peaked caps. By contrast, the Italians looked apathetic and poorly clad in khaki drill or plus-four-type trousers with ill-fitting bluish coats, like cyclists bereft of their cycles.

As Dampier's little group climbed down from their vehicles, wondering how and where to set about obtaining food, the work of unloading the freighter stopped and the stream of Italian soldiers, dusty, shabby and unshaven, collapsed. Bottles were passed round and sausages and bread appeared.

Caccia's throat worked. 'Think we could cadge a bit?' he said. 'My guts are as empty as a last bus.'

After a quarter of an hour a whistle shrilled and the groups of men stumbled to their feet and the work started once more. Dampier's group were just on the point of turning away when Clegg gave a bleat of alarm. 'Morton,' he hissed. 'There's an Italian officer coming over here.'

There was an immediate move towards the lorry but Morton stopped it dead. 'Stay where you are!' he snapped. 'I can handle him.'

The Italian officer, a small fat man with a major's badges and strapped about like a Christmas tree with dangling map case, a pair of shabby binoculars and a pistol, was striding towards them, a look of determination on his face. Two steps behind him was another, younger officer, slender, dark, intense-looking, who wore the uniform of one of the crack Bersaglieri regiments and walked with a limp. Halting

78

in front of Morton, the stout officer gave him a quivering fascist salute with outstretched arm.

'Who are you?' he demanded aggressively.

Morton looked down on him with his cold stare. '*Unità di Riparazione*,' he said. '*Veicoli Leggeri. Numero 64.*'

The Italian seemed a little disconcerted and stared along the line of dusty vehicles. 'Those are British,' he said.

'We've been engaged in collecting and repairing abandoned enemy transport,' Morton explained.

'Where are your own?'

'Coming up behind. I'm looking for a site for my workshop. I'm Tenente Mortoni. Ugo, Conte di Barda. At your service.'

The major's head jerked up at the title Morton had awarded himself; he stiffened and adjusted his tunic. It was a well-pressed bush jacket which had probably originated in South Africa and had doubtless been part of the loot from the recent disaster at Mechili when Gambier-Parry's divisional HQ and the 3rd Motor Brigade had been overwhelmed.

'Scarlatti, Giulio. Major.' His manner changed as he introduced himself. 'Town major, under the immediate command of Commandante di Brigata Olivaro in Derna, and Commandante di Brigata Marziale, who has this area. I have command of No. 7 Base Stores and Resupply Dump, all ancillary services in the town, the harbour, the refuelling depot at the fort, the Arab labourers and the furniture factory, whose products it will eventually by my duty to commandeer for the war effort. This is my assistant, Sotto-tenente Faiani.'

The younger man saluted smartly, his eyes searching Morton's face. He looked puzzled. 'Count,' he said in greeting. 'I didn't recognize you.'

'We've met?' Morton's heart thumped.

'No, count.' Faiani's eyes were bright and shrewd. 'But I've seen your pictures in the magazines. You're taller than I expected.'

Morton was momentarily disconcerted. Recognition was something he hadn't expected and he didn't like the look in Faiani's eye.

'Lost a lot of weight,' he explained quickly. 'Being thinner makes you look taller.' He decided it might be a good idea to change the subject and nodded casually to the barbed-wire compound nearby that surrounded a group of large huts. He affected to be totally unimpressed by what was clearly Scarlatti's pride and joy. 'That your dump?' he asked.

'Yes.' Scarlatti answered briskly as if Morton was not showing sufficient awe. 'It was an Italian dump the British took over. We've taken it back again. It's my job to refit the army. It's my duty to extend the dump and fill it with spares. I have supplies to unload and could do with every man I can get. Brigadier Olivaro has ordered me to get them under cover before the British planes spot them. He forgets that, unlike Colonel Ancillotti, who has the dump in Derna, I can't call on thousands of base troops.'

'My people,' Morton pointed out quickly, 'are just in from the desert. They're tired and hungry.'

'They look well equipped,' Faiani said quietly.

Morton lifted his eyebrows and the Italian explained.

'Their boots,' he said. 'British boots.' He turned to the Italian soldiers behind him, a long stream of human ants, some of them stripped to the waist, pushing carts or carrying equipment into the dump, and jerked a hand at the ugly boots they were wearing.

'Our people wear the Duce's yellowbacks,' he said. 'Cheap. Made by prisoners in jail.'

Morton gestured. 'We found a captured lorryload and helped ourselves.'

Scarlatti sniffed. 'Some of my men have had to stuff cardboard in where the soles have worn out.' He eyed the British group. 'Your men are quiet.'

Morton was acting like mad to sound casual and indifferent. 'They're tired. And they're from the mountains round Stresa. In fact they're not like Italians at all. Until 1918, of course, they were Austrians. But they know what they want and if they don't get it they make a point of taking it.' It sounded like a threat.

Scarlatti became almost apologetic. 'It won't take long, count. An hour or two. You can feed them with my people as soon as you've finished.'

'We also need petrol.'

'I have plenty. My refuelling depot's at the other side of the harbour near the fort.'

Watched uneasily by the others, among whom only Caccia had any idea what was going on, Morton debated for a while, then he nodded. 'Very well,' he said. 'I'll give them five minutes to get their breath, then bring them over.'

Scarlatti beamed. Morton nodded again, indifferent and supercilious, deciding it was a stroke of genius to promote himself to the aristocracy. Italians found it difficult to resist a title and Scarlatti was already behaving as if he were the junior officer.

'I'm grateful, count. Colonel Ancillotti will not be able to make comparisons as he usually does. A most unpleasant man, Ancillotti. A mere works manager before the war. My family have their own business.'

As he strutted off with Faiani, Morton pointed out to the others what was required; they looked a little startled.

'Work?' Clutterbuck said. 'For the fuckin' Italians?'

'You weren't doing such a lot for the fucking English,' Clinch observed tartly, his round cheeks quivering with indignation.

The unloading took longer than they'd expected and they found themselves stumbling in and out of the wired compound in the heat of the lowering sun until they were exhausted. Rafferty seemed almost to enjoy masquerading as an Italian, but to Dampier it came as a blow to his pride to have to stagger under heavy loads, goaded on from time to time by the sharp tongue of Morton, who kept telling him, almost as if he were enjoying it, to get a move on.

81

Caccia stood close by, wearing the sergeant's stripes, nervous and blank-faced, but ready, in case anybody came near, to step in if necessary with a mouthful of Italian.

Clutterbuck was still muttering his disgust when Rafferty and Morton got their heads together. There were a lot of Italian vehicles near the harbour.

'Not many,' Rafferty said. 'Just anything that's up for grabs.'

He pulled Clutterbuck out of line and explained what he wanted. Clutterbuck's sly face broke into a grin.

'Easy as oiling a bike,' he said.

Half an hour later, Clutterbuck reported that he'd got rid of the two fifteen-hundredweight trucks. 'I got a couple of Lancias instead,' he said. 'Much better condition, too. I couldn't get no more. One of their officers started 'angin' about.'

'Right.' Rafferty was impressed. 'Back to the compound then. And while you're in there, nip around a bit and see if there's anything else we could use. We might be here for longer than we expected.'

When Rafferty explained what they were up to, Dampier was shocked. 'Stealing?' he said.

'Why not?' Rafferty asked. 'It belongs to the enemy.'

'But Clutterbuck! A deserter! A military criminal!'

'Sure, sir, I can't think of anybody more suited. He's already swopped the fifteen-hundredweights for Lancias. If nothin' else, that'll make us look better than we did.'

Clutterbuck appeared like a shadow from behind a pile of crates. 'Booze,' he said. 'Fags. Most of it captured Naafi stuff. British blankets, weapons and uniforms. Italian wine. Radios. Cheese. Sausage. Rice. Tinned meat.'

By the time they had finished, there were several more Italian caps and jackets tucked away under the property baskets in the Ratbags' Bedford, another Italian flag, a portrait of Mussolini, several bottles of chianti, sausages, boxes of cheese, a sack of rice, plywood, Italian money, two wristwatches, a pressure lamp, a pair of binoculars, tools, dixies, several pairs of the baggy trousers the Italians wore, two pairs of underpants, a rosary and half a dozen of the splendid German jerricans for which the mobile units of the Eighth Army would have given their right arms.

'We captured 150,000 of these when Derna fell,' Rafferty murmured. 'And because nobody back at base pulled his finger out, they stayed there and were all recaptured when the Germans advanced.'

As they finished, Major Scarlatti reappeared. This time he was alone and in a well-polished Lancia open-top tourer driven by a chauffeur. He had changed to his best tunic and was obviously anxious to impress 'Count Barda'.

'Now, count,' he said to Morton, 'I suggest you take your men to my cookhouse. It's just over there. You, yourself, however, will perhaps join me in my office for lunch. It's in the former harbourmaster's room.'

Morton was wary. He had decided he didn't trust Scarlatti's assistant, Faiani, and he cautiously tried to find out where he would be.

Scarlatti waved a hand airily. 'Faiani will be busy,' he said. 'I don't share meals which I wish to be private with a junior officer. He'll be dining in the mess. He's an uncomfortable man to have around too much. Because he came from the Bersaglieri and was hit by shrapnel last winter, he feels he's the only patriotic Italian in Italy. Don't worry about him. And I have a fine Orvieto, a tin of parma ham and a bottle of British whisky. You can refuel your vehicles afterwards.'

The cookhouse had been set up in a shed just outside the compound and a long line of Italian soldiers was queueing up with their dixies.

'how do we go about it?' Clegg asked nervously.

It was Clutterbuck, the deserter, who answered. 'Just go and stand in the queue,' he said.

Dampier whirled on him, startled, and he gestured. 'Stand in line,' he said. 'That's all you do. Just stand there, say nowt and act daft.'

So they did. Parking the vehicles alongside the ruins nearby, they stood among the grubby, unshaven, dusty, mutely exhausted Italian soldiers, Morton at the front and to the side of the group like a conscientious officer making sure his men were fed, Caccia at the rear in case anybody addressed them from behind. The rest huddled in a nervous bunch between them where they were safe.

Nobody questioned the assorted British and Italian dixies they offered, and pasta with a meat sauce was dumped into them. Then they all drew a ration of rough red wine and were given a tin of captured British bully beef between every two men. Dampier came away looking slightly bemused.

'They didn't say a word to us,' he pointed out.

'They never do.' Clutterbuck sounded contemptuous of his attitude to crime. 'You only need a bit of nerve. I've been livin' off British cook'ouses like that for months.'

When Morton returned from his meal with Scarlatti, he looked pleased with himself. He and Rafferty had decided a little bribery and corruption was in order and he had gone armed with an excellent pair of X12 binoculars from the stock they had removed from the cavalry. Zeiss binoculars were something Scarlatti had coveted for a long time, and he had almost wept with gratitude, so that Morton had had an excellent meal. 'Splendid wine,' he observed. 'The whisky wasn't bad either.'

'You've got more sauce than a bloody bottling factory,' Caccia said admiringly and, exhausted after the unaccustomed labour in the dump, Dampier gave them a sour look. He had twisted his back and was in a bad temper.

'Never mind drooling over the food,' he growled. 'What did the feller have to say? Didn't he mention their plans? Surely you didn't spend all that time guzzling with him without learning what they're up to.'

Morton smiled. 'Well, he confirmed what the officer in Sofi said. He's got orders to issue everything that's needed. They *are* going to put on a follow-up attack.'

'When?' Dampier's eyes were gleaming.

'With the shortages and the way the Italian High Command works, he thought in about a fortnight.'

'Where?'

'He didn't know.'

Dampier turned to Rafferty. 'What do you think, Mr Rafferty?'

'South, I'm thinkin', sir. Opposite direction, to catch our people off-balance.'

'Doesn't sound like south,' Morton observed. 'That Scarlatti chap's been ordered to direct his supplies along the coast to Sofi. They'd hardly send them there if they were going south.'

Dampier had to agree. 'Very well,' he said. 'Then it's our job to find out when.'

Rafferty didn't like the look in Dampier's eye. 'What are you suggestin', sir?'

Dampier seemed surprised that he hadn't guessed. 'The Italian attack, Mr Rafferty. We could save thousands of lives. It might end in the total defeat of the enemy in North Africa. For want of a nail a shoe was lost, for want of a shoe a horse was lost, for want of a horse a battle was lost.' Dampier's enthusiasm was showing again like a recalcitrant underslip. 'An Italian defeat could result in them withdrawing from Africa altogether.'

''Twould have to be a big one, I'm thinkin', sir. And I doubt if Hitler would let 'em. An' wouldn't we be best pushin' off as soon as we can?'

'I think we should stay, Mr Rafferty,' Dampier said doggedly.

Rafferty wondered if he ought to hit him with something. It was his firm conviction that, as soon as they'd refuelled the lorries and acquired food and water, they ought to disappear immediately darkness arrived. But as the sun sank and the white walls of the town turned bronze-yellow, a German column roared through Zuq. It came along the coast road from the direction of Tripoli, filling the place with rolling clouds of dust. The young men in the vehicles, wearing peaked khaki caps and the briefest of shorts, showed no interest in Zuq, the Italians or Dampier's group and, swinging south, began to head out into the desert. Vehicle after vehicle came past, big Panzer IVs with short 75 mm calibre weapons, monster eight-wheel cars, Panzer IIIs with 50 mm armament, and vast guns with barrels like telegraph poles. They set Rafferty wondering.

'Eighty-eights,' he commented. 'I've seen pictures. They're better than anything we've got.' Spitting out the whirling grit, his eyes narrowed as he watched the tail of the steel column thunder past. 'I'm thinkin', sir,' he observed, 'that with that lot deployed just to the south we might after all be safer to stay where we are for the time bein'.'

'I'm glad you agree, Mr Rafferty,' Dampier smiled. 'Dammit,' he went on, bubbling with enthusiasm, 'nobody looks twice at us. We have Italian uniforms, we look like Italians, we have two Italian vehicles and two people who speak Italian, and the Italians are noted for their lethargy, indifference and laziness.'

'Some of 'em, sir. They're not all mugs.'

Dampier conceded the point. 'Nevertheless,' he said, 'they *are* short of transport and have to use whatever they can pick up. What's to stop us finding out a few things? Numbers. Regiments. Divisions. Plans. What sort of chap this Brigadier Marziale is. Zuq's now only a base area. Let's use it to our advantage.'

Rafferty's idea had been merely to lie low and say nothing and hadn't included anything as dangerous as gathering information, but he allowed Dampier's enthusiasm to carry the day.

'All the same, sir,' he said dubiously, 'I doubt if it's quite time to let the rest of 'em know. I can just imagine their indignation when they find they're staying in Zuq instead of bolting for home at the first opportunity.'

As they climbed into the lorries, it happened that Sottotenente Faiani was heading for the mess and he stopped near the end of the mole to watch them.

Faiani was suspicious. He had, in fact, never heard of Count Barda but there was something about the group just driving away that set his mind buzzing. He had been a policeman – a very junior policeman – in Naples until he had been swept into the army, and he had the sort of mind that was quick to notice anything odd. He couldn't put his finger on anything in particular because he had heard nothing but Italian spoken and they all seemed to be dressed in much the same sort of uniform as everyone else. Even Faiani, like Scarlatti, wore a captured South African bush jacket. No, it wasn't clothing or speech. It was behaviour. They clung together as if they were scared and, Naples having one of the biggest criminal populations in the world, Faiani had come to know something about criminal behaviour.

He lit a cigarette and watched the lorries disappear towards the old fort, then he turned and walked slowly towards the army police post just beyond the end of the mole. It was a square whitewashed building which had once been the office of the Director of Harbour Control.

Captain Bianchi, the officer in command of the post, was a man he'd known in Italy and he explained his suspicions over a glass of grappa. 'It's nothing I can be sure of, you understand,' he said. 'But there's something. Just a feeling.'

The policeman gazed at him over his desk. 'Where are they based?' Bianchi asked.

'I don't know. But I can find out. That idiot Scarlatti has taken them on trust and seems willing to supply them with anything they want.'

'You don't like him?'

There had never been much liaison between Faiani and Scarlatti. Scarlatti considered Faiani dour, un-Italian, ill mannered and obsessed with duty. Faiani considered Scarlatti a fool. It didn't lead to a lot of co-operation.

He explained carefully to Bianchi, who nodded understandingly. 'What do you think these people are up to?' he asked.

'Well, you know what goes on. They may be running some sort of racket.'

'If they are, they could be deserters. We could hit them hard for that. They might even be more. They could be British agents. They wouldn't be the first to operate behind our lines. And they're wearing Italian uniforms, you say? For that they could be shot.'

Blissfully unaware that they had already raised suspicions, Dampier's group were heading for the old fort, where they filled the lorries and all the German jerricans they possessed, and cruised slowly back into the town, Morton, Rafferty and Dampier arguing fiercely about what to do next.

There were few goods in the open-fronted shops, the mosque had a battered look, half the palm trees had lost their fronds to blast, and the awnings outside the bars were torn and lopsided, their stripes pale in the growing dusk. The few Germans they saw were interested only in stripping off their clothes and plunging into the sea to wash from their bodies and hair the dust from the recent storm. A length of beach had been cleared of mines and naked men were disporting themselves in the dark water. Nearby was a bar, the Bar Barbieri, where a few Italian soldiers were drinking. One of them had a mandolin and they were singing to it.

'Time slips by.
Our prime of youth
We'll not see again.
And that's the truth.'

It was a sad soldiers' song they'd heard Italian prisoners singing and one of the men had a soaring tenor that stood out from all the others.

'You'd give your top teeth to sing like that,' Caccia

taunted Jones. '*You*'ve got the sort of voice you can sharpen knives with.'

Jones's lined scruffy face twisted and he was just looking as though he'd have liked to brain Caccia with the jack when a young *sottotenente* arrived on a motorcycle and started shouting. The soldiers in the bar finished their drinks in a hurry and began to shuffle off. As the place emptied, dry British throats worked.

'Think we might take a chance?' Dampier's mind was filled with thoughts of a cold gin and tonic.

As the vehicles drew to a stop, a German sergeant appeared from inside the bar. He was handsome, blond and cheerful-looking and he was dragging by the hand a girl who was obviously Italian. Reaching the street, he turned, swung her round and slapped her behind. She responded with a straight-armed swing at him, missed and fell to her knees. The German laughed, waved and climbed into a *kübel-wagen*. As he drove away, still laughing, the girl was spitting with fury and an empty bottle snatched from a table followed him. An Arab woman filling a *chatti* at a standpipe down the street watched with interest.

As Dampier's group climbed down, the owner of the bar appeared, gave the girl a push so that she disappeared inside out of sight, still spitting with rage, and approached Morton, wringing his hands, his face moist with sweat.

'A little trouble, excellency,' he explained. 'Nothing to trouble you. You know what girls are like. What can I get you?'

'Beer?'

'Alas, excellency. No beer.'

'Cold white wine?'

'Alas!'

When Morton asked what *was* available, the Italian shrugged and launched into a long diatribe.

'What did he say?' Dampier demanded.

'He says they have anisette and red wine – and *poor* red wine at that.'

'He's got whisky and gin on the shelves.'

Morton gave his aloof smile. 'The whisky's cold tea and the gin's water. They're there just for the look of the thing.'

The drinks were brought by the girl. She was good-looking and at that moment still flushed with anger. Slamming the tray down in front of them, she vanished at full speed.

'Bit of all right,' Caccia murmured knowledgeably. 'In a right old tear, too. Playing it big and using both hands.'

'Them Italian bints aren't bad,' Clutterbuck agreed.

'It's nice just to see a woman,' Jones the Song observed gloomily. 'I'd almost forgotten how they were made.' He lost himself in a mental picture of Swansea on a Saturday night, garish with lights, full of women and redolent of the smell of fish and chips.

As they had been warned, the red wine was poor enough to taste of iron filings. As they emptied their glasses and left, the girl was standing in the doorway, watching them, her face sullen. As he passed, Caccia the ladykiller couldn't resist winking and her sulky face immediately broke into a smile which transformed it. Caccia was encouraged.

'*Buona sera*,' he said.

She gestured. '*Buona sera, soldato.*'

'*Come si chiama?*'

'Rosalba. Rosalba Coccioli.'

'*Signora?*'

She gave him a cold look. '*Signorina.* I am not married.'

'Ah!'

'*E Lei? Come si chiama Lei?*'

'Caccia, Arthur.'

'Arthur?'

Caccia coughed and hurriedly changed step. 'Arturo. Arturo Caccia.'

They talked desultorily in Italian for a while as the others strolled towards the vehicles. One of the Bedfords took a lot of starting and Rafferty lifted the bonnet and pushed his head inside, the others grouped nervously round him, their eyes flickering about them for signs of hostility, Morton in the middle, tall, straight and good-looking, alert in case they were questioned. After a while Rafferty lifted his head and Morton swung round to wave to the bar.

The girl eyed Caccia as he turned away. '*Quando ritorna Lei*? When are you coming back?'

'You want me to?'

'Why not?'

Caccia smiled. 'I'll come. *Ciao.*'

As they left, a string of German trucks halted on the asphalt strip edging the beach and dusty men from the desert jumped down. NCOs barked at them and they formed up in three lines. Another bark and they began to undress, neatly fold their clothes and place them on top of their boots, until finally they stood naked, still in three rows facing the sea. A final bark and they broke ranks to run towards the water.

'Our lot,' Rafferty observed admiringly to Dampier, 'would have made a shambles of it.'

The Germans were all in the water now, yelling, splashing and leaping about like little boys in a swimming pool. From the Humber Rafferty eyed the piles of clothing, all placed in neat rows. It was almost dark and suddenly Dampier's idea didn't seem quite so silly.

'Lots of German caps and coats lying about loose,' he commented thoughtfully.

5

By the time the sun rose next morning, a great pulsing disc in an aura of incredible golden light, it was beginning to dawn on Rafferty that they were safer than they'd thought and Dampier's idea seemed to grow better all the time. There were dozens of Italian units of all kinds in and around Zuq now and, thanks to the Italian uniforms they had acquired and Morton's quick thinking, they had got off to a good start. Because of Italian military inefficiency, nobody had even noticed them.

It took twenty-four hours for it to sink in among the hoi polloi that they weren't after all going to head off into the bright blue yonder back to their own lines – the group was so small everybody soon knew when anything was in the wind – and they promptly pushed forward to put their oar in. To most soldiers, the order of battle had God and the generals running the world, with the officers and NCOs administering the law somewhere just beneath, hearing everything, seeing everything, missing nothing, while they themselves, with the lance corporals – who didn't count – hovered in the depths below. It didn't, therefore, normally pay very well to make one's opinions too clearly known but, with nothing to lose but their chains, when the personnel of 64 Light Vehicle Repair Unit finally found out what was going on there was a considerable amount of muttering.

'Stay here?' Jones the Song's high tenor rose almost to a falsetto. 'Behind the enemy lines, man?'

By this time, however, even Rafferty was becoming

enthusiastic. The idea had started to appeal to his mischievous Irish mind. And, as Clutterbuck had pointed out, they were able to draw rations so long as they had Caccia and Morton handy to answer awkward questions. With Rafferty's knowledge of procedure and Morton's knowledge of the Italian army gleaned during his period in Intelligence, they felt they were capable of dealing with all eventualities. All the rest of them had to do was appear to be stupid.

'And,' Morton observed sagaciously, 'as the average soldier, British or Italian, is normally *expected* to be stupid, nobody will bother to enquire any further.'

They found a quiet place not far from the wrecked warehouses where they had hidden on their first night in Zuq. It was handy for the harbour but out of the immediate neighbourhood of any other units, most of which were near the fort, and, to make themselves look as if they belonged there, Clutterbuck recruited the usual Arab labourers to dig slit trenches in case the RAF came over and bombed them by mistake.

As it happened, the plan was very nearly abandoned within the first few hours. Having just escorted a convoy of supplies to beleaguered Tobruk not far away along the coast, the Royal Navy, well fed and feeling their oats, decided it was time they did something spiteful to the opposition to make up for the loss of Zuq and Sofi. They arrived off the little harbour in the early hours of the morning and started to bang away with everything they possessed. The first cracking explosions brought everybody at 64 Light Vehicle Repair Unit bolt upright in their blankets at once.

'What the hell's that?' Clegg demanded.

'Go to sleep,' Caccia said. 'It's the RAF again.'

'That's not bombs, old comrade and boon companion. Listen. There aren't any aircraft engines.'

Caccia sat up again. Clegg was right. Whatever was being flung at them wasn't coming from above. Then, as the coastal batteries began to hammer away, it dawned on Clinch what was happening.

'It's the navy!' he screeched. 'They're making a raid! They're putting troops ashore!'

All thoughts of being heroic by remaining in Zuq were forgotten at once, because if there really were a naval landing there was a good chance of being picked up. To hell with winning the war on their own, they thought – even Dampier agreed – and, dressing hurriedly, they scrambled for the trucks, eager to be first on the deck of a warship. They were just sorting themselves out when they realized they were wearing Italian uniforms.

'They'll fuckin' shoot us!' Clutterbuck yelled, and they all scrambled out again to collect their British uniforms so they wouldn't be shot at by the Eighth Army as it swarmed ashore.

In fact, by the time they reached the town, the navy's spitefulness had worn itself out. The ships were a long way from base and, with the Luftwaffe commanding that particular stretch of sea, it wasn't a good idea to be caught around it in daylight; and, after a few salvos, the warships had bolted. Arriving in a panic, 64 Light Vehicle Repair Unit scrambled from the trucks aware of a sinking feeling in their chests.

'The rotten bastards have gone without us,' Caccia said bitterly.

They stood staring out over the indigo sea, all the sour things they'd heard about the navy churning in their minds. Then, as they turned away, it dawned on them that in the town they could hear cries of rage; they realized that two or three of the navy's shells had struck the furniture factory on which Zuq depended for so much of its prosperity. It wasn't a particularly big factory and didn't employ many craftsmen but it gave work to a lot of people and there was a large woodyard next door. As town major, both the factory and the woodyard came under Scarlatti's wing.

The fire brigade had turned out in a rush with their single rickety fire engine, a dozen scared Italians and Arabs clinging to the sides. But the appliance had a semi-flat tyre, the hoses were perished, and a bucket chain had to be formed from the sea. Half the town and half the Italian garrison was involved, men in uniform standing in line next to women and teenagers and Zuqi Arabs who depended on the factory for a livelihood. For a while they seemed to have the blaze under control and an attempt was made to salvage some of the produce, so that the streets around were full of dark figures hurrying away under the weight of chairs, tables and sideboards.

They were just winning the battle when the wind got up and started to fan the blaze and in no time the place went up properly, because, in addition to wood, the factory contained paint, thinners and varnish which fuelled the flames so that they roared skywards, drawing in gusts of air like a furnace to drag in loose sheets of paper, dust, leaves and scraps of rubbish. The fronds of nearby palms streamed out, the trees themselves bending towards the blaze. Finally the RAF appeared and started to bomb the fire. It wasn't exactly a good night for Scarlatti.

With Zuq a little more battered than it had been, its white walls scorched and scarred, and the charred remains of the furniture factory stark against the sky, 64 Light Vehicle Repair Unit returned to their camp a little depressed that they had not been swept to safety.

Though they didn't know it, they had been lucky because it hadn't been a good night for Faiani either. One of the last shells that had landed had destroyed what had once been the office of the Director of Harbour Control.

Faiani heard about it as he and Scarlatti worked over the returns to find out what damage had been done. Disappearing on the excuse that his leg was giving him trouble and he needed to see a doctor, Faiani headed for the harbour.

The whitewashed building that had housed the police was a pile of wreckage, with the remains of office furniture still smouldering with the papers which had once been records and were now fluttering in the hot breeze among the debris. There was no sign of any of the occupants.

'Shell,' one of the men clearing a path past the ruins told Faiani. 'Last night.'

'What happened to them?'

The soldier shrugged. 'I don't think they were killed,' he said. 'I saw them being pushed into an ambulance.'

Climbing into the little Fiat he drove, Faiani headed for the hospital, only to find that Captain Bianchi had already been put aboard a ship for Italy, and he limped slowly back to his car, deep in thought. It was going to take a day or two before anyone else was appointed to take Bianchi's place and another few days before his successor could set himself up with a base and an office and a squad of men. By that time the group calling themselves 64 Light Vehicle Repair Unit might well have disappeared.

Faiani frowned. It seemed to him that the best thing he could do was make the investigations himself. He'd had the training and, with that idiot Scarlatti sending supplies as if he and the man who called himself Count Barda were bosom friends, it wouldn't be difficult to look around occasionally. In the meantime, he would try to find out something about the so-called Barda. He could, he realized, be wrong and could easily make a fool of himself. And if he did, then he could be in trouble. People with titles had influence and he could well be making a rod for his own back. But Faiani was a dogged young man who had grown up in a poor home in Naples and had a chip on his shoulder that prevented him ever being too fond of people who were fit and whole and wealthy. He decided he would move with care. The first thing would be to contact some old colleagues in the police department in Naples and get them to send him some details about Count Barda, because he still had a feeling that the man he'd spoken to *wasn't* Count Barda.

As the day wore on, Dampier's group began to recover their spirits. They hadn't been hurt and no one had so far shown any interest in them, and they settled themselves once more to wait. Nevertheless it occurred to Rafferty that near the harbour wasn't exactly the best place to be and he found a new site at the other side of the town alongside an old Arab cemetery with its curious coffin-like graves carrying a stone at both head and foot. There were one or two palms nearby and a few spiky-leaved cacti, with here and there bunches of whitened thorn trees and scrubby bushes bearing an aromatic scent. Though they missed the cooler breezes from the sea, it was far from unpleasant.

Their nearest neighbour was a nomad Arab encampment among the dunes, a dozen low, square black tents with dogs, asses, camels, chickens, goats and sheep. The children all had flies round their eyes and nostrils and Dampier's group saw sleeping babies with their faces covered with them. The women peeped shyly at them from behind the men, who came on their flat horny feet to exchange midget-sized eggs, fruit and goats' cheese for coffee and sugar. It was noticeable that inside the Arabs' tents on the usual dusty rugs there were one or two surprisingly new armchairs, a little scorched perhaps but serviceable nevertheless, and that their owners were keeping their chickens in what appeared to be wardrobes that looked very much as if they'd recently been part of Scarlatti's furniture factory.

Rafferty was more than satisfied with their new site. 'There's just one thing,' he pointed out. 'We need some equipment.'

'Equipment?' Dampier's head jerked up. 'Why do we need equipment?'

Rafferty was very patient. 'If we're intendin' to stay here, sir, it's going to be for several days at least now, and in that case we have to have a reason for bein' here.'

'A reason for being here?'

'Sir' – Rafferty's patience slipped a little – 'we're not part of a cup-final crowd. If anybody asks us what we're doin' here, what do we say?'

What he was getting at finally penetrated. 'So what *do* we say?' Dampier asked.

'We tell 'em who we are, sir,' Rafferty indicated the crude notice Dampier had erected to disguise them. '*Unità di Riparazione 64*,' he said. '*That's* who we are, sir. So, I reckon we'd better start looking like one. A bit better notice, for a start, I'm thinkin'. Somethin' a bit more professional. And a line underneath indicating light vehicles only, so there'll be no nonsense about being asked to repair tanks.'

The nearby desert was full of small units supporting the fighting troops – workshops, mechanical, electrical and radio; supply dumps; petrol dumps; food dumps; and a little airfield with its old wreckage of Savoias destroyed at the end of 1940 and its new squadron of Fiats, which had been moved in for the present advance. There was every kind of unit to make an army function – all tucked away in the valleys between the dunes or anywhere they might get some shade, all operating individually, all drawing and cooking their own rations, all with their own discipline, all minding their own business and interfering with no one else's.

In any army – the Italian army as well as the British army – units kept very much to themselves, whether they were regiments, brigades, divisions or merely companies or platoons. Every man lived within his own small outfit and beyond that within the larger family of his regiment, brigade or division. It didn't matter whether they were artillery, infantry, supplies, maintenance and repairs, or whatever, and the fact that 64 Light Vehicle Repair Unit had been accepted as part of the Italian army was recognized at once, as they began to receive visits from Italian soldiers on the scrounge for food. At first Morton tried to discourage them but, as Dampier began to compile a long report headed 'Italian troops, Morale of', he was finally ordered to encourage them.

Wretchedly equipped in their baggy trousers, puttees, vast yellow boots and ill-fitting, board-stiff clothing that chafed the skin without offering much in the way of protection, the Italian soldiers had few comforts and fewer luxuries and were over the moon at the British rations captured at Sofi – chocolate, ham, cheese, tinned fish, the Three Threes Cigarettes instead of their own hated Nazionalis. But they were quiet men on the whole, frugal, disciplined and patient, with a deep sense of injustice, and it didn't take Morton long to discover that they belonged mostly to the Longhi Brigade, so known from its commander, one Colonel Giacinto Longhi, whom they saw occasionally strutting about with visiting officials from the Fascist Party in Rome. In the manner of most Italian units, they bore in addition the more virile title of the Lupi di Longhi – Longhi's Wolves – but it also didn't take Morton long to learn that they'd run away so often all the other Italians called them the Lepri di Longhi – Longhi's Hares.

Unlike the confident, sturdy men of the Alpini and the Bersaglieri, their favourite reading was *Tradotta Libica*, Libyan Troop Train, which was a soldiers' magazine in which grievances were aired; and they lived only for what they called the Shopping Bag – the convoy that brought their rations, the few luxuries they were allowed and the red wine they drank from their mess tins. They were old hands for the most part who had little time for the politicians in Rome with their corruption and inefficiency, or for the authoritative and energetic generals who tried to ape the Germans with their clicking heels, salutes, medals and the *passo romano*, Mussolini's version of the goose step. The new recruits, who had arrived to fill the gaps in their ranks, were even mere boys, badly trained, poor in spirit, lacking élan and initiative and with none of the soundness of the men who had been lost in Wavell's advance in 1940/41; and their chief fear was of being caught in a brewed-up vehicle and becoming what they called '*soldati fritti*'. They were so concerned with their private woes they barely noticed the oddities that existed about No. 64 Light Vehicle Repair Unit.

'An' after all,' Rafferty explained, ''twould be natural enough for a vehicle repair unit to be in Zuq.'

'There are disadvantages,' Morton pointed out. 'Italians eat a lot of pasta. It's something we'll have to get used to.'

Rafferty smiled. 'They also drink a lot of wine, boy,' he said. 'That's something we'll also have to get used to.'

Their first visitor not seeking food was Sottotenente Faiani. He arrived in his small, battered Fiat and claimed he'd come to make sure they had all they needed. It didn't take Morton long to decide he was also more than a little interested in him personally.

'I haven't always been a rear stores officer,' he pointed out. 'I was a front-line man, count, like you. My company was almost wiped out trying to hold the British near Bardia during the winter. Have you been out long?'

'As long as most people,' Morton said brusquely.

Faiani smiled, not in the least put out by Morton's lofty manner. 'I was convinced you were shorter than I am,' he said. 'Strange that I had a totally different impression of you.'

'You seem to have had a lot of strange impressions,' Morton snapped.

As Faiani disappeared, Rafferty stared after him, his eyes narrow. 'I reckon,' he said slowly, 'that he's noticed we aren't quite what we seem. We're short of equipment and he's spotted it. Light aid units have oxyacetylene gear, weldin' gear, a portable generator, a fixed drill. Normally, they also have a truck with a crane, a stores truck, sometimes a six-wheeler with a girder and a pulley for liftin'. They'd have hand tools, gasket sets, tyres, stencils for div. signs, numbers, letters and a stipple brush to use with 'em. They'd have a collapsible bench, a vise, taps and dies, a block and tackle and some sort of sheerlegs, to say nothing of the Italian equivalent of an Aldershot shelter so we could work out of the sunshine and dust.'

'You're suggesting we actually *do* repairs for the Italians, Mr Rafferty?' Dampier asked.

'If we say we're a light aid unit, somebody's going to ask for light aid.'

'But, dammit, Mr Rafferty! Putting Italian vehicles to rights!'

'Can you think of anything better, sir?'

Dampier did a bit of huffing and puffing but he couldn't.

Rafferty nodded. 'At the very least we ought to have a few more tents. One for the office, for instance, and one for the officer.'

'We can get tents easy enough,' Clutterbuck said.

They swung round on him. 'How?'

'Half-inch 'em. Pinch 'em. I could get you a tent easy as winkin'. I know 'ow. The wogs was always liftin' 'em. I once saw a 'ospital marquee got down in an hour. Next day it was sails on a dhow on the Nile. They didn't even find the tent pegs.'

Dampier looked at Rafferty then back at Clutterbuck. 'It occurs to me, Clutterbuck,' he said soberly, 'that at the moment, despite our different ranks and positions, we're all in the same boat and in grave danger of becoming prisoners. We *could* do with a tent or two to make us look more official for a few days and, if you pull your weight and we make it back to our friends, I'm prepared to forget the circumstances in which we met.'

Clutterbuck eyed him warily. 'Straight up?'

'I've given my word. We might need every man. We might even need what few skills *you* seem to possess.'

'I'm good with Lancias, I say it myself.'

Dampier coughed. 'I was thinking more of knowing how to live unofficially as long as you did without getting caught. If we wish to reach our lines in safety, we might have to rely on you occasionally and it's no time to have to wonder if you're going to bolt.'

Clutterbuck stared at him for a while. 'Gawd knows what Dow and Raye'll say.'

'Dow and Raye might well prove more unlucky than you.

101

They might already have been picked up by the Military Police.'

Clutterbuck considered for a few moments. 'Done,' he said. 'Sir,' he added for good measure. He paused. 'I'll need some money.'

'What for?'

'Arabs. Nobody like Arabs for gettin' things done. They'll need bribin'.'

Dampier fished in his pocket and produced the roll of notes from the Italian officer's jacket. 'Do we trust you with it?' he asked.

Clutterbuck's smooth ugly face split in a grin. 'You've got no option,' he pointed out.

As they watched Clutterbuck drive off in the Bedford with Clegg and Caccia, Dampier's eyes were narrow.

'God knows what we've done, Mr Rafferty,' he said. 'We've just given him a great deal of money and a British army vehicle. We'll probably never see him again.'

'Clegg and Caccia'll watch him, sir.'

'Clegg's a music-hall comedian. Caccia was a grocer.'

It took two days for them to return – two nervous days when everybody was on edge; then on the third day just as it grew light they heard a vehicle approaching. As they turned out to see who it was, they realized it wasn't the Bedford. It wasn't even one lorry, but two, both Lancias. Clutterbuck, in the cab of the first, stuck up a thumb.

'Easy as eatin' your dinner,' he said.

They had been to Derna, fifty-odd miles away, and not only had they managed to exchange – unofficially – one British vehicle for two Italian vehicles, they had also acquired an assortment of light hand tools, among them screw cutters, tin cutters and wire cutters, and a marquee and two tents.

'We can 'ave as many lorries as we like now,' Clutterbuck said cheerfully. 'Once we're in business, they'll *bring* 'em to us.'

'That man's growing ambitious, Mr Rafferty,' Dampier observed darkly. 'He'll land us in trouble.'

Clutterbuck had also found out exactly what the dump at Derna contained and exactly where things were kept.

'Everything we want,' he said cheerfully. 'Artillery wheels, cavalry sabres, pistol 'olsters, rifle stocks, anti-aircraft cannon barrels, gas cylinders, acres o' mule saddlery, Mercedes Benz engines – even a 'orse's gasmask.'

'A horse's gasmask, for God's sake!'

'I saw it.' Clutterbuck's sly smile appeared. 'The bloke told Caccia and we went and looked. There's face pow-der – '

'Who in God's name uses face powder?'

'Some of them Eyetie officers is proper poncy.'

They had also seen sugar, scent, cosmetics, corsets, uniforms, cameras, Lee Enfield rifles of the latest mark, which the British army hadn't yet received, soap, dress swords, male and female civilian clothing, ski boots – 'Ski boots, for God's sake!' Dampier said. 'In the desert?' – boxes of guidebooks on Italy and Sicily, several of which Clutterbuck, with a surprising amount of intelligence, had managed to steal, coffee, tinned meat, wine, and British cigarettes by the thousand. They had also noticed a general's dress uniform, complete with polished field boots, silk shirt and hat, all being carefully preserved for its owner's return from the desert, to say nothing of a patent-leather holster which contained not a real weapon but a child's toy pistol, as if the general hadn't enjoyed supporting the weight of the real thing. There was even a register of the prostitutes in Tripoli and Derna, each name followed by revealing photographs, measurements and various other intimate details.

Dampier gasped. 'I'm thinking of the mass of base clerks they'll need,' he said.

'Sure, sir,' Rafferty pointed out, '*I'*m thinkin' that it's obvious why the Italians never win their wars.'

Clutterbuck had also brought back coffee, tinned milk –

103

British, from the disaster at Mechili – a crate of beer, and cartons of assorted tinned foodstuffs from the dump at Zuq.

'How did you get inside, man?' Rafferty demanded.

'Drove in.' Clutterbuck didn't seem to think it odd.

'How?'

'Well, there's this Arab, see – '

'Which Arab?'

'This Arab what organizes papers and things. He's a printer. He's got a nice little business goin'.'

'In Italian?'

'Oh, yes. Caccia talked the lingo, and 'e knew what to do, anyway, because 'e's done it afore. 'E fixed us up with passes and identity papers for workin' in the dump. All 'is pals 'as 'em.'

Dampier was concerned that Clutterbuck might have gone too far, but Clutterbuck wasn't worried.

'Nah,' he said. ''S nothin' to worry about. 'E's runnin' a racket 'isself, anyway, isn't 'e?'

'Who is?'

'Scarlatti. That Eyetie major. There are several of 'em at it. 'E must be fillin' 'is pockets.'

'How do you know?'

'I saw four Lancia engines with the numbers filed off, didn't I? You know what that means.'

'He's stealing them.'

'Exact. Well, you know what they say: if you can't beat 'em, join 'em. If 'e can do it, so can we.'

'Perhaps you'd better explain,' Dampier said coldly, feeling he was on the slippery slope to perdition.

Clutterbuck obliged. 'Well,' he said, 'if we run rackets on our side of the line, so do the Eyeties, don't they?'

'Except that we don't speak Italian,' Rafferty pointed out.

'Two of us do. And that goes a long way. Them Italians the police picked up workin' in Cairo didn't speak much English. There was even one who got a job in a senior officers' mess where 'e 'eard army secrets discussed.'

'How do you know?'

''E told me, din't 'e?'

'You'd better give me the name of the mess,' Dampier said.

'It wun't do no good. 'E 'opped it to South Africa. Got on a ship and went through the Sewage Canal. 'E didn't like the war much.' Clutterbuck smiled. 'I've got a contact who'll 'elp. Found out I did a bit of business with a mate of 'is in Cairo. That's the best of bein' able to speak wog. 'Ad a wog girlfriend, see.'

Dampier eyed Clutterbuck's oily face. He'd often heard it said that the best way to learn a language was in bed from a girl.

'These wogs 'ere is workin' a fast one,' Clutterbuck went on. 'So, if we threaten to tell on 'em, they'll 'elp us, won't they? So long as we 'elp *them*, too, and let 'em 'ave their fair share.' He paused and grinned. 'There's also an Italian lorry in that dump what don't work any more,' he added.

'Did you disable it?'

Clutterbuck grinned again. 'Them Eyeties is careless buggers. They never guard nothin'. I peed in the petrol tank. That'll stop it. Probably miles from anywhere, too. It'll give 'em a right laugh.'

6

By the end of the afternoon, the newly acquired lorries'
numbers and signs had been changed, their engine markings
filed off and, smeared with grease and dirt, fresh numbers
stamped on in their place.

With the new additions, they now had acquired enough
vehicles to indicate a unit of some importance. No self-
respecting repair unit, whether Italian, German or British,
would have been seen dead without spare vehicles to ride
about in. As Dampier, who had been working to bring an
end to this very problem, well knew, it just wouldn't have
looked right.

Unfortunately, older than the others and unused to hard
labour, Dampier was also beginning to suffer from the
effects of the heavy work they'd done at Scarlatti's dump.
His twisted back had given way to something suspiciously
like lumbago and he could hardly move.

'Leave it to me,' Clutterbuck said cheerfully. 'I'll sort it
out.'

Heading into Zuq with Caccia in one of the Lancia trucks
he'd acquired, he returned the following morning trailed by
Caccia driving yet another Lancia.

'No need to get alarmed,' he said. 'Nobody'll find out. I
never take 'em from the same place twice.'

He had also brought back timber, inner tubes, a complete
set of carpenter's tools, two stretchers and a set of pillows,
and, with the help of Micklethwaite, began to build a bed
frame which he stretched across with cut-up inner tubes.

Covering the inner tubes with blankets, he placed a pillow at the head and as they lowered Dampier on to it, he couldn't help letting out a long sigh of relief.

''Ow's that?' Clutterbuck asked with concern. 'Comfortable?' He disappeared and returned with a motor inspection light, which he strung to the tent pole.

'So you can read in bed,' he pointed out. 'I brought you some books, see.'

Clutterbuck's idea of literature turned out to be a set of what were known to the Merchant Navy as 'Blue Books', pornographic publications, some in Italian, some in English, some in French, produced by Arab printers in North African ports before the war for the delectation of frustrated passing seamen, and their contents made Dampier, a stickler for propriety, go hot all over.

Clutterbuck quite failed to notice his shocked expression.

'Fancy a bit of music?' he asked. 'I can get you a wireless set if you like.' He paused. 'I peed in the tanks of two more lorries today,' he ended. 'Doin' me bit for the war effort.'

By the following day they had acquired yet another light truck complete with changed signs and engine numbers. With it came a small lathe and an electric drill, for which, unfortunately, they had no generator. Nevertheless, it all looked very impressive and it had all arrived by kind permission of Corporal Clutterbuck and had the effect of making them look more like what they claimed to be. By this time Dampier was looking a little bemused. In effect, and although it concerned an army that was not his own, he was a party to the sort of stealing he had only recently been trying to halt, and moreover using the skill of an acknowledged deserter and thief. His guilt troubled him.

So that no questions should be asked, Clutterbuck made a red-cross flag out of a sheet and erected it outside Dampier's tent. Outside the tent which Morton claimed should be his as senior officer were the Italian flags they'd stolen, flanked by the portraits of Victor Emmanuel and Mussolini. Though neither Victor Emmanuel nor Mussolini, as Morton was well aware from the prisoners he'd interviewed in the past, was every Italian's cup of tea, to an outsider the little post represented the summit of Italian patriotism. If not patriotism, perhaps, then the cynical pretence of patriotism they'd noticed in a great many Italian prisoners.

Lookouts were organized to warn of the approach of anybody unexpected, with instructions to dig Morton out at once, and they all stood back to admire their handiwork, feeling reasonably safe from anything but too searching an investigation. And, since all armies had small detached units scattered about the desert and the Italians had plenty in and around Zuq, there was no reason why anyone *should* investigate them too closely.

'After all,' Rafferty pointed out, 'if those Eyeties they picked up in Cairo could get away with it behind *our* lines, there's no reason why we shouldn't get away with it behind *theirs*.'

'All the same,' Dampier said, 'it troubles me, Mr Rafferty. You and I are surrounded by some very strange people. Actors. Singers. Deserters.'

'Sure, it takes all sorts, sir, to make an army, and it takes all sorts to win a war.'

'We've certainly got all sorts here.'

Rafferty smiled. 'And, thanks to that chap Morton, we're using 'em to good advantage, sir.' He eyed Dampier's bed. 'You seem to have a rare comfortable perch there, sir,' he added slyly.

Dampier frowned and avoided his glance. 'Has it occurred to you, Mr Rafferty,' he asked, 'that we are suddenly in a unique position? We can pinpoint for the RAF or the navy the Italian supply dump, the refuelling depot and the ammunition compound. Moreover, with Corporal Morton – ' He paused and Rafferty could see that Morton's behaviour still stuck in his throat a little. ' – With Corporal Morton on excellent terms with Scarlatti, the town major, there might also be a few other things we might discover which would have value behind our lines.'

There was something in what Dampier said because almost every day brought fresh supplies and fresh troops into Zuq, and, with a constant stream of vehicles moving in and out of Scarlatti's dump and Scarlatti issuing equipment as if there were no tomorrow, it didn't require an expert to realize that the rumour about a follow-up attack was genuine. Notices indicating the road to the east were being erected and desert-worn units were arriving in numbers to re-equip.

In the hope of recouping some of their losses of the previous winter, the Italians were putting everything they'd got into the planned attack. As the ships arrived under cover of darkness, what they brought was never in the quantities the Italians needed to feel safe, but units *were* building up their strengths again and it didn't take much effort on Morton's part to confirm that they'd been told to prepare for another move forward.

And with the continuing build-up, it was obvious that every lines-of-communication officer in the area was busily taking advantage of the fact to expand his own unit as fast as possible. There wasn't an officer or NCO in the Italian army – or any other army, for that matter – who wasn't aware that an increase in his establishment could mean an increase in his chances of promotion: so many more underlings and a corporal became a sergeant, a lieutenant a captain, a major a colonel. The confusion of the desert war made it even easier and Scarlatti was as eager as anyone for promotion.

He arrived in the Lancia, trailed by Faiani in the little Fiat, and he produced forms, indents and inventories, to say nothing of a bottle of captured whisky for Morton, tins of pilchards, a box of grapes, a case of captured British beer. Faiani seemed less eager to please, and his eyes were constantly flickering about the still somewhat threadbare set-up that was meant to represent a light aid unit. By this time they had got rid of all their vehicles except the Humber, and in their places were Lancias of various weights.

'I see you've lost your British vehicles, count,' Faiani observed.

'Sent to Derna, Morton explained. 'For examination and appraisal.'

'What a pity you didn't bring them to me.' Scarlatti sounded faintly reproachful. 'As it is, I expect Colonel Ancillotti will extract one or two for his own use, probably even sell them quietly in the Arab quarter. He's like that, isn't he, Faiani? I wouldn't trust him as far as I could throw him.' His dark eyes moved about the camp. 'It's strange, count, that you don't have the honour of commanding a fighting unit.'

Morton smiled. 'My hobby before the war was motor racing,' he said. 'We all do in war what we did best in peacetime. Perhaps you, too, with your storekeeping.'

Faiani's glance went to Morton's face and he smiled to himself, but Scarlatti wasn't sure whether the comment was meant to be praise or a snide remark. Because his connections *were* with an unglamorous family business in Milan, he changed the subject hurriedly before they could go too deeply into a background that couldn't hope to match that of a count and a racing driver.

Faiani interrupted. Naples had come up with a few of the details he'd been wanting and he was all set to catch out the man he felt sure was an impostor. 'I expect you used to practise on your estate, count,' he said. 'Did you have a circuit near your home? In the Alban Hills, isn't it?'

Morton glanced sharply at Faiani. Fortunately he knew his facts too well. 'No, it isn't,' he said briskly. 'It's north of Florence.' For good measure he offered a detailed run-down on the place both inside and outside, with a mention of all the neighbouring villages and a brief description of the surrounding countryside. Because he'd more than once

110

visited the real Count Barda's home, there was no hesitation.

Faiani looked crushed but he was far from beaten. 'The Bardas have a good reputation, count,' he said.

'I trust so,' Morton snapped. 'Our motto is "Honour with Courage".' That should convince the sod, he thought maliciously. A phoney wouldn't be expected to know that fact.

Scarlatti was showing signs of impatience. He didn't like being thrust out of the limelight by a subordinate, especially when the subordinate appeared to know more about the nobility than he did himself. 'What a pity your heavy equipment hasn't yet arrived,' he said.

Morton smiled. '*Il mondo è di chi ha pazienza*. The world is his who has patience. It'll turn up. I heard from my friend Baron Malaparte, of the Alpini, that it was seen by the Marchese Fulco in El Adem.' He shrugged and produced a long story about being attached first to the Trieste Division, then to the Liguria Division and finally to the Ariete Division – all of which he knew from his period with Intelligence to be in the desert – until now, with the last move, he wasn't sure what division they belonged to.

The name-dropping impressed Scarlatti. 'You must be attached to me,' he insisted at once. 'You must draw rations, petrol, water, everything you need, from my dump. I'll send you timber, paint, stencils and brushes for your signs. You can then make it clear who you are.' He cleared his throat noisily. 'And might I suggest, count, that beneath the information you state that you're part of my own 7th Base Stores and Resupply Depot.' He beamed, showing a mouthful of gold teeth. 'So that there'll be no difficulties if questions are asked. Indeed, count, why don't you move alongside my dump? It must be most uncomfortable for you here. We'd welcome you into our mess and we'd be delighted to have your company, wouldn't we, Faiani?'

Morton's excuses had been prepared long since. He was there to work not with base troops but with the men in the

111

desert and, though he appreciated the major's interest and concern, patriotism had to come first. The Duce had demanded virile attitudes to the war, had he not?

Scarlatti didn't take quite such an astringent view of his duties but he was more than prepared to supply them with what they needed. As he climbed back into his car, Faiani climbed into the Fiat. He was looking puzzled. With the information he'd received from Naples, he'd felt he could trip up any false Count Barda, but Morton had offered more information on him than even Naples knew. He still wasn't satisfied but he knew he was going to have to think again.

That afternoon a lorry sent by Scarlatti brought paint, stencils, brushes, cartons of pasta, tins of meat and tomatoes, cheese, bread, flour, fruit and wine. The man who drove it had heard the rumours of a new advance and – like his comrades – wasn't relishing the idea. He didn't like the desert and was scared stiff of the RAF and the Long Range Desert Group, the new British outfit which had taken to prowling far behind the Italian lines. Mainly recruited from the teeming cities of central Italy, the driver and his friends were baffled by the vast empty spaces where the war in Africa was being fought, and they knew that, if the Italian army advanced, without doubt they'd be following it – away from the comparative security of Zuq and the ships that linked them to Italy.

In no time the little camp sprouted a forest of white-painted, black-lettered notices, one of them firmly stating their identity: UNITA DI RIPARAZIONE DI VEICOLI LEGGERI 64.

'If it moves, salute it,' Clegg said. 'If it doesn't, paint it white.'

The following day two of Scarlatti's lorries appeared for servicing. Faiani brought them, driving ahead of them in the little Fiat. He hung about the camp as the lorries were unloaded, his eyes alert, as usual saying little but always watchful. For safety, Morton never moved from his side and, because of his knowledge of Count Barda and the knowledge of the Italian army he had acquired in Intelligence, he was able to counter every carefully worded question.

It troubled Faiani. So much so he'd even tried to discuss it with the despised Scarlatti. But it had got him nowhere. Scarlatti had lived too long with the effects of influence and had too many irons in the fire of which he hoped to take advantage. It had made Faiani frustrated and irritable. He felt he *ought* to be able to trip up an impostor and the fact that he couldn't left him short-tempered and finally silent.

Under tarpaulins in the lorries were tyres and spare parts, and on Dampier's instructions the drivers were given food, with plenty of wine, and encouraged to talk. It wasn't difficult because one of them, an avowed communist who'd been in the Italian disasters in Greece, was loud in his contempt for that profitless campaign, which he condemned as an example of political improvidence, military incompetence, petty ambition and strategic and tactical shortsightedness.

'Started out of pure pique,' he said. 'Mussolini just wanted to show Hitler he could conduct a *blitzkrieg*, too.'

When Scarlatti himself appeared, Morton thanked him with a bow.

'Faiani tells me you come from Organo in the Apennines.' Scarlatti had also obviously been doing some homework. 'I have interests there. My father-in-law has a business that covers the area and I am a partner. But we've never been able to attract much attention. Perhaps the count might pass the word among his friends.'

Morton's face was blank. 'It could be possible. After the war. Providing, of course, the Duce has chosen the right side and we win.'

Like many Italians aware that Mussolini wasn't the man he claimed to be, Scarlatti wasn't sure how to answer. He knew the failings of the Italian army only too well, how conscription had produced nothing because there were never enough uniforms or equipment; how divisions had been reduced from three regiments to two – a piece of legerdemain that enabled the Duce to claim he had sixty divisions instead of the twenty-odd he really had; how, to bolster his claim of motorization, the police had to lend their vehicles to be painted in army colours for the military parades and hurriedly had to repaint them again on their return.

Scarlatti's driver, a lugubrious private called Mondi, who had been brought in out of the desert with jaundice and given the job of driving Scarlatti about until he recovered, echoed his thoughts. Like most private soldiers, he loathed the desert.

'Sometimes when you dig fortifications,' he said, 'it's as hard as rock and a pick or shovel makes no mark. At other times, it falls away beneath your feet.'

The wind, the disembodied silence, had scared him and he talked with horror of the khamsin, the drying wind which surrounded everybody in a cloud of fire and whirling sand.

'Two men lost last time,' he told Caccia. 'We found them shrivelled up like mummies. One had stones clutched in his fists. The other had shot himself through the head. Their eyes were dry as prunes and their mouths were full of sand.'

He had a fondness for English gin and was always on the cadge for it. 'It scares away the bullets and makes you forget the war,' he claimed. 'I just hope when I'm killed they bury me deep down so the jackals won't get me.' He sighed. 'Mussolini's filled Rome with fasces, flags, fine phrases and fancy claims,' he went on. 'But he never did much for me.'

'May the Lord protect us,' Caccia intoned piously.

'Will the Lord really protect us?'

'Of course He will.'

'What about the ones who are dead?' Mondi's face contained all the good cheer of an elderly bloodhound's. 'He didn't protect them.'

114

7

Even the Germans seemed to have accepted them. After all, they wore Italian caps and Italian tunics with Italian insignia on them, even some of them the ugly Italian trousers. And they used Italian tools on Italian vehicles. *They had to be Italians*.

The grumbling from the hoi-polloi died and apart from a doubtful wariness the nervousness disappeared. They were tucked well out of the way of the main traffic, which was largely round the fort, and they were rarely bothered. Dampier's idea began to seem not only possible but even very practical.

From time to time a German vehicle stopped alongside them, its driver asking the way or offering to barter rations for wine. The Germans were suffering from dysentery and, almost as badly off for food as the Italians, were always on the lookout for supplies. They ate the same tinned meat as the Italians, from tins marked AM (Administrazione Militare) but known to the Italians as Asinus Mussolini (Mussolini's Donkey) or Arabo Morte (Dead Arab) and to the Germans as Alter Mann (Old Man). Occasionally a little cheese or olive oil came their way but never any potatoes, which they loved, and they drooled at the thought of captured British rations.

Among them was the German sergeant they had seen tormenting the Italian girl outside the Bar Barbieri near the harbour. His name was Schwartzheiss and he worked as a chief stores clerk just to the west of Zuq where the Germans

115

had set up tank workshops far better than anything the British possessed. Embedded in concrete under canvas were big lathes and a heavy smithy, and they had tank precision instruments by the truckload, boxes of periscopes, 50 mm guns, sheets of armour, tracks, tyres, woodwork and steel parts.

'We could build tanks from scratch if we had to,' Schwartzheiss told Morton. 'In fact, we did when we first arrived. Dummy ones. Wooden, on old car frames. But then' – he grinned – 'we always did have a few extra tricks up our sleeve, didn't we, *tenente*? When we landed, there weren't many of us so we marched several times round Tripoli to make it seem there were more of us than there were.'

He had an engaging personality, with a wide smile, an infectious laugh, and an obvious sense of mischief that was tickled by any suggestion of outrageous fraud.

'It was a funny time, that,' he went on. 'While we were building up, the Tommies thought there were only a few disorganized Italians to face. And, while we thought the Tommies were going to come down on us like a lot of ravening wolves, we found out later that all the experienced ones had gone to Greece and been replaced by an inexperienced lot newly out from home.'

He offered a cigarette – a British Gold Flake, Morton noticed. 'Still,' he went on. 'It didn't matter much, because old Mussolini had already messed it up, hadn't he? He's already lost half his navy, the war's being won without him and his adventure in the Balkans has gone sour. He not only deluded Italy, he deluded himself, which is worse.'

'You don't think much of fascism, sergeant?' Morton tried.

Schwartzheiss smiled enigmatically. 'I'm just a German soldier fighting for his country,' he said. 'And your army doesn't contribute a lot, does it, *tenente*? Artillery that came from Austria after the last bunfight. No anti-aircraft guns

116

at all. And those tanks of yours – *Himmelherrgott!* Most of them come to a grinding halt whenever they're used.'

Morton listened with a faint growing indignation. He had heard it all before from captured Italians while in Intelligence but now it was with a vague sense of resentment at the German's smug self-satisfaction. He could only put it down to the Italian tunic and cap he was wearing. He thrust his thoughts aside and tried probing. 'I'm surprised your Führer allied himself to us,' he said.

Schwartzheiss grinned. 'I expect he knows as much about it as most politicians.' He gazed at Morton. 'I suppose a lot of Italians feel the same about what goes on in Rome.'

'Most of us are aware.'

Schwartzheiss frowned. 'It's the flies that get *me* down most about this place,' he said. 'Always wanting first bite at your food. *Afrika ist Scheiss*. Africa is shit. Come to that, *Krieg ist Scheiss*. War is shit, too.'

Morton smiled and Schwartzheiss went on with the arrogant contempt of all Germans for all Italians. 'All Mussolini's after is glory. We're only here to enhance his prestige.'

Morton smiled again. 'And *we*'re only here to make up your numbers.'

Schwartzheiss laughed. 'It's a marriage of convenience, *tenente*,' he agreed. 'Not one of joy. Still, why should I worry? The real estate's Italian not German. At the moment, though' – he shrugged – '*Nichts klappt*. Nothing works. And I'll bet nobody knows it better than your boys.'

Though Schwartzheiss was friendly enough, No. 64 Light Vehicle Repair Unit were glad to see the back of him. The Germans were twice as alert as the Italians and twice as shrewd, and their Intelligence, unlike Italian Intelligence, which was reputed to spy less on the enemy than on doubtful friends, was efficient. After his departure, with their eyes constantly straying towards the road in case a squad of German field police appeared, it took them the rest of the day to calm down.

They had just begun to feel safe when two Mercedes cars

appeared over the brow of the slope. Micklethwaite was on lookout, sitting on the edge of the wadi nursing a split finger he'd caught in one of the lorry doors and dreaming of the bestseller he intended to write when he returned to the British lines. He was just wondering how to spend the royalties when he became aware of the two cars and of high-peaked long-visored caps such as German officers wore.

'Oh, my God,' he croaked and scuttled at once to Dampier's tent, where Dampier, Rafferty and Morton were holding a conference.

'Visitors!' he bleated. 'They look like Germans!'

Convinced they were German field police sent by Schwartzheiss, they waited nervously. Unaware of what was going on, in one of the tents Jones the Song was shaving in the mirror of a Lancia truck. Dampier had told him to smarten himself up because he looked scruffy even for the Italian he was supposed to be impersonating and he was consoling himself with a verse or two of 'Land of My Fathers':

'. . . Ei gwrol ryfelwyr, gwladgarwyr tramâd,
Tros ryddid collsant eu gwaed,
Gwlad, Gwlad . . .'

Jones thought a lot of the land of his fathers and his splendid high tenor soared up to scratch at the sky.

As the cars slowed in a drifting cloud of yellow dust, Morton stepped forward, smart in his Italian officer's tunic. Following the drill they had devised, somebody had also warned Caccia and he waited nearby with Clegg, ready to supply Italian chatter in case anybody was listening who might understand.

As the cars stopped, a tall German officer with a general's badges and a thin sensitive face, climbed out, followed by a younger officer who was obviously his aide. The general was dressed in drill slacks and jacket. The younger officer wore shorts.

Morton drew a deep breath. Ordinary, brutalized Italian

soldiers, not too well educated and knowing nothing of the rest of the world, were one thing; Schwartzheiss, shrewd, clever, a German with a German's efficiency, was another; this man, a general, knowing everything, a man with authority who knew what made an army – any army – tick, was still another.

The German general, however, seemed less interested in 64 Light Vehicle Repair Unit than in the offside-rear tyre of his car. '*Il pneumatico si è –* ' He stopped and looked enquiringly at the younger officer.

'*Sgonfiato*,' the younger man prompted from a dictionary he held.

'So!' The general turned again to Morton. '*Il pneumatico si è sgonfiato. Per favore –* '

As he paused, Morton smiled. 'I speak German, excellency,' he said.

The German smiled. 'So? That makes it much easier. I am General Erwin, 4th Light Division. The tyre needs air. Is it possible to inflate it?'

'Of course, excellency. We have compressed air.' They hadn't but Morton had no doubt someone – probably Jones, who was least likely to object – could be bullied into doing the job manually. 'It's punctured, perhaps? Perhaps the general would like me to check it?'

Erwin glanced at the aide. 'Why not?' he said. '*Räder mussen rollen für den Sieg*. Wheels must turn for victory, eh? One of Dr Goebbels's latest slogans. Some people might call it one of the German atrocities we hear so much about. Please fix it. We have plenty of time.'

For a moment he stood with his head cocked listening to Jones, who was still in full spate.

'. . . Trwy deimlad gwladgarol, mor swynol yw si
Ei mentyff, afonydd i mi,
Gwlad, Gwlad . . .'

Clegg caught Morton's frantic look and gestured at Clinch. 'Shut that bloody fool up,' he hissed.

Having disposed of the land of his fathers, Jones was now into 'Guide me, O, thou Great Jehovah'.

'. . . Dal fi pan bwy'n teithieo'r manau
Gierwon yn fy ffordd y sydd:
Rho imi fanna,
Fel no bwyf yn llwfrau . . .'

As Clinch arrived and the song stopped abruptly, the German officer shrugged.

'*Che peccato*,' he said. 'What a pity! He has a splendid voice. He is a professional, perhaps?'

'No, excellency,' Morton said. 'He just sings because he likes singing. They all do. They aren't *Berufssoldaten* – regular soldiers – just peasants in uniform. From the mountains. Mountaineers always sing. You'll have heard the Swiss, I expect.'

'You should encourage him,' Erwin suggested. 'There's little enough beauty in the world. Especially these days. But that's surely not Italian he's using? My Italian isn't good but I can recognize it when I hear it.'

Morton thought fast. 'A dialect, excellency.'

'Of course. He comes from the mountains.'

'Near Stresa.'

'So! Austrian territory originally. I expect it's a crude form of German. I thought I recognized one or two of the words.'

You were clever if you did, Morton thought. Nobody but the Welsh understood Welsh, and not all of them.

Erwin smiled. 'I'm going out into the desert there,' he said. 'Stracka' – he gestured at the aide – 'and I are water-colour enthusiasts. We've noticed that from there you can get a glimpse of the roofs and palm trees of Zuq. It's a splendid subject.'

'I have little to offer in the way of refreshment, excellency, but perhaps – '

Erwin waved away the offer. 'Don't bother, *tenente*. We've brought food for the day.' He gestured at the driver of the second car. 'Obergefreiter Bomberg there has prepared something. We'll pick up the car on the way back.'

Confident of his skill with Erwin's language, Morton decided it might be wiser if he didn't. Jones the Song might well be singing 'I'm Dreaming Of A White Christmas' by then. 'I'll bring it to you, excellency,' he said. 'As soon as it's repaired. An hour or so, no more. Perhaps I might be permitted to see your work. I've always been interested in watercolours.'

Erwin was flattered. '*Wunderbar!* Splendid. Do that. I'll be pleased to show you.' He dabbed at his face with a handkerchief. 'What a pity it's so hot. The washes don't run as they should. The paper's brittle and tinder dry. It soaks up the colour. And the sand – ' He gestured vaguely.

Easels and drawing boards and boxes of paints were transferred to the second car and Erwin and Stracka climbed in with them. As Erwin settled in his seat, he gestured to the tent where Jones's voice was suddenly ominously silent.

'You should never stop your men singing, *tenente*,' he said reproachfully. 'That man has a splendid voice.'

'He should be giving his attention to his work, excellency.'

Erwin smiled. 'He should sing, too, *tenente*. Let him have the pleasure of his voice. I'd like to hear more of him. Italians are so lucky. Their climate makes for clear chests and splendid vocal cords.'

As Erwin jabbed the driver in the back and the car moved off, Rafferty and Dampier appeared warily from the tent.

'What did he want?'

Morton grinned. 'He wanted to listen to Taffy Jones singing,' he said.

When they had repaired the punctured tyre and the indignant Jones had been bullied into blowing it up, Morton climbed into the car and, followed by Caccia in Dampier's Humber to bring him back, drove it into the desert. The scene that greeted them was bucolic and peaceful. Erwin and Stracka were seated on camp stools with easels erected

121

in front of them, a large striped sun umbrella leaning over their heads. Alongside them a portable gramophone – once British – was playing. Erwin had discarded his peaked cap and wore a wide-brimmed straw hat tilted over his eyes and was busy sloshing colour on to the paper in front of him. In ochres and blues, a passable reproduction of the desert with the roofs and palms of Zuq just appearing over the horizon was emerging. Stracka was sitting alongside doing the same, though his painting was considerably less skilful than Erwin's. Both men were utterly absorbed and thoroughly enjoying themselves.

As the car came to a stop, Erwin went on painting for a moment. The gramophone finished playing and Bomberg, the driver, replaced the record with another and rewound it. Morton recognized the music as Mendelssohn.

'A Jew, excellency?' He couldn't resist it.

Erwin grinned, an honest mischievous grin. 'We keep that one for Italian generals,' he said. 'They worry about what to do, what to say, where to look, because they're puzzled yet they're afraid of offending. Are *you* afraid, *tenente*?'

'I like Mendelssohn, excellency. His music is kind. But, then, I like Mozart and Puccini and St Saëns and Elgar.'

Erwin smiled. 'All preferable to *"Deutschland Über Alles"* which sounds like ten thousand Lutheran choirs trumpeting a protest. Or the *"Horstwessellied"*, which only reminds us of a thug killed in a street brawl.'

'You're not a Nazi, general?'

Erwin's smile came again. 'I shouldn't be painting deserts if I were,' he smiled. 'I should be painting good Nazi supermen with strong faces and bronzed arms. Perhaps even good Nazi superwomen with full breasts and buttocks and a fanatic look of hope in their eyes that they'll produce good Nazi superchildren.'

Morton's face was blank. This was one for the book, he was thinking. A German sergeant who didn't think much of fascism and a German general who enjoyed Mendelssohn.

'We Germans are a strange race,' Erwin continued. 'We

have all the virtues except the arts. Our arts are leaden. The British produced Shakespeare. The Italians Puccini. What did we produce? Our beloved Führer.'

He looked at Stracka and laughed. 'Art's so important,' he went on, bending over his easel. 'Especially here. The desert saturates the mind and makes it as sterile as itself. Which is why we must keep up with the things that make us use our intelligence.' He frowned at his work. 'I could do better in oils. Perhaps you'll take a drink, *tenente*, with my thanks for the repair work.'

Clicking his fingers, Erwin directed Obergefreiter Bomberg forward. He held a bottle of German wine, frosted with cold.

'We managed to get ice,' Erwin smiled. 'It's our day off and we like to get away from time to time.' He passed the glass to Morton and gestured at Caccia. 'See the sergeant gets a beer, Stracka.'

He was studying Dampier's car. 'An English car?' he said. 'A Humber?'

'Captured, excellency,' Morton agreed. 'Everybody uses what they can get.'

'Soon it'll be impossible to identify each other,' Erwin admitted. 'We shall all look alike. As it is, we all wear khaki drill shirts and khaki drill shorts or trousers. The only difference is in the caps we wear.'

'Even our boots are British, excellency.'

'You're wise, *tenente*. The British have splendid equipment even if their weapons are inferior. They still have nothing to touch our 88 which, as you'll know, is anti-aircraft, anti-tank and, for the British, anti-social.' He laughed, then his smile died as he went on in the same vein as Schwartzheiss. 'But otherwise we're sadly lacking in many things. Our German corps here was a child of chance so that our food leaves a lot to be desired.'

He gestured with his glass. 'At Mechili there were stacks of canned beer, huts bursting with white flour, cigarettes, tobacco, jam, gallons of Scotch whisky, Indian tea, *Bohn-kaffee* – bean coffee, not ersatz – tinned food of all kinds.'

It seemed that, as with the Italians, food was a favourite topic of conversation.

'And the clothing,' Erwin went on. 'So tough, but so cool to wear. I was terrified my men would be seduced into indiscipline. A distinctive trait of the German is his capacity for envy, and British clothing is enough to make a saint break the Tenth Commandment. And when a German soldier loses faith in his army he finds it hard to face reality.'

The smile grew wider. 'We're taking advantage of the quiet spell. Stracka and I thought we'd spend a few days enjoying ourselves. We expect to be on the move again soon but unfortunately your general doesn't move very swiftly.'

Morton smiled, confident of Erwin's friendliness. 'I've heard it said that the only thing that stops the Germans getting to Cairo is the Italian general staff.'

Erwin gave a bark of laughter. 'And loose bowels,' he agreed.

They laughed together and Morton bent over Erwin's painting to admire it.

'It's not very good,' Erwin said modestly. 'I think it is another German atrocity. Every nation has them. With the British it's bagpipes.'

They laughed once more, then Erwin became serious. 'Still,' he said, 'we must count ourselves lucky here in the desert. We have none of the hard-eyed zealots of the Gestapo in this theatre. War brutalizes and battle has many bestial by-products, but out here, thank God, it's a war without rancour and there's not the sad destruction of beautiful things that war normally brings.' He smiled. 'There aren't even too many bad frights – only about one every week or two. And still human virtues and good manners and a little of what's been lost lately in Europe: *Ritterlichkeit und Kameradschaft* – chivalry and comradeship. It's the only thing that makes war endurable.'

Morton found himself actually liking the German. He was

a sophisticated, urbane military man of the type he thought only the British army with its amateur attitudes could produce. Despite an inclination to talk too much, he had a sense of humour and clearly saw through the sham of dictatorships. And, though it was clear he despised the Italian High Command, he was treating Morton, whom he believed to be Italian, with considerable courtesy.

He was gesturing with his glass again in a sweeping movement. 'This spot is full of pictures, *tenente*. The light and shade in the afternoon are splendid. The desert itself – pink, purple, grey, yellow, blue – and just to the east there, the dunes catching the light. One day I shall hold an exhibition of my desert paintings.'

Morton tested the water. 'When the British are driven out of Africa,' he said.

Erwin gave him a sidelong glance and in it there was doubt. 'Yes,' he agreed. 'When the British are driven out of Africa.'

They exchanged a few more pleasantries, then Morton drove away with Caccia. As they disappeared, Erwin stared after them.

'A good young man that, Stracka,' he said. 'But strange.' He glanced again at the disappearing cloud of dust. 'I wonder who he is.'

8

Though no one was keen to see General Erwin again – 'Generals know too much about the army,' Rafferty said – Scarlatti seemed too concerned with his own affairs to worry anybody much.

Despite his bounce, he was an anxious little man whose thoughts were always with his family back in Italy, and it was easy to draw him out. By talking about his children, it wasn't hard to get him worrying about the outcome of the war and from there to his hopes for the new push. By discovering what he was issuing, in what quantities and to where, it then wasn't hard to build up the sort of picture Dampier was seeking. As Morton reported what he learned, Dampier, still confined to his tent with a back that stubbornly refused to improve, put it all down on paper. And while Dampier occupied himself with gathering information, it became Rafferty's job to preserve their anonymity.

They had already effected simple repairs to one or two vehicles, but since they had had to turn away others more seriously damaged, the wary Rafferty thought that Clutterbuck should put his skills to use once more.

'The notice out there says 64 LIGHT VEHICLE REPAIR UNIT,' he pointed out. 'So, unless we want somebody to surround the place with storm troopers we've got to look as if we really are a light vehicle repair depot.'

Clutterbuck saw his point at once. 'Leave it to me,' he said.

The following morning, Clutterbuck, Clegg and Micklethwaite, dressed in galabiyahs from the Ratbags' property basket and wearing a lot of brown No. 7 from the make-up box, set off for Zuq in Dampier's car with Morton and Caccia. Morton was done up to the nines in his Italian officer's jacket and cap. Caccia, wearing his sergeant's stripes, was armed – just in case – with a bundle of the requisition forms they had found on the night they arrived, filled in by Rafferty and completed by Clutterbuck – who, it seemed, could add forgery to his other skills – with a fair facsimile of the signature of Brigadier Olivaro.

Morton dropped them near the dump and Micklethwaite was left outside the wire fence, squatting by a ditch clutching a sack.

'You just sit there, old mate,' Clutterbuck said. 'When Cleggy 'ere appears, you pick up what 'e drops and shove it into your sack. Got it?'

'Won't anybody want to know what I'm doing?' Micklethwaite's plump face was worried under its make-up.

'Arabs is always sittin' in the sun thinkin',' Clutterbuck explained patiently. 'Sometimes they're even just sittin'. Nobody takes no notice. If anybody comes along 'oo looks suspicious, just 'old out your 'and an' say, "Backsheesh." That's beer money. If they start gettin' stroppy, pretend you don't understand. You wouldn't, o' course, them bein' Italian, and you bein' a wog. If they try to kick your arse, beat it. It's safer. You can always come back when they've gone.'

'Suppose they find out I'm *not* an Arab. Won't they think I'm a spy and shoot me?'

Clutterbuck considered the possibility. 'Well,' he admitted, 'they might.'

Leaving a distinctly worried Micklethwaite sitting by the wire, his sack stuffed up a culvert under the road, the other three strolled into the dump, Clegg and Clutterbuck in their dusty robes, Caccia carrying the Italian forms they'd acquired. As they passed the gate, Caccia gestured at the other two, and the private sitting at a desk checking in the native workers nodded.

Five minutes later Clutterbuck was carrying a brush and Clegg a bucketful of dirty water, both neatly removed by Clutterbuck from alongside a hut where an Arab labourer, who had disappeared round a corner for a smoke, had left them.

'Tools of the trade,' Clutterbuck explained. 'I expect 'e's usin' 'em for the same thing we're goin' to use 'em for.'

Nobody looked twice at them as they moved about the dump because they looked exactly like an Italian soldier with his two Arab helpers making sure the drains were working.

'It's a well-known fact,' Clutterbuck reassured the nervous Caccia, 'that if you're carrying a piece of paper you're on office business. You've got a 'ole sheaf of 'em there.'

Under Scarlatti the dump had become an extensive one and they remained there the whole day. Every hour or so, Clegg carried his bucket to the perimeter and emptied it over the wire, at which point Micklethwaite rose from the ditch where he was squatting and shovelled into his sack the assorted spanners, wrenches, pliers, screwdrivers, wire, screws, nuts and bolts which the dirty grey water had hidden.

'It's an old dodge,' Clutterbuck said cheerfully. 'Them Arabs what work in the camps round the Delta are at it the 'ole time. They caught one old bastard with a sack containing a 'undred and sixty spanners, twelve pressure gauges and fifty spark plugs.'

As they left late in the afternoon, the Italian private on the gate eyed them but said nothing, and they strolled down the road towards the town. They were well pleased with the day's work, especially Clutterbuck, who had also done the rounds of any unattended petrol tanks he had seen. Micklethwaite was waiting for them by the wire, obviously encouraged by their success.

'What I tell you?' Clutterbuck said. 'They didn't shoot you arter all, did they?'

'One Italian tried to kick me.' Micklethwaite seemed quite pleased that the Italian had thought him worth kicking. 'An Arab spoke to me too.'

'What you do?'

'What you told me. Acted daft. Morton came past,' he went on. 'He said he'd pick us up near the mosque.'

They waited close to the Arabs drowsing with their animals near the white dome among the trees. It was impossible for Caccia in his Italian uniform to squat down with them, so he wandered down the street, keeping one eye on the others so he could pick up the car when it appeared.

As he reached the corner, he recognized the standpipe in the road and the Arab women carrying *chattis* and gossiping in a group round a muddy pool. They reminded him of the Bar Barbieri and he found it only fifty yards further on. As he approached, he was presented with the same performance he'd seen a few days before – Rosalba Coccioli swiping with a cloth which looked as though it was normally used to wipe the floor at Schwartzheiss, the German sergeant he'd seen with her on his last visit to the bar.

The sergeant was hooting with laughter as the girl began to pick up empty bottles and hurl them futilely at him. As he climbed into his *kübelwagen*, she turned away and savagely began to wipe the tables. As she saw Caccia, however, her expression changed and she waved enthusiastically, pleased to see him.

'Eh, *soldato*,' she said. 'So you came back after all!'

'I said I would.'

'And your friends?'

Caccia waved a hand vaguely.

'Is our army staying in Zuq this time? I'm tired of going out into the desert every time the place changes hands. So is everybody else.' She gestured after the German. 'That Sergeant Schwartzheiss,' she snapped. 'He's always here. He wants to get into my bed.'

129

Caccia eyed the girl. She had a good figure, long legs, a good behind and, as he could see down the front of her blouse when she bent forward to wipe the tables, a good before too.

'I would, too,' he said. 'If I could.'

She swung at him with the grey cloth but there wasn't the anger in it with which she had swung at the German.

'*Eh, soldato,*' she said. 'You have a large mouth.'

'Noted for it,' Caccia agreed.

'You going to Cairo? After the English?'

Caccia shrugged. 'Mussolini'll never get to Cairo,' he said. Nobody had ever explained the strategic or tactical situation to him. It was just a feeling he had.

The girl pulled a face. '*Mamma mia,*' she said. 'It's certain *you* won't if that's how you feel. You might as well pack up and go home to Italy. I expect you'd like that, *eh, soldato?*'

Caccia shrugged again and she went on in a bitter voice. '*I'*d go back,' she said. 'Tomorrow. There's nothing to keep me in Libya – only a bar with nothing in it except Sicilian wine, vermouth and anisette.'

'Why did you come here?'

'My mother died. And then my father died. That frog-faced clown Mussolini put him in prison for speaking his mind and he never came out. I couldn't stay in Rome. I'd have ended up on the streets. There are plenty of dirty old men who'd have helped me to. So I came here to join my uncle. My aunt had run off with a sergeant in the army and he needed a woman about the house.'

'Why did *he* come here?'

She gestured. 'The government had schemes to help people. Surely you've read about them in the papers. He fancied himself as a farmer. Only he didn't know anything about farming so he ended up doing what he did in Rome. Running a bar. He's out looking for petrol. We need wine. We need beer. But to get wine and beer you have to go to Derna or Tripoli, and to go to Derna or Tripoli you have to have petrol for the car. But there *is* no petrol. It's needed for the Duce's war machine, they tell us. Also, I suppose, for the Duce to drive round in a big car with his generals to impress Hitler. Hitler?' She spat. 'He looks like a plumber come to fix the drains.' She shrugged again. 'All the same, perhaps we're better off here than back home in Italy. Italy will come out of this war worse than she went in. If the English win, they'll be all over Italy. If the Germans win, it'll be the Germans.'

He fished. 'Which would you prefer?'

Her shoulders lifted. 'I worked in England once. I speak good English. Listen: "Pass down the bus, please. No standing on the platform." How about that? And "What is your choose?" when you ask someone to have a drink. And when one has had a triumph, "Bob's your ankle." Who is this Bob, I wonder.'

'Nobody in particular,' Caccia said. 'It's just a phrase. "Bob's your uncle." '

'Ah! I visited many places in London. Waterloo Square and Trafalgar Station. Named for battles when the English beat Napoleon.'

'You mean Trafalgar Square and Waterloo Station. Trafalgar Square's got a big column in it with a statue of Admiral Nelson on top.'

'*Si*. A proud nation, the English. I've also seen the Arco di Marma. The Arch of Marble.'

'The English call it the Marble Arch.'

'Such wealth!' She turned the words over on her tongue. 'Is it really of marble? I wish I'd stayed in England. They'd probably have put me in prison when Italy came into the war but I think I'd rather be in prison in England than free in Italy. There isn't much difference. Except that they get fed in England. Meat several times a week, they say. Even with a war on. And they don't have that loud-mouthed stallion Mussolini shouting at them.' She sighed. 'It was better here when the English soldiers were here. They don't pinch your bottom like the Italians. It's always better when there are soldiers here. Most of the civilians are gone.'

'No other Italian girls?'

'One or two. I have a friend, Teresa Gelucci. But most of them work in the officers' hotels. Some of them have even become officers' groundsheets. *I* wouldn't work for them.'

'The Italians are their allies.'

She sniffed. 'I am not truly Italian. I'm a cosmopolitan. I've been to London. I stopped a day in Paris on the way home, and I have worked in German Switzerland.' She paused for a moment and sighed; in the sigh was all her longing for the romance of big cities.

'It's dead here,' she went on. 'I think they take the sidewalks in after dark. No clothes – where would you buy clothes in Zuq? No lipstick, no face-powder. No perfume nearer than Derna. The ships carry only shells and guns.'

Caccia remembered what Clutterbuck had seen. 'I can get you lipstick,' he offered. 'I can get you perfume.'

'I'd like that.' She looked sad. 'I wish my mamma hadn't died. I'd still have been in England. I might have married an Englishman like my cousin, Cecilia Neri. She thought they'd put her in prison but she had a couple of children and they couldn't put the wife of a soldier and the mother of his kids in prison. They're not like Hitler over there, you know. She's all right, too, because there are plenty of other Italians round her. Well' – she gestured – 'not *Italian* Italians. *English* Italians. They look after her. It used to be easy for Italians to go to England. They set up in London. Soho. That's where this cousin of mine lives. Her husband has a big house with lawns and gardens. In Dean Street.'

'There aren't any big houses with lawns and gardens in Dean Street,' Caccia said. 'It's all shops and offices and restaurants.'

'You know London?'

Caccia did a little quick thinking. 'Worked there before the war. A month or two. In a restaurant.'

'Harrods?'

'Harrods isn't a restaurant. It's a big store.'

She sighed again. 'My cousin Cecilia was lucky. She was going to pay a visit to her family in Rome but she found she was having another baby and couldn't go. She was lucky. The war started and she'd have had to stay. Her husband's family have a food store called the Continental Market. Angelo Donatello her father-in-law's called. Her husband's called – '

'Max.'

Her eyebrows shot up. 'You know him?'

Caccia had spoken without thinking and he hurriedly backed down. 'No, no.'

Her eyes narrowed. 'You've been to Soho? You know the Donatellos?'

'No, no.' Caccia's automatic response to a familiar name was getting him into trouble. The unbelievable coincidence that this girl was a cousin of the wife of a man he'd known all his life, who'd attended the same school, chased the same girls, gone to the same dances, seemed impossible.

But he'd been to Max Donatello's wedding and kissed the bride because Max Donatello was the son of a grocer like Caccia himself, working in and living above a shop redolent with Italian scents and hung with sausages and peppers and Italian vegetables. He'd even been called up with Caccia but, because his interests had always been with filling his stomach, he had managed to get into the Catering Corps and was now a sergeant chef in an officers' mess in England, able to get home at regular intervals to his wife, the Italian girl who was cousin, by God, to this girl who was leaning on the counter of her uncle's bar, staring at him with large, dark, suspicious eyes.

He was still considering how to convince her when he heard the car outside. He was glad to bolt.

'*Ciao*,' he said. 'See you again!'

She didn't answer and as he appeared outside the door Clutterbuck stuck his head from the car. He was still wearing his galabiyah and make-up but like the others was smoking a British Players.

'Jesus Christ,' he said. 'Look slippy!'

Caccia glanced at the girl, who was staring at him with hostile eyes as he scrambled aboard. But as Morton revved the engine her expression changed and she started to wave.

'*Eh, soldato!*' she screamed. '*Ritornate! Ritornatevi!* Come again!'

9

That night the RAF came. It was fairly well understood at the other side of the lines that the Italians were up to something, and with Zuq among the entry ports for their army's supplies it was inevitable that the RAF should turn their attention to it.

As the bombs whistled down round the harbour, the fire brigade turned out as usual and, despite their frightened eyes and wild cries of alarm, they did sterling work. They had no sooner put out a fire near the harbour, however, than the fort was hit. A wall collapsed but, apart from two lorries which went up in flames, little other damage was done. Even as the fire brigade headed towards it, though, they were caught up by a dispatch rider with the information that a corner of the hospital had also been hit.

Scarlatti, the town major, had called out the troops and the place was surrounded by soldiers in trucks and cars, and a whole string of them started carrying out patients and equipment and laying them on the lawns. To aid the ancient fire appliances, the usual bucket chain was started from one of the ponds supplying water to the fountain but it was never sufficient and, as they struggled to douse the flames, other soldiers were putting up marquees to house the rescued patients.

While all this was going on, a stray salvo of bombs from one of the last aeroplanes over the town hit Scarlatti's dump. The first bomb brought down the gatehouse and part of the fence. A second fell inside, bringing down a corner of the food store, another demolished part of the heavy tool store, and the last two removed the fence at the far side. Immediately, as the news shot around the town, every Arab and Italian who wasn't afraid to be out in the bombing descended on the place to grab what he could.

Clegg, who had taken to sleeping under one of the lorries for safety, lifted his head sharply at the sound of a vehicle roaring into camp and hit it sharply enough against the axle to bring tears to his eyes. Crawling out dizzily, he saw it was Clutterbuck who had been in the town searching for beer. He had just arrived back and was yelling blue murder.

'The whole bloody place's wide open and up for grabs!' he was screaming. 'The wogs are in there already! Scarlatti's doing his nut, yellin' for 'elp, and they've turned out all 'is staff and labourers and 'alf the Italian police to get the stuff away before it's either burned or pinched! But you can't tell who's rescuin' it and who's pinchin' it and, in any case, as soon as they dump it outside, it gets pinched again! If we get in quick we can get everything we need to set us up!'

The whole area was chaos. Two palm trees, caught by the blast and uprooted to cant at an angle of forty-five degrees, had brought down telephone wires which hung in loops over the road to cut communications with anywhere outside the town. There seemed to be hundreds of soldiers and night-shirted Arabs about and they all seemed to have their arms full. The military police kept stopping them but the Italians said they were rescuing the stuff and all the Arabs apparently had passes to indicate they were on the staff of the dump.

'Half of 'em false,' Clutterbuck said. 'Never mind usin' your 'ands. Just drive the lorry in.'

They were stopped at the gap in the fence where the gate had been by a frightened young soldier with his rifle at the ready.

'Get out of the way, man,' Morton shouted at him. 'This whole business is ridiculous! People are carrying things out

136

one at a time. We should be saving it in lorryloads, not handfuls.'

The soldier seemed to agree that it was a good idea and waved them through.

'The heavy tools, Clutterbuck,' Rafferty demanded immediately. 'Where are they?'

'Over 'ere,' Clutterbuck said. 'They got acetylene burners an' the lot.'

The end of the heavy tool store was lying in a pile of splintered planks and, because most people were after the food and the lighter articles which could easily be carried away, the immediate area was deserted both by looters and guards. A generator went into the back of the lorry first, followed by a block and tackle, acetylene burners and gas cylinders. Then Clutterbuck spotted a heavy-duty drill.

'We could do with one 'o them,' he said. "Ang on. I'll get another lorry.'

As the rest of them grabbed tools, tyres and spare parts, he disappeared into the flame-lit darkness to return five minutes later with a Lancia truck.

Directed by Rafferty, who knew exactly what they required, they began to fill the second truck. One eye on the future, Clegg had found a crate of beer. Food, clothing, camp equipment followed. By this time they had been joined by other Italian soldiers and a few Arabs. Most of them were helping themselves, on the principle that if it were going to be destroyed why not enjoy it?

Morton spotted Scarlatti in the distance, standing in the back of his car screaming orders at a group of soldiers, and Faiani, on foot, limping painfully about, flourishing a fistful of papers as he marshalled Arab labourers into carrying things to safety outside the main gate. As soon as he'd disappeared, Morton stepped from the shadows and ordered the Arabs to stuff what they'd rescued into the lorry Clutterbuck had appropriated. Then, as he found the liquor store and was just helping himself to a case of Italian brandy, he became aware of another man in the shadows. His heart thumped, but, as the spill from a searchlight fell on the other figure, he saw it was Sergeant Schwartzheiss, staggering under a case marked JOHN WALKER AND CO., SCOTCH WHISKY.

For a second they stopped dead, facing each other, the light playing on their faces. Schwartzheiss grinned.

'*Guten Abend, tenente,*' he said, his teeth gleaming in the glow of the flames.

'*Buona sera, sergente,*' Morton replied.

'On business, *tenente*?'

'You, too, I see.'

Schwartzheiss nodded at the case Morton was carrying. 'Two of mine for two of yours,' he said.

They switched bottles quickly and Schwartzheiss's teeth gleamed.

'*Gute Nacht, tenente.*'

'*Buona notte, sergente. E buona fortuna.*'

'*Das Glück.* Good luck to you, too, *tenente*. Funny how you can get involved in this sort of thing and see so many people without recognizing a soul.'

Morton laughed. 'Not a soul, sergeant. Not a soul.'

As Morton returned to the lorry, people were tossing blankets, bedding, tents, flags, anything they could get hold of into it from any salvaged pile that was handy. Coats, shirts, shorts, military plus-fours, socks, jerseys, scarves, caps, overcoats, boots – most of them originally British and, like the whisky, the beer and the cigarettes, the spoils of the disaster at Mechili. Belts, packs, ammunition pouches, bayonet scabbards, rifles laid down by their owners to make the fetching and carrying easier. Tins of food. Bottles of wine. Looted British rum.

The first lorryload had already disappeared, driven off by Caccia, when the panic began to subside. As some sort of order began to be brought into the affair, Rafferty decided to leave while it was safe. A squad of military police brought up by Bianchi's successor were starting to search the Arabs but, with Morton standing on the running board shouting,

'*Aprire la strada!* Make way, make way,' nobody stopped them and they arrived back at their camp undetected and elated by their success.

Twisted by his lumbago, Dampier could only grind his teeth with frustration that he hadn't had the pleasure of being there too, and try to console himself with the thought that at least it had been *his* command which had done the work. When he saw what they'd acquired, however, he was aghast, thinking of investigations, enquiries, even courts martial – all conducted in Italian.

'It's ridiculous,' he said. 'We're beginning to look like a *heavy* duty unit!'

Aware that, after British army parsimony, even he had been overcome by the excitement and the joy of robbing the enemy, Rafferty managed to look sheepish. 'It was there,' he explained.

'So we had to steal it!' Dampier was shocked. 'Because it was up for grabs.'

'You couldn't just leave it,' Morton said.

'And we can't give it back,' Clegg pointed out. 'We could mebbe bury some of it – '

'Or flog it in Derna,' Caccia suggested.

'Or even,' Rafferty suggested, 'make it official. Properly issued, accounted and signed for.'

'Italian army forms D3801 and C2947!' Morton grinned.

Despite Dampier's alarm, there was no point in not putting what they'd acquired to good use, so they started work at once. Working all night, they changed the signs and the paintwork on the lorry they'd acquired, filed off the engine number and stamped on a new one, unloaded tents, bedding, clothing, the generator and the oxyacetylene welding apparatus, and filled in – from Rafferty's experience of stores and Morton's knowledge of Italian procedure – the blank inventory forms they'd picked up from the bombed convoy the first night in Zuq. To complete the picture, all that was necessary was for Clutterbuck to add his version of Brigadier Olivaro's signature, which, until they felt safe to move east, would make them officially part of the Italian North African army.

It was a satisfying feeling as they breakfasted off looted and re-looted British bacon, sausages and tea. As he pushed away his dixie, Clinch held out a packet of cigarettes to Jones the Song.

'After all,' he said, 'what *is* loot? Anything that's left lying around. Have a smoke. These are better than them bird shit and camel dung Indian Vs they issue us with. We got enough tents now to start a circus. Old Clutterbuck knew what he was doing.' He stopped abruptly and sat up slowly. 'Incidentally, he said slowly, 'where *is* Clutterbuck?'

In the excitement nobody had noticed Clutterbuck was missing and, as the news flew round the camp, they stared at each other, edgy and concerned again.

'He doesn't speak much Italian,' Morton pointed out. 'Suppose they've arrested him.'

'More likely hanged him,' Dampier growled.

All the same, when Clutterbuck hadn't turned up by lunchtime they began to grow nervous. But nobody else turned up either – neither the Italian service *carabinieri* nor the German *feldpolizei* – so that, while they made preparations for a quick departure just in case, they decided to risk it and wait a little longer.

During the afternoon, Clegg, boiling his spare socks in a dixie as he sat on a hump of sand on lookout, became aware of a truck heading towards him. It was an Italian Lancia and he recognized the driver at once.

'It's old Buttercluck,' he grinned. 'He made it after all.'

As Clutterbuck jumped down, he looked indignant. 'Got copped,' he explained. 'Got arrested, din't I? That bloody Sub-lieutenant Fanny. Caught me with a bottle in me fist.'

'Did he ask who you were?'

'Asked all sorts of things. I just acted daft.'

'Did he recognize you?'

'Naw, it was dark. But he got a couple of Libyan

conscripts to guard me. Shoved me in a shed, the bastards did, and locked the door. Thought I'd had it. Only they forgot about the window. It opened from inside, and I nipped out at the back. I expect they're still guardin' the door.' Clutterbuck's grin reappeared. ''Alf the bloody dump's disappeared into wog town.'

'Old Scarlatti'll cop it in the neck.'

'Not 'im.' Clutterbuck was full of contempt for Clegg's naivety. ''E was at it as 'ard as the rest, shiftin' what 'e could for 'is private use every time that Fanny feller turned his back. It'll all be locked up now and he'll probably even 'ave a sergeant o' police 'e can trust to guard it. 'E'll 'ave written it all off as "lost due to enemy action" by now, and what 'e can't sell in town'll go to civvies in Derna an' Tripoli.' He paused. 'I got a surprise for the Old Man.'

He moved to the back of the lorry. Inside, lying on looted bedding, was a sleeping man wrapped in a blanket.

'Who's this?' Clegg demanded.

''E reckons 'e's an Australian. I once thought I'd like to emigrate to Australia.'

'Which part?'

'All of me, you stupid sod! 'E says 'e's a company sergeant major. I found 'im wanderin' about at the edge of the town.'

Clegg took another look at the sleeping man. 'How do you know he's not an Italian spy?'

Clutterbuck grinned. 'No Italian spy I ever 'eard of could 'ave swore like 'e did.'

As they talked, the man in the lorry opened his eyes and sat up. He was unkempt, thin-faced, unshaven and dressed in tattered khaki drill. He was staring puzzled at Clegg's Italian jacket.

'This is one of my mates,' Clutterbuck said.

The Australian stared. 'An Eyetie?'

''E's not a proper Eyetie. 'E's English like me.'

The Australian looked bewildered as they helped him from the truck, staring round at the Italian flags, the Italian lorries, the portraits of Mussolini and Victor Emmanuel.

'Well, if you're Poms,' he said, 'what the hell are you doin' here?'

'I sometimes wish I knew,' Clegg admitted. 'What are *you* doing here?'

'I got out of the compound at Sofi, didn't I? Where am I? I thought the Italians were in this place.'

'They are.'

The Australian looked blank, so Clegg took him by the arm and drew him into the nearest tent. Caccia, who was sitting on a roll of blankets daydreaming about the girl at the Bar Barbieri, looked up.

'Get Morton,' Clegg said. 'And bring a bottle of beer back with you.'

As Caccia vanished, the Australian stared after him.

'That's Caccia,' Clegg explained.

'He Italian or a Pom?'

'A Pom.'

'He had an Eyetie name.'

'Some Poms do. Some have French. What's yours?'

'Irish, I think. It's Fee. Athol Fee.' The Australian looked suspicious. 'What the Christ's goin' on here?'

'We got stranded behind the Italian lines when they put on their push. We've been here ever since.'

Fee gestured. 'That feller who went out – he was wearing an Italian cap – '

'That's right.' Clegg picked up his own cap. 'I've got one, too.'

'What the hell for?' Fee's voice became a bleat.

'So the Italians'll think we're an Italian vehicle repair unit.'

'And what *are* you?'

'Well, I'm part of a concert party but we got a bit mixed up with an equipment recovery unit under a colonel. He's done his back in unloading Italian stores.'

The Australian was looking completely baffled now, but as Caccia returned with a bottle of beer, he stared at it in delight. 'I'm not suffering, am I?' he asked. 'I'm not seein' mirages?'

Clegg tried to make him understand. Fee looked so bemused, he was glad when Morton appeared with Rafferty and Dampier.

'Escaped prisoner of war,' Clegg introduced.

'Where from?' Dampier asked.

'The compound at Sofi,' Fee said. 'I dug me way underneath the wire.'

'Good God! How far did you walk?'

'About four thousand bloody miles! To Cape Town and back! All round Africa! I dunno. Too bloody far. I know that.'

'Good God, it must have been hot!'

'Hotter than you think, mate.' Fee began to pull his shirt off. Underneath it, wrapped round his waist, he had a Union Jack. 'Wore that all the time,' he said. 'Ever since they put us in the bag, Couldn't let the bastards have the old flag, could I? She was carried when we marched through Sydney on our way to the troopship and she's goin' to be carried through Sydney when we go home after this lot's over.'

'Saving the flag! A very commendable action.' It was the sort of pointless, old-fashioned military gesture of which Dampier heartily approved. VCs had been awarded for similar actions before now. 'Anybody else with you?'

'No. "Where the hell do you run to when you're out?" they asked. We knew the Italians were holding the coast and the Germans were directly to the south. It only left the desert. I decided to chance it. But I hadn't any food or water and it only took me twenty-four hours to decide I'd made a mistake and the only thing I could think of then was to turn north and head for the coast. I thought I might steal a boat and sail it back to Alex. By the time I got here, I'd decided I'd be wiser to give meself up. What happens now?'

'We take you with us.'

'Where to?'

'Back to the British lines. That's where we're intending to go. Eventually anyway.'

'Holy Jesus Christ!' The Australian's gaunt face broke into a grin. 'Then I didn't make a mistake after all.'

10

Company Sergeant Major Athol Fee's arrival in the camp of 64 Light Vehicle Repair Unit caused few ripples. He was in far better shape than they'd thought and with two days' food and drink inside him soon began to sit up and take notice.

He had a great deal of information about Sofi and knew roughly what units were in the area around. He had picked up a little Italian and, Italian guards being as garrulous as they were, had managed to learn what tanks and what guns they possessed and roughly what they intended. He had also been careful to count the Australian prisoners who were still at Sofi.

'Two hundred and seventy-nine,' he announced. 'Exactly. And every one of the buggers wantin' to know what's goin' to be done about him.'

Two hundred and seventy-nine extra men – especially Australians who were not noted for their affectionate natures or for their fondness for the enemy – were a godsend to a man like Dampier, eager to imprint himself on the war. With a group that big, he felt, he could take over Sofi, radio the navy to pick them up, and hold off the opposition until the job was done. At the very least create another Tobruk to be a thorn in the enemy's side.

It was a pleasant enough thought but, without weapons and supporting artillery or armour, he knew it was nothing but a dream. He was well aware that they ought long since to have moved east, but somehow the feeling that they were living under the noses of the enemy intrigued him. Still nobody had investigated them and they all, even Jones the Song, felt safe now.

Morton and Rafferty, however, hearing of Faiani's arrest of Clutterbuck, were nervous, and only the thought that the imminent commencement of the new Italian attack would allow them to disappear reassured them. Despite his suspicions, Faiani had made no move against them and they persuaded themselves that he'd stopped asking himself questions.

The only snag was that the camp had now grown so important-looking with all the tents and vehicles and painted notices they'd acquired, they felt they could expect a visit at any moment from some important Italian politician, who everybody – even the British – knew liked to slip across the Mediterranean on a visit to collect the ritual silver medal that was given for service overseas. At the very least, an inspection by Brigadier Marziale, the area commander, or Brigadier Olivaro, the quartermaster general from Derna.

By this time Clutterbuck had a group of Arabs operating for him in and around the German workshops at the other side of the town where Sergeant Schwartzheiss worked. Despite their vaunted efficiency, it seemed the Germans were no cleverer at protecting their matériel than anybody else.

'That Germany sergeant's workin' a racket, too,' Clutterbuck said. 'Got 'isself appointed Director of Native Labour for Zuq, din't 'e, an' 'e's takin' bribes to give jobs and paddin' the rolls somethin' terrible.'

'Are you sure?' Dampier was wondering if the information might possibly contribute to the winning of the war.

'It don't take more'n a coupla glances to see what 'e's up to, does it?' Clutterbuck said. 'They're supposed to be buildin' a new pipeline between Zuq an' Jeniffa, and 'e's the bloke what's 'irin' the labour and indentin' for the material. Steel, cement, petrol, rations for the workforce, 'uts, beddin', tents. Only there isn't a pipeline between Zuq and

Jeniffa. I 'ad a look. Everythin's goin' to Arab and Italian contractors in Derna and that Schwartzheiss feller's linin' 'is pockets with the proceeds, to say nothin' of the wages 'e draws for wog labour what don't exist.'

Clutterbuck knew exactly where the enemy units in the desert were because he was careful to study the direction forms he saw about Scarlatti's dump and, to Dampier's surprise, he found they were building up a remarkably clear picture of the enemy's order of battle, because Mondi, Scarlatti's driver, was also never slow to air his grievances.

He still hadn't got over his jaundice. He was as yellow as a lemon – even his eyes were yellow – and it had left him low in spirits, sentimental and full of nostalgia for home, so that he liked to talk of girls, bowls, wrestling matches and hunting hares in the fields outside Naples where he lived to add to his family's rations. He often listened to the officers of the ships arriving in Zuq and he was worried about the news they brought because Italy was expecting to be bombed and food was scarce so that there were queues at all the shops and his family were being driven into the black market.

'It's as bad as here,' he said.

Due to inefficiency and corruption, in the desert he and his friends had been existing on biscuits, captured bully beef and beans, and, because there was a shortage of pasta, had been issued with rice which they loathed, while at times they had even been driven to netting migrating birds.

'And that's no diet for a sick stomach,' he said. 'But what do you expect? The ships only carry things for the fighting, and there are so many sinkings our own Mare Nostrum's nothing but a swimming pool for Italian sailors.'

Even the fuel situation was sinister, he claimed, because the ships that managed to cross to North Africa had to have so many escorts, as much fuel was used as was brought across, while, with Tripoli, the only really workable port in North Africa, always a bottleneck because of lethargy and indifference, when they arrived the ships had to wait to be unloaded and became sitting ducks for the RAF.

The activities of 64 Light Vehicle Repair Unit had produced remarkably useful information that couldn't have been bettered by a paid spy, though they did seem to Dampier to give Clutterbuck, the thief and deserter, a surprising hold over them. He had become indispensable, and, what was more, he had realized it, and these days he and Morton, with help from Rafferty, were almost running the little unit. Occasionally – almost, it seemed, with condescension – they took Dampier into their confidence and told him what they planned next.

It was, Dampier decided, an extraordinary situation they were in.

Morton was on easy terms with Scarlatti, and Clutterbuck had set up an arrangement with the leader of an Arab gang that was milking Scarlatti's stores for all it was worth. A lot of what they stole disappeared into hidden passages and rooms in the Roman amphitheatre. Nobody wanted the place and most of the Arabs considered it haunted, so Clutterbuck had set up a stores of his own in one of the chambers at the back that was full of items from Scarlatti's warehouses. In another he had opened a canteen where an Arab boy dispensed stolen coffee and it actually seemed to be making money.

'I'd never have believed it,' Dampier admitted. 'Not without first seeing it in Cairo.'

'It takes all sorts.' Clutterbuck's face was cunning. 'Scarlatti's got a 'ut full of stuff he's nicking and 'e's fitted a bloody great padlock on the door. But what 'e don't know is that I've got the same padlock on my door. Anything you want,' he encouraged in fatherly tones, 'just ask for.'

To Dampier it sometimes seemed that, while the governments of Europe were beggaring their countries to provide for their troops, those same troops were busy robbing them hand over fist. The only consolation he could find was that the looting he had struggled so hard against in the British army went on in the enemy's camp, too. At least, one cancelled out the other.

By kind permission of Clutterbuck, Jones the Song had acquired a portable gramophone – like Erwin's once part of some British officers' mess – together with a set of records of popular English ballads. Their repetition drove everybody mad.

'It's for after the war,' Jones insisted. 'I'm learnin' 'em, see. Thought mebbe I'd go on the stage.'

'You have to wash to go on the stage,' Caccia pointed out.

'If you want to move into the top bracket,' Clegg agreed, 'you have to behave as if you're already there. Washing's important.'

Jones wasn't the only one who had profited. Conscious that he was sitting on a tremendous scoop, Micklethwaite was writing on stolen paper with a stolen typewriter reams of notes for when he was in a position to make use of them in the story he was going to publish as soon as he was free. It had always been his ambition to write something sensational and in his notes he had the scoop to end all scoops. Drama and comedy – even a touch of scandal.

Even Clinch had acquired a German radio receiver that was twice as good as anything the British possessed and had collected reams of information for Dampier to collate. Since Clutterbuck had stolen a code book from Scarlatti's signals office, they knew exactly which signs meant which units and Clinch was busy pinpointing where they were on Dampier's map.

Nevertheless – Dampier was suffering from a mixture of nerves and guilt – the thing had gone wrong. They had arrived in Zuq intending to return to the British lines with the Italian plan and order of battle, to say nothing of a few additions such as notes on German weapons and Italian morale. With Dampier's full approval, they had even stolen Italian equipment to improve their disguise, while Morton

149

had prostituted – Dampier couldn't think of a more apt word – his skill at languages to pick Scarlatti's brains. But now, he realized, the thing was out of control. The tail was beginning to wag the dog. Clutterbuck had pushed them further than they'd intended so that they were now stealing Italian equipment merely because it was there, and Morton was behaving with the arrogance of a subaltern in the Brigade of Guards. It was affecting the lot of them.

Only Dampier, it seemed to Dampier, had failed to get much out of their extraordinary circumstances. Then he remembered the bed strung with inner tubes and covered with Italian army blankets, the stretcher pillow, the inspection lamp that enabled him to read – even the English copy of *The Pickwick Papers*, found by Clutterbuck among the loot of a defeated British column in Scarlatti's store to replace *Le Raggazze, Il Amore* and the other books he'd originally produced. When he thought of them, Dampier's shame was almost enough to overwhelm him.

If only, he thought in a depressing moral scour-out, they could move from their passive role to an active one. If nothing else, it would ease his feeling of guilt.

'It seems to me,' he said to Rafferty, 'that we ought to try to put someone across the lines with the information we have.'

He frowned at the map stretched on the table near the bed Clutterbuck had built for him. He still moved with difficulty and it irked him that he couldn't do the gathering of information himself.

He produced a file – looted – and from it took a bundle of paper – also looted – on which he had scrawled his views, and they began to consider what they had collected.

They had seen nothing of Scarlatti since the raid on his dump and could only assume that, busy sorting out his inventories, he was covering himself to account for what had disappeared – ''E's at it like a bloody market trader fiddlin' 'is income tax,' Clutterbuck said – but, though he himself didn't appear, Scarlatti clearly had no intention of losing his grip on the man he thought was Count Barda, and Mondi appeared regularly with titbits for Morton's pleasure. And, though he was apathetic enough about the war to be depressing, Mondi had a deep insight into the attitudes of the ordinary Italian soldiers.

Wavell's shattering advance at the beginning of 1941 had destroyed Italian confidence and for the most part they were men without hope. With their poor weaponry and a government that bred cynicism, they considered themselves to be despised by their allies and a laughing stock to their enemies. This was all useful information that went down under the heading of 'Morale', to be passed on, like all the other items they'd collected, when 64 Light Vehicle Repair Unit returned to the British lines just ahead of the Italian advance.

'But,' Dampier demanded, 'when are they going to *make* their advance?'

'According to Scarlatti's estimate,' Morton said, 'in about seven days. They've got to open the minefield first and they haven't started yet.' He picked up Dampier's map and jabbed with his finger. 'He said it would be about there.'

'And the Germans?'

'More than willing to take advantage of any success.'

'You're sure of this?'

'Scarlatti likes to talk. His dinner parties are a great success.'

Dampier gave him a bitter look. 'I wouldn't mind sharing them with you,' he growled.

'I could always,' Morton smiled, 'take you with me as an orderly, sir. They'd probably give you something in the kitchen.'

As Morton disappeared, Dampier stared after him sourly. 'Mr Rafferty,' he announced to the warrant officer, 'any minute now that damned man'll start ordering me about.'

'Perhaps, sir,' Rafferty said, 'we should be grateful that he's pretty good at it.'

A thought occurred to Dampier. 'Why isn't he an officer, Mr Rafferty? The boy's a born leader.'

'Those are my sentiments entirely, sir.'

'The fact that we're still free – if you can call free being stuck behind the Italian lines and subject to every alarm that arises – to say nothing of an acute case of lumbago that refuses to go away – is entirely due to his quickness of mind. And' – Dampier looked sheepish – 'let's admit it: the deserter Clutterbuck's skill at removing things that ought not to be removed.'

'A quare feller that one, sir,' Rafferty agreed. 'If we get out of this, I think we should recruit him into our organization. They always say, "Set a thief to catch a thief." '

Dampier frowned. 'As a matter of fact, Mr Rafferty,' he admitted, 'that's something that's already occurred to me. He could clean up the Middle East.'

11

Dampier's need to do some damage received a fillip a few days later when Clutterbuck informed him that he'd discovered that Scarlatti's refuelling depot near the fort at the other side of Zuq was guarded at night by only two men and an officer.

'An',' he added, 'the men are Libyan levies and the orficer's got a bird at the other side of town so 'e's never there.'

Dampier eyed him warily. 'What are you suggesting, Clutterbuck?' he asked.

Clutterbuck's eyes widened. 'Blowing the bugger up,' he said bluntly. 'I thought that was what you wanted.'

It was indeed what Dampier wanted but it irked him that the idea had come, not from himself, but, of all people, from Clutterbuck, the deserter and thief.

More forward-thinking, cleverer, wilier and more deeply conscious of the dangers, Rafferty was inclined to be wary.

'It sounds all right,' he said. 'But won't they immediately start askin' who did it?'

'Libyans,' Dampier suggested. 'Obviously.'

'The Libyans don't go in for that sort of thing, sir,' Rafferty said. 'For one thing, they don't have the explosives, for another they don't have the know-how, and for a third. they're *pinchin'* the stuff.'

'Even the bloody Libyans?' Dampier sounded as though there were no longer anyone trustworthy in the whole world.

'They take it on camels to sell in Derna and Tripoli, so it's to their advantage to keep it intact, not blow it up.'

Dampier frowned. 'Could we let it be known it was the Long Range Desert Group?'

They all knew of the Long Range Desert Group. It seemed to be officered entirely by young men of good family who were used to telling other people what to do and, when they'd been called up for service, so little enjoyed taking orders that they had organized themselves a murderous little private army in which they could all be generals.

'If it's goin' to be thim boys, sir,' Rafferty said, 'somebody's got to see 'em.'

'Why not us?'

'Because if *we* saw 'em, somebody'll ask why didn't they blow us apart? It's a habit they have. And anyway, we have no explosives.'

'We have those percussion grenades we found in the lorries when we first arrived.'

Rafferty still wasn't keen. 'If it's going to be done at all,' he said, 'it's got to be done when the RAF are over, so they'll think *they* did it.'

Dampier bowed to the warrant officer's greater experience. 'What do you suggest?' he asked.

'Have the grenades handy, sir,' Rafferty smiled. 'And nip along the next time they appear.'

Dampier made his plans carefully. They had wire cutters and getting into a wired compound didn't present much difficulty. All it required was instant readiness.

Unfortunately, it didn't quite work out like that.

Dampier and Rafferty weren't the only ones in the group who were interested in what the dumps in Zuq contained. Nobody wanted a horse's gasmask or an Italian general's uniform but everybody was concerned with coffee, sugar and food.

'And how about some of that scent?' Caccia suggested.

''Ow much would you like?' Clutterbuck asked.

Caccia grinned. 'Just enough to sweeten a bird, that's all.'

Two days later, Caccia was outside the Bar Barbieri, his Italian sergeant's uniform tarted up to make him look smart and, for safety, with a heavy Webley .45 revolver belonging to Dampier which he'd lifted when its owner wasn't looking. Acquired by Dampier in 1914, it was big enough to bring down an aircraft and, he felt, was enough to make anyone who started being awkward back away at once.

Rosalba Coccioli's wariness dissolved immediately as he produced a bottle of *Fragranza di Violette*.

'*Mamma mia*,' she said. 'Where did you get it?'

Caccia shrugged, the sort of shrug he'd employed just before his call-up as he'd slipped an extra piece of rationed sausage into the shopping basket of one of his father's prettier customers, and she pushed him towards a table and made him sit down.

'What will you drink?' she asked. 'Vermouth? Anisette? There's some wine. Castelli Romani.'

Caccia beamed, feeling at home. Rosalba Coccioli wasn't the first Italian girl he'd chased. Cairo and Alexandria were full of them and every time the Italians or the Germans made an advance, no matter how insignificant, word always got around and they came out from under the stones. They were reputed to wear knickers in the Italian national colours and one woman, as bombastic as the Duce himself, had wrapped herself in the Italian flag and sworn to drink British blood. The Military Police were always very patient and merely told them to go home.

With his ability to speak their language, Caccia had got to know many of them. Most of them were living in a world devoid of Italian men and, because of his looks and his name, despite his British uniform they had welcomed him with open arms, sometimes half hoping to direct him towards the Italian cause. Caccia wasn't interested in causes, however, just in getting them into bed and, with his black brilliantined hair and an ability as a dancer gained over many visits to the Hammersmith Palais de Danse, he had acquired a considerable skill at picking up girls.

With the perfume in her hand, Rosalba sat alongside him. 'You wish to kiss me?' she asked.

Caccia obliged.

'You think I'm pretty?'

She was prettier than Max Donatello's wife, her cousin, and had a better figure too, and Caccia held up his hand, making a circle with his forefinger and thumb in a sign of approval. '*Prima*,' he said. 'First class.'

She looked pleased. 'I think perhaps you're hungry,' she said. 'I'll find you some food. My uncle's in Derna again. There's plenty to buy in Derna. Some of it comes from Tunisia and Morocco. He bribed a sergeant to sell him petrol for the car. He'll be back before dark because the RAF will be over again to drop bombs on the harbour.'

'Do they scare you?'

She shrugged. '*È destino*. It's fate. Mostly they just sink the ships they've already sunk. Come.'

She led the way into a room at the back alongside the kitchen. On the mantelpiece was a family group photograph – 'My cousin Ansaldo,' she said. 'When he was called to the colours' – and on the wall a map of the Italian colonies of Tripolitania and Cyrenaica and the western border of Egypt. Small red, white and green flags had been marked on it, rubbed out and put in again.

'What's that?' Caccia asked.

'My war map,' Rosalba said proudly. 'Every unit in the Italian army. Some of them contained my boyfriends. But not many. Italian soldiers don't make good boyfriends. They have no money. And most of them were captured in 1941, anyway.'

'How about the Germans? You got them down, too?'

Her finger indicated small swastikas.

'If they found that, they'd think you were a spy.'

She gestured, quite unperturbed. 'Nobody comes in here.

156

That German sergeant tried once but he got the floor cloth in his face.'

'How did you find them all out?'

She shrugged. 'Zuq's the dispatching point for supplies, and soldiers talk. And when we have anything to drink they come here to drink it. There are also four brothels in Zuq and I know the girls. You'd be surprised what they're told. Let's sit outside. It's cooler.'

The back of the bar faced a minute dusty patch where she'd planted flowers in small stone-enclosed circles. Red geraniums flared among the spiky leaves of cacti and there was another patch beneath a pergola where a vine gave shade to a rickety table and a long bench. Beyond, Caccia could see the dark shapes of trees and, beyond that still, white houses, the dome of the mosque and a glimpse of the indigo sea.

She poured the wine and a few moments later, he heard her clattering dishes and pans in the kitchen. A ginger cat rubbed against his leg and he lit a cigarette – by kind permission of Corporal Clutterbuck a British Players from Scarlatti's dump – and sat back to enjoy himself. Almost before he was ready, she slapped a plate in front of him.

'Spaghetti napolitano,' she said. 'There is no meat. But there is cheese.'

She banged a bowl of grated parmesan alongside it and produced another bottle of wine. 'You'll enjoy this, Arturo,' she said. 'Eat.'

The sun vanished in a flare of crimson and amber, streaking the blue-green sky with fiery sword-strokes. The shadows lengthened and the dusty patch at the back of the bar grew yellow in the lowering sun.

'You're not very busy here,' Caccia said. By this time he had Rosalba on the bench with him and had backed her into the corner, one hand round her waist under her breast. She pushed it away occasionally but she wasn't defending herself too vigorously.

157

'Why not shut the shop?' he suggested.

'Now?'

'Italian soldiers have no money to buy anything and you've nothing to sell, anyway. Nobody'll come and bother us.'

'My uncle will come. He'll probably shoot you.'

'I'm not scared.'

'I am.'

He pushed her up against the wall. 'How long will he be?'

'He usually comes back after dark.'

'We've plenty of time then.'

'For what?'

'You know for what.'

'I think, like the German, Sergeant Schwartzheiss, you're trying to get into my bed.'

'Better me than him.'

'Better nobody at all, I think,' she said spiritedly. 'I'll allow into my bed only the man I'm going to marry.' She paused. 'On the other hand,' she admitted, 'you're a hand-some man, Arturo Caccia.' She was studying him shrewdly, her mind working at top speed. 'Perhaps – ' she said. Then she stopped.

'Perhaps what?'

'Perhaps – ' She stopped again and Caccia took it as a strong hint that he wouldn't be unwelcome despite what she said.

Close to the kitchen there was a stone staircase lined with red tiles for easy cleaning, and he rose and pulled her towards it. She didn't seem more than normally unwilling and he'd actually got her halfway up when they heard a car stop outside. She pushed him down again at once and into the kitchen.

'It's my uncle,' she said. 'He's back.'

Barbieri appeared in the doorway, a sack over his shoulder. 'Unlock the store shed,' he said. 'We're loaded. Sausage. Pasta. Rice. Wine. Anisette. *Dio*, always anisette!'

'Where did you get it?' Rosalba asked.

'Where do I always get it? The black market. Always I have to go to the black market. How else am I supposed to get supplies? Walk with them on my head like the Arab women? Perhaps I should wear a robe and a veil and worship Mohammed instead of the Lord Jesus Christ, son of the Virgin Mary.' Barbieri flung his head back and started to wail in the manner of the muezzins in their high towers, '*Lah illa Lah Mohammed rassoul Allah*. There is no God but Allah, and Mohammed is His prophet.' He suddenly noticed Caccia and stopped dead. His head swung to Rosalba. 'Who's this?'

'This is Arturo Caccia, uncle,' she said. 'He came for a drink.'

'And what else?'

'Nothing.'

'Then there must be something wrong with him. No young man visits a girl when she's alone unless he's after something other than a drink. Why isn't he fighting the war?'

'My day off,' Caccia said.

'You have days off?' Barbieri's eyebrows danced. 'When Italy totters and the British are preparing to wipe us off the face of the earth?'

'Oh, shut up,' Rosalba said sullenly. 'The British have been driven back.'

'They'll come again. The British always come again.'

'The Germans will stop them.'

'Always it is the *Germans* who will stop them!' Barbieri slapped himself on the forehead. 'Why don't the Italians stop them? Because they have days off. Tell him to go!'

Rosalba pushed Caccia to the door. Under a cyclamen-coloured sky a convoy of trucks carrying a batch of new recruits was just debussing in the road. The soldiers, under-sized boys in ill-fitting uniforms, were staggering under kitbags. They looked poorly equipped and a few were even shouting anti-war slogans.

There was a sad motherly look in Rosalba's eyes as she watched the column disappear between the ever-hopeful hawkers offering lemonade for sale, then she turned and gave Caccia a quick kiss. 'Come again,' she whispered.

'Next time,' he said, 'I won't take no.'

'My uncle will be there.'

'It gets dark.' An idea occurred to Caccia. 'You got any girlfriends?'

She stared angrily at him. 'So! Because I am not available you want the addresses of my friends.'

Caccia grinned. 'Tell him one of them's coming to visit you. To talk. About clothes. About scent. Girls do, I know. I've got sisters. Tell him one of them's got some for you on the black market. I'll bring some.'

'And you'll entertain us both?'

Caccia grinned again. '*I'll* be the girlfriend. I'll dress up. I've got a wig.'

The sad motherly look had gone and she stared at him with eyes full of mischief. 'This is something you do often? Where did you get it? Where will you get the clothes?'

He gestured vaguely in the direction of the dump. 'There's everything we need in there. Even a horse's gasmask.'

She looked blank. 'We shall need a horse's gasmask?'

She caught on eventually. 'You'll need somewhere to change,' she said. 'You can't walk through the streets after dark. You'll get dragged down an alley and raped.'

'Some rape!'

She giggled. 'There's the hut behind the house. My uncle uses it as a store. I'll see the padlock's unfastened. There's a lamp and a mirror. I used to sleep there in the summer before the war when he let my room off to tourists.'

'I'll be there just after dark.'

'And I'll tell him there are soldiers billeted in Teresa Gelucci's house and her father's worried they're trying to get into her bed, and she wants to stay with me.'

Caccia grinned. He couldn't believe his luck.

12

The following evening Caccia headed into town again. He was shaved to the bone and slung over his shoulder was an Italian side-pack which contained the dress he'd used in the Ratbags' female-impersonation act. They'd often found that the soldiers they entertained, despite the fact that they knew full well what was under the dress, were more interested in Caccia than all the rest of the company put together. With it was a linen handbag, a wig and, for safety, Dampier's heavy revolver.

It was a warm night with a sky full of stars all glowing like headlamps. Somewhere a man was singing in a light tenor voice.

'Kennst du das Land
Wo die Zitronen blühn,
Im dunkeln Laub
Die Gold-Orangen glühn. . . .'

Caccia had no idea what it meant but it sounded sentimental and the thought of Rosalba was pushing his voltage up so much he felt about to burst into flames.

A lorry pulled up alongside him with a low squeak of brakes and he saw the driver was Clutterbuck.

'Dampier said we'd all to stay in camp in case there was an air raid and we 'ad a go at Scarlatti's refuelling depot,' he pointed out cheerfully.

'If that's the case, how is it *you're* out?'

Clutterbuck pulled a face. 'They couldn't keep me in if they tried.'

As he climbed into the passenger seat, Caccia decided that perhaps he ought to have written to the Air Officer Commanding the RAF.

'Dear AOC, Could you possibly hold off your boys tonight? I've got this date with this bird. Yours faithfully, A. Caccia.' Or why not the Commander of the Eighth Army, whoever he was? Why not Auchinleck, the Commander-in-Chief, Middle East? Or for that matter, Churchill? Why not go right to the top? The thought made him grin.

'What time are you coming back?' he asked.

'Midnight. About that.' Clutterbuck laughed. 'I've got a few petrol tanks to pee into.'

'See you outside the Bar Barbieri.' Caccia paused. 'Unless there's an air raid. If there is I'll be outside as soon as the sirens go.'

As Caccia made his way to the bar, in the Italian cap and jacket no one looked at him. It was almost dark when he arrived and he walked up and down for a while, his blood thumping in his veins at the thought of Rosalba's warm flesh under his hands. Then, as the outlines of the buildings faded in the blue dusk, he slipped through the cactus hedge and into the garden at the back.

As Rosalba had promised, the shed was unlocked. The shutters were already closed and his feet were silent on a floor covered with wood shavings. He struck a match and found the lamp, then, his heart thumping, began to strip off his shirt. Adjusting the padded brassière he had used to sing 'Olga Paulovski, The Beautiful Spy,' he hitched at the football shorts he wore as underwear and slid into the red and yellow dress and the pair of size 9 women's shoes for which they'd had to search every shop in Cairo. Carefully putting on the wig, he began to apply make-up round his eyes and lipstick on his mouth; then, reaching for a shawl, he draped it over his head to hide his face and, picking up the handbag, slipped into it the lipstick Clutterbuck had acquired for him and Dampier's revolver.

Feeling full of oats, he looked around him. The shed contained flour and cartons of pasta, to say nothing of two cases of anisette and one or two bottles of Italian brandy, one of them unsealed. To give himself courage, he took a swig from it and, grasping the handbag, was just moving down the side of the bar when he heard the crash of glass and Rosalba's voice screaming.

'*Via! Va via! Che faccenda sporca!*'

He pulled back quickly into the shadows as the door was wrenched open and the German, Sergeant Schwartzheiss, appeared. He was holding his head but, as usual, he was laughing. As the door slammed behind him, he leaned against the wall, still laughing softly, then he jammed his peaked forage cap straight on his head and was just about to walk away when his eye fell on Caccia in the shadows.

'So!' He straightened up, grinning. 'What have we here? *Che è? Come si chiama, tesoro?*'

He leaned against the wall, his arm outstretched, his hand flat against the brickwork, making it impossible for Caccia to bolt.

'*Cara mia! Carissima! Buona sera!* Don't be afraid!'

Caccia *was* afraid – very afraid – but for a very different reason from the one Schwartzheiss was imagining.

'*Non trovo più la strada!* I'm lost. *Non so parlare italiano.* I can't speak Italian.'

Caccia was crouching back into the darkness as Schwartzheiss's face drew closer.

'*Parla tedesco?*'

Caccia shook his head. No, he didn't speak German. How the bloody hell, he thought, did he get out of this one?

'*Che bella ragazza. Dove va?*'

Schwartzheiss, Caccia decided, had learned off by heart all the best phrases from a tourist's phrase book.

'*Quanti anni ha?* How old are you?'

The German had Caccia pinned against the wall now.

His breath smelled of beer and Caccia guessed he'd been enjoying the evening in the German soldiers' canteen and was after anything he could get. Caccia was in a panic. From his own experience, he knew exactly what the next step would be and he knew it mustn't take place.

There was a distant burst of firing from the desert, a faint thud-thud-thud, almost too far away to be heard. But Schwartzheiss heard it as plainly as Caccia. His head turned and, as it did so, Caccia saw his chance. There was no time to fish the Webley out of the linen handbag so he brought up the handbag itself and swung it as hard as he could against the back of the German's head.

As the heavy revolver inside clunked against his skull, Schwartzheiss dropped like a felled tree. Caccia stared down at him, startled by his success, and was just about to bolt for Rosalba when it occurred to him that Schwartzheiss had to be convinced there was no connection between the 'girl' he'd met and the nearby bar, or he'd come searching for his attacker as soon as he recovered consciousness. Dragging him into the shade of the trees, Caccia dropped him with his head among the bushes and, turning him over, fished in his pockets. He found a penknife, a notebook, a length of string, a grubby handkerchief and a large bundle of notes. Tossing everything aside but the money, which he stuffed into his pocket, he headed for the bar. When he woke up, Schwartzheiss would assume he'd been attacked and robbed. He might even, Caccia thought with some pleasure, come to the not very difficult conclusion that the 'girl' he'd waylaid had been a bait. He might even consider himself lucky not to be dead.

Reaching the bar, Caccia banged on the side door. Rosalba was waiting for him and it opened so sharply he almost fell into her arms.

'*Fate presto!*' he muttered. 'Quick! *Disopra!* Upstairs!'

She didn't ask questions and pushed him up the red-tiled steps at once. As they reached the top, Caccia twisting his ankle agonizingly in his haste as the high-heeled shoes he wore threw his foot over, they heard Barbieri's voice.

'*Chi è la?* Who's that?'

Rosalba turned. 'It's Teresa, uncle. She doesn't feel very well.'

'Tell her not to be sick in my house,' Barbieri growled.

'Oh, it's not that bad,' Rosalba said. 'She needs to lie down a little, that's all. I'll lie down with her and keep her company.'

Pushing Caccia into her room, she slammed the door and collapsed against it, her hands to her mouth to stifle her laughter.

'He'll not come up,' she said. 'Don't look so scared. He sleeps in the room behind the bar in case anybody tries to break in and steal anything. Who'd want to steal anisette?' She realized he was still leaning against the wall, frozen with fear. 'What's the matter? What happened?'

As he told her, her hand flew to her throat and, peeping through the shutters, she signed to Caccia to join her. Schwartzheiss had staggered to his feet and was stumbling away into the town.

'He'll think your boyfriend did it. It's happened before. Arab girls have been known to lure soldiers round corners where there's a man waiting. What did you hit him with?'

Caccia fished in the linen handbag and produced the revolver.

'No wonder his head hurts. Did he try anything?'

'Yes.'

'*Una fornicazione straordinaria*, I think.' She giggled. 'He was in the bar. He tried to get me in a corner. I had to hit him with a bottle. He's had a bad day today, I think.'

She stopped and studied the dress Caccia was wearing. 'You look good,' she said. Then she stared at him, suddenly alarmed. 'You're not one of *them*? There are men who –'

Caccia laughed. 'I wouldn't be here if I was, would I?' He fished into the handbag. 'I brought you something.'

She stared at the small tube he put in her hand. '*Rosetto?* Lipstick?' She flung her arms round him and clutched him tightly. 'I haven't had a lipstick for months.'

Snatching the wig from his head and throwing it on to the bed, he kicked off his shoes and slipped out of the dress. Turning, he found Rosalba curled up with laughter.

'What's so funny?'

'*Le cami-mutande.*' She pointed to the football shorts. 'The cami-knickers.'

He kicked his shoes off and, as she tossed a towel at him, wiped the lipstick and rouge from his face. Standing in front of her, wearing nothing but the football shorts and his socks, he reached for her. She turned in his arms and, kissing her, he started to unbutton her blouse. She put a hand on his chest. She had stopped giggling and looked scared.

'No,' she said.

'There's nothing wrong with it.'

'I'm afraid.' She looked at him with large worried eyes. 'I've never done this before. My mamma always told me to save myself for my husband.'

'Who says you're not doing?'

Her eyes searched his face. 'You mean that, Arturo? You mean you want to marry me?'

She wasn't the first girl he'd promised and it cost him nothing to say he did.

She had backed away from him but now she allowed him to put his arms round her once more, and this time she raised no objection as his hand lifted her blouse. She giggled again, as if it had dawned on her that apart from the football shorts he was naked and she was only half clothed herself, then suddenly she threw all caution to the wind and flung herself at him, her lips fiercely seeking his.

As he clutched her, Caccia found himself thinking of Dampier's instructions to remain in camp in case there was an air raid. Cocking his head, he listened. There was no sound outside. They weren't coming tonight. It was going to be all right and he gave his full attention to the task in hand.

Rosalba also seemed to have thrown aside her doubts and was wrenching at the rest of her clothes.

'*È destino*,' she chirruped and, dragging at the football shorts, she pushed Caccia back on to the bed and yanked them over his feet with all the delight of a full-blooded girl who had been kept too long from men.

As he came up for air, Caccia was just savouring the situation when the siren went.

Sitting bolt upright, he stared at the ceiling. The blasted bombers had come after all! And he was supposed to be out at the camp of 64 Light Vehicle Repair Unit, ready to form a commando or something to blow up Scarlatti's bloody refuelling depot! In spite of the letter he'd written to the AOC, the leader of the Eighth Army, the Commander-in-Chief, Middle East, and Churchill, the Desert Air Force was about to bomb Zuq after all, and he, Arthur Caccia, the great lover, the Napoleon of North Africa, was in the wrong bloody place!

He was still staring at the ceiling as if he could see through it and pick up the approaching aeroplanes when Rosalba clutched him.

'It's all right,' she said. '*Per me è lo stesso*. I don't care.'

Caccia fought free. 'I do,' he said.

Assuming that like most Italian soldiers he had been subject over the past months to the ministrations of the Royal Air Force and didn't fancy being on the receiving end of a stick of bombs, she tried to reassure him. 'They won't come here,' she said. 'They only bomb the sunken ships in the harbour.'

As she made another grab at him, he backed away. 'I've got to go!' he yelled.

'*Codardo!*' she yelled back. 'Coward! It's because you're afraid!'

'No, it's not! It's duty! I'm supposed to be in camp when

there's an air raid. If they find I'm not – ' Caccia stopped, wondering what Dampier *would* do if he found out where he was. He could hardly confine him to camp, but perhaps he could have him flogged or staked out over an ant heap or something. Caccia was uncertain on the subject. As he grabbed for the football shorts, Rosalba stared at him furiously.

'You're going to leave me to be bombed on my own!' she said. 'I tell you, you're quite safe here!'

But, even as she spoke, she became aware of a whistling sound that grew in intensity to a shriek.

'*Mamma mia!*' she screamed, leaping at Caccia; as he clutched her in his arms, they fell backwards on to the bed. There was a tremendous crash outside that rattled the shutters, then the banging of an anti-aircraft battery. Voices sounded in the street and Barbieri's voice came up the stairs.

'Rosalba! Are you all right?'

'We're all right, uncle. Teresa's scared but we're all right.'

The blast had put out the lamp but there were lights flashing in the street as people with torches moved about. Caccia heaved at the football shorts.

'I've got to go,' he said. 'If I'm missed, they'll murder me!'

He dived frantically for the door but Barbieri was still at the bottom of the stairs and he drew back in panic.

'Through the window!' Rosalba had forgotten her complaints in her desire to help. 'It's not a long drop!'

At the camp of 64 Light Vehicle Repair Unit, the bombs had brought them out at once. Wincing against his lumbago, even Dampier fought his way to the door of his tent.

'It's an air raid,' he yelled. 'They've come! Turn everybody out, Mr Rafferty!'

Snatching at Italian jackets and caps, they were just emerging from the tents when the Lancia came hurtling round the corner, with Clutterbuck yelling that their opportunity had come. Nobody noticed that Caccia had arrived with him and, scrambling aboard, they rocked over the ruts back on to the road with creaking springs and a lurch that threw them all in a heap. Clutching the box of percussion grenades, Micklethwaite slid across the steel floor of the rear of the truck to slam against the back of the driver's cabin. 'Do these things go off easily?' he asked nervously.

As they disappeared, Dampier stared after them sourly. It was his idea, he thought bitterly, but he was the one who, because of his lumbago, had to be left behind to guard the camp. Without a single bloody Italian speaker, too, if the SS decided to pay them a visit!

As Clutterbuck had promised, there were only two guards, both Libyan conscripts, at the refuelling depot and they were both in a ditch with their heads well down. Their officer, his jacket buttoned in the wrong holes, was still trying to skirt the wreckage caused by a couple of bombs that had landed on his route across town. It took no more than a minute to cut the wire and scramble inside the compound. The din over the town was tremendous now, the crash of bombs mingling with the iron rumble of aeroplane engines. The flash of explosions lit the square flat-roofed houses, the dome of the mosque and the white walls of the fort.

Shoving several drums of petrol together, Rafferty unscrewed the cap of one of them and tipped it on its side. As the petrol poured out, he gestured to the others to disappear. As they scrambled into the ditch, he pulled the pin of one of the grenades and, placing it carefully in the pool of petrol, hurtled after the others.

They were all crouching with their heads down as the grenade exploded. It went off with a crack and a flash of flame, and almost immediately the stack of drums went up, less with a bang than with a whoof. A whole series of explosions followed, as if a giant were blowing breathy belches across the desert, and in seconds the whole area of the refuelling depot was sending huge black clouds of smoke into the sky. The heat was enough to create a whirlwind and they could feel the air roaring past them to feed the flames. Dust and uprooted bushes went with it, to disappear as cinders into the heavens with the smoke. Almost at once, lorries appeared from the fort. Imagining it to be an attack by the Long Range Desert Group, the officer in command had given orders to evacuate the place and the lorries were pouring out, one after the other, to head for the safety of the desert, the faces of the drivers lit up by the glare of the flames.

It was Rafferty who came to life first. It was a long time since he'd enjoyed himself so much. 'Come on, bhoys,' he said, his accent thickening in his excitement as it always did. ''Tis time we were off.'

Caccia followed in a daze. It was only twenty minutes since he'd been in Rosalba Coccioli's arms.

13

When Scarlatti finally appeared at 64 Light Vehicle Repair Unit, it was noticeable that Faiani had surfaced again. They had seen nothing of him for some time but on this occasion he was with Scarlatti in the Lancia and Clutterbuck promptly disappeared to the stores tent and kept his head down.

Scarlatti's face was as mournful as Mondi's behind the wheel. His plump features seemed to droop and he was full of woe. 'First the furniture factory,' he complained. 'Then the dump. And now, last night, the refuelling depot. Why is it always me and never Ancillotti? The RAF have bombed Derna again and again and his dump is always spared. I begin to think the Holy Father in Rome doesn't pray hard enough for us or that his prayers aren't answered, because nobody deserves success less than Ancillotti. The way he's filling his pockets is disgraceful.'

'Perhaps,' Morton said mildly, 'you should report him to Brigadier Olivaro.'

Scarlatti had no intention of reporting anybody in case a general enquiry should be set in motion to cover *all* dumps, including his own. 'Those damned bombers are becoming too accurate,' he said, changing the subject. 'Or else some *traditore sporco* – some filthy traitor – is signalling to them. I think I shall have to have a few heads blown off by a firing squad.'

Morton didn't take him very seriously because he'd long since realized Scarlatti was a soft-hearted man longing only to return to Italy and his plump wife and three daughters.

The jeremiad continued for a while, then Faiani's sharp eyes detected that there were more tools about 64 Light Vehicle Repair Unit than previously and he turned sharply, his eyes narrow.

'I see your equipment turned up, count,' he said suspiciously.

'Not mine.' Morton smiled. 'That appears to have disappeared somewhere near Sofi. Commandeered, I expect. You know what soldiers are. These ' – he gestured about him – 'these are all new issues. I signalled Brigadier Olivaro. He's an old friend of my family. I pointed out that we couldn't function without equipment. It arrived during the night. At the height of the air raid.' He flourished the inventories, all sporting Clutterbuck's version of Brigadier Olivaro's signature.

Faiani nodded. 'There have been some disastrous happenings in Zuq lately,' he observed shrewdly. 'Funny you should be here to see them all, count.'

'Fortunes of war,' Morton said. 'Some people have doubtless gone through the war without hearing a shot fired in anger.'

Scarlatti said nothing. He suspected the signatures were false, and it was common practice in the army, he knew, to help yourself to what you needed if the opportunity arose. If you lost something, you helped yourself to the next man's, while *he* replaced what you'd taken from the possessions of the person next to him in line, and so on. The last man started it all over again by helping himself from the possessions of the first. It was an army adage that only a fool allowed himself to remain without. Nevertheless, even though he suspected that what he saw in front of him was his, Scarlatti had already, as Clutterbuck had predicted, followed another army adage and was protecting his own rear by writing it all off as 'lost due to enemy action'. And, having done so, he had no intention of making an ass of himself by suddenly discovering that it hadn't been.

All the same, Scarlatti thought, considering the amount

of help he'd given to 64 Light Vehicle Repair Unit, the advice he'd offered, the food he'd supplied, it was nothing less than base ingratitude, and the Italian nobility clearly wasn't what he'd always thought.

Though Scarlatti didn't worry them much, Faiani was another kettle of fish, while Schwartzheiss was yet another. And when Schwartzheiss arrived within a couple of hours of Faiani's departure, it had 64 Light Vehicle Repair Unit alarmed.

He was driving a *Kübelwagen* and there was a large plaster on his head where Dampier's revolver had contacted it. Seeing him from his tent, Caccia bolted for the marquee where Morton was standing with Rafferty.

'It's him,' he said frantically. 'That German I bonked over the conk.'

Rafferty was nervous but Morton was confident he could handle things.

'I'll attend to him,' he said.

As the *Kübelwagen* stopped, he stepped forward. 'Good morning, sergeant,' he said. 'Your car is in need of repair?'

Schwartzheiss smiled. 'If it were, I'd get it serviced at our own workshops.' He was looking about him, his eyes shrewd. His comment was the same as Faiani's. 'I see your lost equipment turned up, *tenente*.'

Morton smiled. 'During the air raid that destroyed Scarlatti's dump.'

'Pity you weren't here to welcome it.'

Morton smiled again. 'But I was, sergeant. I'm always careful to remain in camp at night. To guard against pilferers. Doubtless you were doing the same.'

Schwartzheiss's smile didn't waver. 'Of course.'

'Have *you* acquired much new equipment, sergeant?'

'It requires sharp wits, *tenente*.'

'Especially in our army, sergeant. We have nothing else to sharpen.'

Schwartzheiss laughed. 'That's the worst of wars.'

'They're always with us. The only way to get rid of them is to have them.'

Schwartzheiss's eyes seemed to be everywhere, flickering about the camp as he talked. Apparently hard at work for the Italian war effort, everybody kept their heads down, Rafferty bent over an engine, Dampier busy over the stove, Caccia hiding with Clutterbuck behind the boxes in the stores tent. Schwartzheiss seemed loath to go and, working the accelerator of the lorry he was occupied with, Rafferty kept deliberately drowning his voice as he revved the engine.

In the end Morton handed over a couple of bottles of chianti and Schwartzheiss seemed satisfied. They stared with relief after the plume of dust trailed by the *Kübelwagen*.

'Think he suspected?' Dampier asked.

'He's no fool,' Morton said.

'Think he and Faiani are in touch with each other?' Rafferty asked. ''Tis only two hours since Faiani was here.'

'If they start exchanging suspicions we're in trouble. Especially if they include Scarlatti.'

Rafferty frowned. 'I'm thinkin' neither of 'em comes here just for a change of air,' he said. 'It's time we moved.'

Almost without orders, almost as if they'd all thought of it at the same time, they started to pack the vehicles, and in a matter of an hour and a half they were heading away from the town.

Rafferty sought a place that was far from people who might ask questions and eventually settled on a spot on the south side of the town, close to a deep gully called the Wadi Sghiara. The site was not on the main road and the traffic was thin. The wadi itself rose in the hills near the coast and opened southwards into the desert at a point where there were several ridges of sand dunes, one or two of them lifting as high as sixty feet to catch the evening sun. In parts it was ten feet deep and the wide entrance had steep walls of sandy soil marked by scrubby yellow flowers where black-striped hoopoes darted. Further south was only

174

the desert, burning in the sun, the dunes like white sugar in the glare. There were no immediate neighbours but there was also no water, which would have to be brought from Zuq, and the only moisture would be their own sweat, while the flies would be more troublesome than ever.

'This will do,' Dampier said confidently.

Rafferty wasn't half so sure. 'I'd rather disappear altogether,' he said.

'In good time, Mr Rafferty.' Dampier had his eyes on thwarting the Italian attack when it came and a solid British victory resulting from the information he'd collected. He could even see a little glory in it for himself. 'All in good time. We'll set up camp here.'

Because of a nervous feeling that Rosalba was suspicious of him – the same sort of edginess they all felt – Caccia didn't go into Zuq for several days, but when he finally succumbed she welcomed him with open arms and a flood of tears.

'I thought you'd forgotten me.'

'Never,' Caccia insisted. 'Never!'

She swung on his neck and, because Barbieri had bribed more petrol out of an Italian transport sergeant and was asleep after a trip to Derna, within half an hour Caccia was in her bed and, over the sound of the radio, which was playing martial music from Radio Rome to drown their voices, he told her about Schwartzheiss's visit.

'All Germans are not bad.' Flushed and happy, Rosalba was in a forgiving mood. 'Some are even well mannered. But not many. They think we are an inferior race.'

'I'm not an inferior race,' Caccia said.

'You should be an officer, Arturo. Have you fought in many battles?'

'You ever heard of Addis Ababa?'

'Of course.'

'I took him prisoner.'

She giggled and, reaching out a slender arm, poured wine into a glass. Caccia swallowed it at a gulp.

'Amazing how thirsty it makes you,' he said.

'A pity it isn't champagne.' She giggled again. 'I always wondered what it would be like to drink wine in bed with a man. I think you plotted this all along. From the moment you saw me. Did you fall in love with me at once?' Rosalba had been brought up on romantic magazines. 'Perhaps you shouldn't go back until tomorrow.'

'I can't do that. There's work to do.'

'Not much. I've seen you.'

Caccia flashed her a startled look and she explained.

'I drove out in my uncle's car and watched you with binoculars, British binoculars that a German corporal gave us in exchange for wine. He stole them from the dump. That German sergeant followed me but I dodged him. I thought you might have girls out there. I was jealous.' She began to wheedle. 'It's a long way to go back, Arturo. Send a note to say you have a bad back.'

'You don't send notes in the army.'

'Not even in the Italian army?' She took the glass from Caccia's hand and carefully placed it on the dressing table.

'What are you up to?' Caccia asked warily. 'I don't like the look in your eye.'

'*Mamma mia*, it's not the look in my eye you should worry about, Arturo Caccia.'

The old shy Rosalba was giving way to a new saucy one who was more than willing to be adventurous; giving a hoot of laughter, her legs waving whitely in the faint light that came through the window, she made a dive for him that flung him back on the pillows. The bedsprings creaked as she pulled his head down to her bosom.

'Rosalba – ' he began, but his voice came out only as a croak.

She squirmed under him, running her fingernails up and down his back. His breath coming faster, he pretended to fight her off but – signed, sealed and delivered, a victim of love – he wasn't over-enthusiastic about it.

'Steady on,' he said feebly. 'Whoa!'

*

Lying back, half asleep, a dew of perspiration on his body, it occurred to Caccia that Rosalba had been quiet for a long time.

'What are you thinking?' he asked.

'I'm thinking about you.' Rosalba lifted herself on to one elbow and stared down at him. Her large slanting eyes, jetty hair and smoky lashes had a deadly effect on him, and as she reached across him for a cigarette, her soft white bosom touched his chest. Her flesh was warm and Caccia drew a deep breath and moved uncomfortably. Then he noticed there was a strange look on her face, puzzled and suspicious at the same time.

'Who are you?' she asked unexpectedly.

'Caccia, Arturo. At your service.'

'Where do you come from? Rome, like me?'

Caccia decided that if she came from Rome it was better that he shouldn't. 'No,' he said. 'Not Rome.'

'Florence? You're not from Florence. You don't look like a Florentine. You don't speak like a Florentine.'

'No, I'm not from Florence.'

'Then where? You're not a Sicilian either, I think. Savoia? Trieste? It's a Trieste way of speaking, perhaps, that you have. Or is it Naples? I think perhaps it's Naples.'

His origins were something that had never been brought up before, but Naples seemed as good a place as any. 'Yes,' Caccia said. 'I'm from Naples.'

She paused, studying him. 'Where? The Via Roma area?'

'No.' The Via Roma area sounded as if it might be dangerous ground. 'Not there.'

'Near the funicular?'

'No, not there either.' Caccia was busy racking his brains. It wasn't easy to answer because he'd never been to Naples and was just guessing.

'I know where. Near the Piazza Vanvitelli.'

'Yes, that's right. Near the Piazza Vanvitelli.'

Rosalba beamed, her eyes suddenly bright. 'Down by the harbour. Close to the sea on the flat land?'

'That's it. Near the Piazza Vanvitelli close to the sea.'

'By the Porto Santa Lucia.'

'That's it exactly.'

'Well, it isn't then!' Rosalba's eyes blazed and her voice rose. 'You're lying to me, Arturo Caccia! Because the Piazza Vanvitelli isn't near the Porto Santa Lucia! It's up near the Castel Sant' Elmo! At the top of a lot of steps! As high as you can get in Naples!'

'Yes, well – ' Caccia was floundering.

'Who are you?'

'Caccia, Arturo. That's me.'

'I bet it isn't. Why do you speak English from time to time?'

Caccia's heart went cold. He couldn't remember speaking any English.

'You said, "Steady on! Whoa!" You didn't notice, I think. But then I remembered. It's something I heard on the London buses. When they say, "Tickets please. No standing on the platform. Pass down the bus." I heard it often when the bus started with a jerk. The people who are standing say, "Whoa" and "Steady on." These are English words.'

'What's all this?' Caccia was beginning to feel twinges of alarm. 'Bed's a stupid place to ask questions.'

'Bed's an excellent place to ask questions,' Rosalba snapped. 'My mamma told me so. She always questioned my father when he'd been out late and she always knew what he'd been up to. Why did that man speak to you in English?'

'Which man?'

'The Arab. When you climbed into the car the first time you came back here. He said, "Jesus Christ, look sleepy." Why did he speak to you in English? And why did he tell you you looked tired?'

'He didn't tell me I looked tired. He told me to – '

She gave him a shrewd glance. 'You see? You understood what he said. You understand English well, I think. And why do you ride in cars with Arabs? Italians don't ride in cars with Arabs. They kick them out. It is pride of race. What the Germans call "*Rassenstolz*". And why do you speak Italian differently from me? Perhaps you come from the Argentine. There are many Italians in the Argentine. The patriotic ones came to fight for the Duce. The sensible ones stayed where they were. Are you a patriotic Italian from the Argentine?'

She was throwing questions so fast Caccia was bewildered. Snatching up Dampier's revolver which he'd brought as usual and laid on the dressing table in case he needed it, she pointed it at him.

'Why do you carry an English gun?'

'That's not an English gun.'

The revolver waved under Caccia's nose. 'I know about guns. I've been surrounded by soldiers for two years and I know what an English gun looks like.'

'I got it from an Englishman,' Caccia said desperately. 'You know how it is. You capture them. You take their wristwatches and their guns.'

He managed to get the revolver off her but she was far from finished with him. Sitting up, stark naked, she lifted her hand and made a circle with her forefinger and thumb. 'Why do you make this sign?' she asked. 'That isn't an Italian sign for a beautiful girl. It is this.' She closed her fingers to a fist and made a sign with her forearm that was obvious in any language.

'There's much that puzzles me about you,' she snapped. 'Why do you possess a wig? Italian soldiers don't carry wigs in their packs.'

'There are some funny things in the dump here,' Caccia said weakly.

'Are there football shorts also?'

'Football shorts?'

'Germans don't wear football shorts. They're too busy winning the war. Italians don't wear them either. That oaf Mussolini never thinks they might want to play football. He dresses them in uniforms that are too big or too small or too out-of-date. Only the English and the Australians and the South Africans and the New Zealanders wear football shorts. They think more of playing football, I think, than fighting the war.'

'I got them – '

' – from an Englishman!' She snorted. 'When you captured him. Like the revolver and perhaps the sign and the wig.'

Caccia was staring at her like a rabbit mesmerized by a snake.

'You have shared my bed,' she said. 'You've done to me things which should only be done to a wife. I've allowed you to because I thought you loved me. Tell me the truth! Do you learn all these things you know in the two months you worked as a waiter? And why only *two* months? You must be a very bad waiter, I think, to get the sack after only two months.'

Caccia tried to protest but she brushed his objections aside. 'You know about Waterloo Station and Trafalgar Square with the statue of Admiral Nelson on top. You know about the Marble Arch, about Dean Street and Harrods and of this Uncle Bob they talk about. I didn't discover so much in the time *I* was there. But maybe you are cleverer than me, *eh, soldato*? Perhaps you're a spy!'

Caccia began to grow alarmed. She'd have him in front of a firing squad before long. 'I'm not a spy!' he bleated.

'Then you're a fascist agent and you're about to arrest me and accuse me of saying dreadful things that I've never said, of insults that I've never uttered, all the things that people would like to say and daren't about that fat-bellied goat, the Duce.'

Caccia was wildly reminded of the British sergeant who had once roared out to a neglectful soldier on church parade, 'You silly bugger, take your 'at off in the 'Ouse of God!'

'I'm not a fascist spy,' he insisted.

'A *German* spy?'

'No!'

'Then if you're not a German or an Italian you can only be – ' She paused and stared at him, her eyes growing wide. 'You're – ' She stopped dead again and when she spoke once more she spoke in English, slowly and with emphasis. 'You must be *Inglese*. You are Anglish? Of course! You speak Italian like an Anglish!'

She was looking scared, then the look changed to one of anxiety. Finally, when Caccia was just wondering when she'd call the police or her uncle, and which of them would shoot him with Dampier's revolver, she suddenly began to look awed.

'I have it!' she said. 'You're one of these people who frighten our soldiers so much – what do they call them? – the Far Distance Desert Gruppo.'

She was actually smiling, excited and interested, and Caccia, who was quick to spot a green light if there was a glimmer of one around, was unable to resist.

'That's it – ' He, too, had switched to English now. 'Long Range Desert Group. There are a lot of us about.'

To his surprise, she flung her arms round him and hugged him. 'If I was a good Mussolini Italian,' she said, 'I should take your revolver and shoot a shot at you. But I am not and you have come to rescue me.' Her grip loosened enough for him to breathe and she stared intently at him. 'Why did they pick you? Because you speak Italian? Because you're an Anglish Italian perhaps. Like my cousin's husband?'

'Yes.' Caccia began to talk about his family and his words came out in a babble. 'My grandfather was Italian. We still speak Italian.'

'All the time?'

'At home. Not in the shop.'

'You have a shop?'

'Yes.'

'A big one?'

'As big as Max Donatello's.'

'You know him! You know my cousin Cecilia's husband?'

181

She clapped her hands delightedly. '*Magnifico! Meraviglioso!* What do you sell?'

'Food. Italian food. Peppers. Sausages. Pizzas. That sort of thing.'

She was eyeing him shrewdly. 'You have many brothers and sisters?'

'Three sisters. All married. One to a feller who runs a restaurant in Dean Street. One to an importer. Food and that sort of thing. One married to a feller who's got a warehouse.'

'Food?'

'Mostly.'

'Your family has much food?'

Caccia grinned, at ease again. 'We know what's good for us.'

'And you have no brothers?'

'Just me. I was just starting to run the business when they called me up.'

'And when the war is over' – she sounded awed again – 'the business will be yours?'

'The girls don't want it. They've got plenty of money and they never enjoyed serving in the shop.'

'I would,' Rosalba said fervently. 'I would always enjoy serving in a shop. Especially a food shop.' She flung her arms round him again and hugged him. 'Come. Let us go and tell my Uncle Barbieri.'

Caccia backed away in alarm. 'He'll hand me over to the army!'

'Not he! He hates the army. He served his time with the class of 1899. He fought on the Piave in the other war. He hates the Duce. He hates *all* Italian governments. They made him fight and they make him pay taxes when he doesn't want to. He hates many people.'

'He won't want you to fall in love with an Englishman, then.'

'He loves England!' She flung her arms wide. 'He speaks Anglish also! He worked in England. For many years. Many

182

Italians did. Because we were allies in the last war. It's only because Mussolini's mad that we aren't in this one. He always wanted to go back and when my aunt died he was going to. But it was too late. The war started. Come! He will look after you.'

'Jesus!' Caccia was finding things were moving too fast for him. 'Hadn't we better put some clothes on first?'

Barbieri appeared from the room behind the bar. He was wearing only a shirt, under which his vast belly stuck out, and he was scratching at his beard.

Rosalba flung a pair of trousers at him. By the time he'd put them on he was more or less awake. He suddenly became aware of Caccia.

'What's he doing here?' he demanded.

'He has been in my room,' Rosalba said defiantly in English.

Barbieri's eyes widened and he replied in the same language. 'Teresa? *This* is Teresa?'

'Yes, yes.'

'She has changed, I think.' Barbieri made 36–24–36 movements with his hands.

'No, no. He has not changed shape.'

'Then I think Gaspare Gelucci must have been under a misapprehension for many years. I wonder if he knows she shaves.'

'No, no, no!' Rosalba pounded on his chest with her fists. 'This is not Teresa. This is my man. I love him.'

Barbieri studied the Italian sergeant's jacket Caccia was wearing and the Italian forage cap he clutched in his nervous hands. 'Why *him*?' he said contemptuously. 'Why don't you pick yourself someone with a good future.'

'He has a future! *Mamma mia*, what a future!'

'An Italian soldier?' Barbieri made a spitting movement with his mouth. 'Italian soldiers have *no* future. If they're not starved to death or killed by the stupidity of the Duce, they're starved to death or killed by the stupidity of their

183

generals. In the last war they dressed us in puttees to which the mud clung so that we marched about with two great balls of clay at the ends of our legs. Italian soldiers *never* have a future. You should pick yourself a German.'

Rosalba made a spitting gesture. 'You think *they* have a future? With that monster Hitler?'

'At least they wear good boots.'

'They will be beaten by the Anglish.'

'All right then!' Barbieri gestured wildly. 'Why not an English? Your cousin Cecilia found an English, and nowadays she has a big house in the country and a Rolls-Royce.'

Max Donatello's family, Caccia decided, had either suddenly started doing well or Cecilia Neri had been spinning some tall yarns.

'There is much money in – ' Barbieri stopped dead and slapped his forehead. 'Why are we speaking in English?'

Rosalba made a sweeping gesture at Caccia. 'Because Arturo is my *innamorato*. My lover.'

'So what has that to do with speaking English?'

'Arturo *is* Anglish.'

Barbieri's jaw dropped and his eyes bulged. 'English? He's an English?'

'Part of the Great Distance Desert Gruppo.'

Barbieri's head was swinging from right to left in alarm, his eyes staring, as if police were pouring in at every door and window. '*Mamma mia,*' he wailed. 'Get him out of here! They'll find out! They'll shoot me! They'll shoot you! Him, too, I expect! If the Germans find out, they'll send the Gestapo to tear out our fingernails.'

'Shut up, uncle,' Rosalba said coldly. 'He's going soon.'

'Tell him not to come back.'

'Arturo *will* come back. He speaks perfect Italian. He *is* Italian. Well – Anglish–Italian. His family are very wealthy. They have the big food store in London. They have many lorries to carry the food about the city. They deliver to all parts of the country. They are never without food. Not even in wartime. They drink wine – good Italian wine – with every meal.'

Barbieri calmed down abruptly. 'They do?'

'Arturo is the only son. He will inherit all. Think of it, uncle: a vast store. A fleet of lorries.'

'*Mamma mia!*'

Barbieri swallowed, then slowly he began to smile. 'Perhaps it will be all right,' he said. 'Perhaps, if we're careful and say nothing, nobody will find out.' He paused, scratching at his beard. 'Perhaps we should celebrate. Have we not another bottle of that white Sicilian wine somewhere?'

'It's gone. Arturo drank it.'

Barbieri gave Caccia a sour look, but it only lasted a second. 'No matter. When I went to Derna I brought back some more Castelli Romani. And why not make us some spaghetti? I think we should celebrate.'

Part Three

1

When Caccia slipped back into camp the following morning, he was looking worried. After a while, he sought out Clegg, who was sitting on a toolbox drinking a dixie of coffee with Company Sergeant Major Fee. The Australian was recovering rapidly and even beginning, like the rest of them, to enjoy the situation in which they found themselves.

'Cleggy,' Caccia said. 'I want to see the Old Man.'

Clegg looked up. 'Fancy a spot of leave then?'

'I want to see the Old Man,' Caccia said stubbornly.

Clegg put down the dixie. 'What's up, wop? Something wrong? What you been up to? That girl you been seeing?'

'I think I'd better see the Old Man.'

'You sound like a gramophone record. Okay, go and see him.'

'I'm trying to do it right,' Caccia said indignantly. 'You're supposed to go through the sergeant, aren't you? You're a sergeant.'

Clegg grinned. 'I hardly ever noticed it. That's only so there was somebody to speak up for the Ratbags.'

'Well, stop looking at me like I'm something hanging off your boot. Start speaking. For me.'

Clegg looked puzzled. 'All right,' he agreed. 'I'll go and see Morton.'

'Not Morton. He's not the Old Man.'

'He behaves as if he was.'

'I want to see the proper old man. Dampier. Morton's just a corporal.'

189

Clegg eyed him, glanced at Fee, and began to head for the colonel's tent. 'All right, then: Dampier. I'll go and see Rafferty. He'll know what to do.'

Caccia looked gloomy. 'I'll bet he won't know what to do this time,' he said.

A little later, Rafferty strolled over to where Caccia was waiting. 'There's something on your mind, lad,' he said. 'Spit it out.'

'I'll talk to the CO, sir.'

'I'm a warrant officer. I'm supposed to be here to save him work.'

'Sir, Colonel Dampier hasn't got any work to do. He hasn't done any work since we came here. Because of his lumbago. I want to see him.'

Rafferty studied him warily. 'All right, lad. Follow me.'

Reaching the tent where Dampier lived, Rafferty signed to Caccia to wait and disappeared inside. A moment or two later, his head appeared, gesturing to Caccia to step inside after him.

Dampier was sitting at a table, writing what looked like a report.

'Well, Caccia,' he said. 'What's the trouble?'

Caccia's throat worked once or twice then he drew a deep breath and blurted out his request. 'Sir, I want to get married.'

Dampier had been listening with only half his attention, his eyes still on the report he was writing. His lumbago was nagging at him again and, in addition, he had a feeling that he was going to have a lot of explaining to do when he finally managed to return to the British lines and he had been giving a lot of thought to his words. He looked up sharply.

'You want *what*?' he said, wincing heavily as pain jabbed at him like an assegai.

'I want to get married.'

Dampier stared. 'Good God, man,' he snapped, 'this is

no time to be worrying about getting married! It can wait until we get back to our lines, can't it?'

'No, sir. It can't wait.'

'Dammit, there's nothing we can do about it here, stuck out in the blue, with the girl back in England.'

'She's not back in England, sir.'

'She's not? Cairo? Who is it?'

Caccia drew a deep breath. 'Her name's Rosalba Coccioli.'

'She sounds Italian.'

'She *is* Italian, sir.'

Dampier frowned. 'I think you might have difficulty over this, Caccia. The authorities would never wear it. They're none too fond of the Italians just now. After all, they're a pretty treacherous lot.' Dampier coughed, realizing his gaffe as he remembered Caccia was almost more Italian than English. 'Well, shall we say they don't like *Italian* Italians. There are a lot of *British* Italians, of course. In London. I expect you're one. Splendid chaps. Run excellent restaurants. Eaten there meself – ' He realized he was running on unnecessarily without improving the situation and changed direction hurriedly. 'However, whatever the authorities think about the Italians, I can't do anything about it here.'

'I think you can, sir. You've got to.'

Dampier's eyes narrowed and his brows came down again. 'What do you mean? I've *got* to.'

In a mass of stumbling sentences, Caccia tried to explain. When he'd finished, Dampier looked at Rafferty, whose face was as blank as his own. Then, as it finally dawned on him what Caccia was trying to tell him, the balloon went up.

'You mean this girl's *here* somewhere? Here? Good God, man, do you realize what you're saying?'

'Yes, sir,' Caccia said wretchedly.

'There's a war on, man! We're facing the whole bloody world armed with not much else but our teeth and fingernails and you go off chasing enemy females. What in God's name have you been up to? Have you been seducing the girl?'

Caccia looked miserable. He had begun to realize that Rosalba Coccioli was a very determined young woman. 'I don't know which way it was, sir,' he admitted. 'It seemed a bit as if she was seducing me.'

'Good God! Dancers! Singers! Comedians! Deserters! Now seducers! What have we got mixed up with, Mr Rafferty?' Dampier glared at Caccia. 'Where is this girl?'

'In Zuq, sir. She lives at the Bar Barbieri.'

'And you've been sneaking in there? Into Zuq, at night? Without a pass?'

'Sir, I didn't know anybody was issuing passes.'

Nobody was, so Dampier cleared his throat noisily. 'You've been consorting with the enemy, Caccia. That's a criminal offence, isn't it, Mr Rafferty?'

Rafferty, as usual, seemed to find it all highly amusing. 'Sure, they usually shoot 'em, sir,' he said.

Caccia threw him an alarmed look and Dampier gestured angrily. It jabbed at his lumbago again and he finally lost his temper. 'Put this bloody man under arrest, Mr Rafferty!'

'Sir!' Caccia's voice rose to a bleat of protest. 'I think you should listen!'

'Good God! Desertion's bad enough! Consorting with the enemy's about the most severe crime you could commit!'

'But, sir – !'

'He's confined to his tent, Mr Rafferty, until we decide what to do with him.'

Rafferty walked with Caccia back to his tent. He was a calm man and he had a lot of experience. Instead of merely leaving Caccia to himself, he leaned on the tent pole.

'You said the colonel should listen,' he said. 'Why? Have you something that might be an explanation?'

'Not half I haven't, sir,' Caccia complained. 'What I've got's enough to make your hat spin round. I just didn't get a chance to say so.'

A few minutes later, Rafferty reappeared in Dampier's tent.

'I think, sir,' he said, 'that mebbe we should talk some more to Driver Caccia.'

When Caccia reappeared in Dampier's tent, the colonel was in a more subdued mood. Morton was also there this time, alongside Rafferty, almost in the guise of the prisoner's friend at a court martial.

'I've been thinking about your case, Caccia,' Dampier said. 'And I'm assuming that your conduct is explained to a certain extent by the fact that you have Italian blood in you. But you're still a British soldier. Can't you just ignore her? Soldiers have done it before, y'know. Got a girl into trouble and then asked for a posting to the other end of the country.' He was itching to know what was on the map Rafferty had told him about, but in his pompous way he felt he first had to go through the rigmarole of reading some sort of lecture. 'Not that we can give you a posting from here. But we'll be away soon. Corporal Morton has information that the Italians are about to start clearing a strip of the minefield.'

Caccia drew another deep breath. 'It's not as simple as that, sir.'

'Soldiers have always found it simple before. It's something I very much deplore. Putting a girl in the family way – is she in the family way?'

'No, sir.'

'Then, what the devil are you worrying about? You've heard of the Soldier's Farewell, haven't you? And shotgun weddings never work. Just forget her.'

'I can't, sir.'

'Great gold teeth of God, man! Don't start being all intense with us! Of course you can forget her!'

'I didn't mean that, sir. This time it concerns all of us. You, sir. Mr Rafferty, sir. All the others. She's found out.'

'What do you mean, she's found out?'

'About us.'

Dampier glared. 'Did *you* tell her?'

193

'No, sir. I swear. But she says if I don't marry her, she'll go to the town major and tell him who we are. We won't half catch a cold.'

'Good God!' Dampier looked at Rafferty for guidance but the warrant officer's face remained blank. 'Can she?'

'She knows where we are. She said she drove out in her uncle's car a few days ago to watch. She had a pair of binoculars. British ones. Captured British ones. Stolen from the dump.'

'Good God,' Dampier said again. 'Everybody's at it.' He paused. 'Look, tell her to come out here to see me. It's usual for the CO to see the girl. Then we can just hang on to her. Keep her prisoner until we're ready to go – it'll only be a day or two now – then we can let her go free.'

'It won't work, sir,' Caccia explained. 'If she didn't return, a word from her uncle would bring the whole of the Luftwaffe down on us. She's got us by the short and curlies. Besides' – Caccia frowned – 'she says *I*'ve got to turn up. Me. Complete with ring and the lot. She wants to be married. In Zuq. I think she wants her friends to know and I don't think she trusts me. There is one thing – '

Dampier glared at Caccia. 'Ah! So there's another angle, eh?'

'Yes, sir. Extenuating circumstances, you might say. She seems to have the battle order of the whole Italian army. Every division. Every regiment. Every battalion. And she knows exactly where they all are. She doesn't want to hand us over, see, sir. She wants to help.'

Dampier chewed at his lip for a second before looking up again. 'How do we know she's not a German agent?'

In reply, Caccia fished in his pocket and handed over a map. It had come from the kitchen of the Bar Barbieri and it had been cut in half. But it was marked with Italian and German regiments, brigades and divisions and the assembly areas for tanks. Dampier's eyes widened.

'Good God,' he said as the others crowded forward to

look. 'She's got the lot! Hand me my map, Mr Rafferty, please.'

They placed the two maps side by side. The positions they had discovered with the help of Clutterbuck, Morton, Scarlatti and the chatter of people like Mondi were all there on Rosalba's map – and there were a great many more besides.

'It seems genuine.' Dampier looked at Caccia. 'And the girl – this girl of yours – she's got the other half?'

'Yes, sir.'

Dampier was interested. 'Well, at least, my lad, I'd say you've found yourself a very resourceful and determined young woman.'

'Yes, sir,' Caccia admitted ruefully. 'I think I have.'

'Is she attractive?'

'Very beautiful, sir.'

Rafferty was studying the map again. 'Where did she pick up all this information?' he asked.

Caccia explained. 'She said it was dead easy,' he ended. 'Some of it came from the girls in the brothels.'

Dampier's eyes narrowed. 'Is she one?'

'Blimey, no, sir!' Caccia looked alarmed. He had a very formidable mother and could guess what she would have said. 'Not her! But there aren't all that many Italian girls left in Zuq, so she knows them all. The Italian soldiers like to talk. They like to show off. I'm Italian, sir, so I know. She says when the attack comes there's to be no barrage. No warning. The tanks are going through with aircraft overhead to drown their engines and there are going to be trucks fitted with aero engines and propellers to the south to stir up clouds of dust so it'll look like a panzer attack from that end. They're going to give our lot a doing. It's going to be a right old ding-dong. It's to be a surprise.'

'It will be too,' Rafferty observed. 'To the Italians. If we get this information to the right quarters.'

'When's it all to take place?' Dampier asked.

'She says Thursday.'

'That's what I heard,' Morton said. 'So that's correct.'

'She got the regimental numbers because her uncle goes into the stores dump to buy army rations. It's all illegal but it goes on – '

'So I've noticed,' Dampier said coldly.

'There's an Italian sergeant who sells him petrol on the side and he gets to see the indents, the amounts, and where it's going, and he can tell from the quantities roughly how many vehicles there are.'

Dampier was growing interested and he leaned forward. 'They seem very anxious to assist us.'

'She's very pro-British, sir.' Caccia's keen awareness of when a green light was showing told him that Dampier was coming round a little. 'It was very dangerous, sir. But they're on our side. Her father was arrested by Mussolini and died in chokey. They want to help.' He stopped and drew a deep breath. 'But,' he ended, 'they also want *me*.'

'Do you want *her*?'

Caccia considered. Despite the trap he had fallen into, it occurred to him that in Rosalba there was a great deal that was in his mother, who had not only brought up a family of four but had also managed to run the family business when his father had been out enjoying himself. She could well be a treasure.

'Yes, sir,' he said firmly. 'I do.'

Dampier frowned. 'But what would you do with her afterwards? When we head back? You'd have to leave her behind.'

'She wants to come with us, sir. She says if she can get to Cairo she can get herself sent to England.'

'What in God's name would she do in England?'

'She'd be all right, sir. Her cousin's married to a pal of mine.'

Dampier was beginning to see the point at last. 'I think we're going to have to take her with us, Mr Rafferty,' he said slowly. 'If only for her own safety because, if it got out that she'd supplied us with information, they'd probably shoot her, imprison her at the very least.' He looked baffled. 'But what do we do about the wedding?'

Morton interrupted. 'There are military priests in Zuq,' he said. 'Scarlatti would find one. He might even consider a marriage in his diocese romantic. I can arrange everything and attend the wedding service.' He smiled sardonically. 'Good officer type, concerned with the welfare of his men. I'm sure you'd approve, sir.'

Dampier gave him an old-fashioned look. 'And then?'

Morton smiled. 'Perhaps they could be allowed their *luna di miele* – their honeymoon – with me picking them up later with the car.'

'I suppose' – Dampier was still faintly hopeful – 'there's no way we could leave her behind.'

'No, sir.' Caccia had finally made up his mind. 'There isn't.'

Dampier looked helplessly at Rafferty and flung up his hands. 'How did I get into this?' he said. 'They'll crucify me when I get back.'

Rafferty smiled. 'You never know, sir,' he pointed out. 'They might recommend you for promotion.'

2

As it happened, it turned out to be more difficult than they'd imagined, and a series of unexpected events rather changed their plans.

Morton returned from an interview with a subdued and an at first none-too-willing Scarlatti – with lunch all the same, however, of pasta, parma ham and *lacrimae Christi* – to say that the second Italian push *was* due to start on Thursday. Unable to forget that Morton now apparently commanded a unit whose equipment was almost totally his, Scarlatti had been inclined to be wary but had finally been won round by promises of a helping hand for his family's business after the end of the war – or even before – and a strong hint that the equipment he assumed had come illicitly from *his* dump had in fact come illicitly from the dump run by his old enemy Colonel Ancillotti, in Derna.

'And there was no air raid on at the time it disappeared,' Morton pointed out cheerfully. 'He's going to have a lot of explaining to do.'

He was surprised how delighted Scarlatti was at the news. The idea of one in the eye for his old enemy pleased him enormously, and after that it took only a brandy or two before he unwittingly confirmed the date they'd picked up.

He made no bones about his doubts, nevertheless. 'The Duce,' he said lugubriously, 'fixes dates, postpones them and abandons them, then picks them up again as if he had a smoothly working military machine, which we all know it isn't. Last time we came to a standstill because there was a shortage of shells and our so-called armoured divisions consisted of nothing more than a regiment of Bersaglieri, a regiment of artillery and three battalions of sardine tins on wheels.'

'At least, sir,' Rafferty pointed out as he listened to Morton's report, 'it proves the girl can be trusted. What about the other feller? Faiani? What did he have to say?'

'Nothing,' Morton said. 'He hardly said a word. He's given up, I think.'

'And when do we get the other half of the map?' Dampier asked.

'After the wedding,' Morton announced. 'I've seen the girl.' He smiled. 'She wants to marry Caccia. In fact, I'd say she was *determined* to marry Caccia. But Scarlatti's turned up trumps and offered to take her into his dump and let her choose a dress from some he's got there. They were about the only things that weren't pinched or destroyed during the raid. Some of them are rather splendid, I gather. Belonged to mistresses of various senior Italian officers who got snatched up in our push last year. Nobody's ever claimed them so he says she can have one as a wedding present. He's also offered a bottle or two of champagne for the reception.'

Dampier's eyebrows shot up. 'They're having a reception? Who're the guests, for God's sake? Hitler? Mussolini?'

They were still discussing the arrangements when Clegg stuck his head through the tent door.

'Sir. Trouble. There's a car on the way. I think it's that German general again.'

Morton shouted for Caccia and headed out of the tent. The car came down the hill trailing a cloud of yellow dust. As it stopped Morton saluted, briskly at attention.

Erwin's smile was friendly as he climbed out. 'So, *tenente*,' he said. 'We meet again. We thought we'd lost you. We hadn't seen you in your usual place in the town.'

'Instructions to move into the desert,' Morton said

smoothly. 'To be nearer the troops. What can I do for your excellency?'

Erwin gestured. 'You might call it a favour. As you doubtless know, we shall be on the move again on Thursday.'

Morton nodded, noting that Erwin was also unwittingly confirming what Caccia's girl had said.

'I feel like a last little celebration,' Erwin went on. 'When we spotted you just now, the idea occurred to me. I've enjoyed our stay near Zuq. It's been what might be called a touch of civilization after the desert, and Captain Stracka and myself are intending to do a last little bit of painting at the end of the wadi before we leave. Obergefreiter Bomberg has undertaken to make it worthwhile and has acquired wine and a few extra rations. A cold collation eaten as we paint. Perhaps you'll join us for a drink before we start?'

'I'd be delighted, excellency.'

'One final thing.' Erwin smiled. 'Our gramophone's given up the ghost. Sand in the works. It gets everywhere, as I'm sure you've discovered. Aeroplane engines. Tank turrets. Gramophone motors. Mozart begins to sound like a cat with its head caught in a set of railings. Then Stracka had an idea: your splendid singer. Could you arrange for him to sing for us?'

Morton's knees went weak. He could just imagine Jones the Song serenading a German general. If anything would bring on one of his headaches, that would.

'We have a gramophone, excellency,' he said hurriedly. 'Perhaps we could lend it to you.'

Erwin waved a hand. 'No, no,' he insisted. 'Portable gramophones are no good anyway. They always sound tinny and I expect yours is no better than ours. We'd prefer your singer.'

Great God in the Mountains, Morton thought. Aloud, he said, 'He doesn't sing in German, excellency. He's not a professional. Just an Italian who has a voice.'

'Then let him sing in Italian. Surely there are Neapolitan songs that he knows. Stracka and I want only to be enter-

200

tained for a while before we disappear into the desert again. This time we either reach Cairo or else we get nowhere and I suspect it might go on for a long time.'

'Wouldn't the general be happier with a German orchestra?'

Erwin eyed him quizzically, then he gestured. 'I know German orchestras,' he said flatly. 'Fiddles, drums, piano accordions, guitars and clarinets. Everything they play sounds like a victory march. Around 6.00 p.m. tomorrow then,' he went on firmly. 'We'll arrive around 4.00 p.m., do a little painting – we still have to get the southern view of the desert over that pink gravel – and then two hours later, when we're in need of a break, you must join us for your drink, and your singer can entertain us.'

Jones the Song put on a fit of hysteria to beat all fits of hysteria.

Company Sergeant Major Fee, listening with interest, put his bewilderment into words. 'A bloody German general?' he said.

'No worse than an English general,' Clegg observed. 'Probably neither of 'em knows anything about it.'

Jones the Song was in full spate. 'What's a good Welshman doing, bach,' he yelled, 'singing to a German general? Why, aye, I shall lose my voice with nerves, see, and he'll want to know what's happened, and will come and look!'

Dampier interrupted the indignation. 'Couldn't you have put him off?' he asked Morton.

'Would *you* have tried to put off a German general?' Morton said sharply. 'Under the circumstances.'

Dampier had to concede the point.

'Dhu, I shall have one of my headaches,' Jones wailed. 'Sure of it I am.'

'You'd better not,' Dampier warned. 'There's a lot hanging on this concert of yours – if only to keep the swine from investigating us too closely.'

201

'Can't we just up sticks and bugger off?' Clegg asked.

'What about Caccia?'

'We could hit him with something hard.'

Dampier had to admit that it sounded much more sensible than what was being planned. But he was a man of uprightness and integrity – more important, he was a realist, a good soldier and a patriot, who believed in putting first things first.

'No,' he said. 'We must honour our promise. Besides,' he added, 'we need that map. It contains the information we need.'

Jones flapped his hands. He looked like an excited and rather grubby gnome. 'What'll I sing? I don't know any German songs.'

'He's not expecting German songs,' Morton pointed out. 'He's expecting Italian songs.'

'Dhu, I don't know any of them either!'

'You sang "*Ave Maria*" in Italian. I bet you known "*Santa Lucia*".'

'My mam used to sing it. She called it "Bright Stars of Italy".'

'I'll write the words down for you. Erwin's Italian's as limited as yours.' With the walking stick he had taken to carrying, Morton slapped the smart Italian field boots he'd obtained from Scarlatti's dump. 'Can you read music?'

Jones drew himself up to his full scruffy height. 'All Welshmen can read music, man.'

'Right then. I'll get Scarlatti to find something.'

Jones desperately sought an escape. 'What about accompaniment?'

'Clegg'll help. We've got a piano accordion among the Ratbags' effects.'

Clegg shied like a startled foal, but in the end he agreed and, as Morton had expected, Scarlatti was able to produce a book of popular Italian songs, of several of which Jones discovered he knew the English version.

'There's just one thing, boyo,' he said. 'I'm not going to stand up in front of him and sing.'

'What the hell *are* you going to do?' Morton snapped. 'Lie on your back?'

Jones's grubby little fists clenched. 'I'm a Welshman,' he protested. 'Llewelyn ap Iorwerth wouldn't stand up in front of an invader and sing.'

'I'll bet Llewelyn ap Bloody Thing never served in the Western Desert,' Clinch said.

Jones gave them an agonized glance. 'Look you,' he admitted, 'it's not that exactly. I'd be scared. I'd lose me voice.'

Morton had an idea. 'Suppose,' he said, 'that we arrange for you to sing out of sight?'

Dampier studied Jones. Tatty wisps of greasy black hair stuck out from under the oversize Italian cap he was wearing, his shorts fitted where they touched and there was a rent in the sleeve of his shirt. 'It might be better if he *were* out of sight,' he observed. 'No self-respecting general would want anyone as scruffy as he is singing alongside his table.'

Jones looked indignant but Morton grinned.

'You can just imagine it, can't you?' Dampier went on. 'Jones leaning over to croon in his ear and a button dropping off his trousers into his soup.'

'And suppose he found out he was British?' Clegg added. 'We'd probably lose the war as a result.'

It was going to be a tight programme for Morton with Caccia, the only other Italian-speaker, occupied with getting married, but Rafferty, as usual, was ready with the answer. 'I've worked out a schedule,' he said, his sly shadowy smile appearing to mock them all. 'The Humber will take Driver Caccia and Corporal Morton to the wedding. In the morning, of course, because the bridegroom is due to go to war that evening. Corporal Morton will attend the reception, returning here for when Erwin arrives around four. He'll then dance attendance on the Germans until the singin's finished, when he'll return to collect Driver Caccia and his girl after their wedding night. Held a little earlier than normal, of course, but under the circumstances I presume they don't need it to be dark.'

'He's going to be pretty occupied,' Dampier growled.

Nevertheless, he thought, despite the rushing around, Morton was going to have all the fun. Drinking champagne at Caccia's reception and German hock at Erwin's little celebration down the wadi. In spite of being a full colonel, he, Dampier, hadn't got much out of the adventure except a bad back.

3

The RAF came over again that night, but apart from a few bombs on the airstrip near the Wadi Sghiara and a few in the harbour as usual, 64 Light Vehicle Repair Unit were never in any danger. It kept them awake for a lot of the night, however, and Clegg decided it was going to be a busy day. Fortunately for him, he had no idea how busy.

With the aid of Clegg's hairbrush and comb, one of Clutterbuck's many spare shirts and a spot of shoe polish borrowed from Dampier, in no time they had Caccia tarted up to meet his bride.

'Pity you have to wear the bloody King of Italy's uniform instead of the King of England's, old comrade, bosom friend and pot companion,' Clegg observed critically as he walked round Caccia, tugging at his jacket.

Sergeant Major Fee watched them as if they were mad. 'You really mean it?' he grinned. 'He really *is* going to marry a wop sheila?'

'Why not?' Clegg asked. 'Wop sheilas have the same complement of legs, arms, eyes and odds and ends as any other sheila.'

'But, Jesus, wops are bloody useless!'

'It won't make much difference either way. Marriage hardens the arteries whoever you're married to.'

'Stone me eyes right and fours about,' Caccia said indignantly. 'It's the girl I'm going to marry you're talking about!'

'I know,' Fee agreed. 'That's why I'm talking about her.'

'Yes, and you're going at it like a load of mad dogs, too! All that about Italians being useless.'

'Well, they are, cobber,' Fee said. 'We all know that. We've been fighting 'em ever since we came into the war. What do you want to go and marry an Italian sheila for?'

'She's got class,' Caccia snarled. 'Italian or no Italian!'

'It's a sort of diplomatic gesture,' Clegg pointed out. 'She's got a map with the Italian order of battle tattooed on her chest. All their gun emplacements, minefields and what have you.'

'Which she won't let him see,' Clinch added, 'unless he makes her an honest woman.'

'Don't *you* start,' Caccia snorted.

Jones the Song joined in delightedly. After all the tormenting he'd suffered from Caccia, he was overjoyed at his predicament. 'Greater love hath no man than this, boy,' he said.

Despite the teasing and embarrassment, when it came to the point, however, and now that the moment had come, Caccia wasn't very worried about his future. 'She'll be good in the shop,' he said.

Morton appeared, decked out in his Italian lieutenant's uniform. Producing a small bunch of red, white and green ribbons, he solemnly pinned it to the breast pocket of the Italian sergeant's jacket Caccia was wearing.

'Sorry there aren't any carnations,' he said. 'But I suppose this will do.'

'Perhaps they don't wear carnations when they're married in Italy,' Clinch observed.

'Perhaps they carry a bust of Mussolini in one hand,' Clegg suggested. 'And a few sticks of spaghetti in the other.'

'Now I've seen everything,' Fee said as they pronounced Caccia ready. 'A Pom dressed in a wop uniform going off to marry a wop sheila behind the wop lines.'

'Oh, there's more to come,' Morton said cheerfully. 'Tonight, remember, we have Jones the Song serenading a German general.'

*

Wearing a red, white and green sash, a small man with dyed hair and a big belly met them on the steps of the battered Palazzo Municipale.

'I am Carloni, Gianpiero, *avvocato*,' he announced. 'I am the mayor.'

He stood framed in the large splinter-pitted doorway, between two carved stone fasces and beneath a carved Italian eagle. On the walls on either side someone had painted stalwart slogans from Mussolini's speeches, and there were a few sombre printed notices for locally born Italians who had been killed pasted to the walls as signs of mourning.

But the sun was out, the wind was not blowing to fill everybody's eyes with grit, and the mayor shook hands with Caccia and Morton. Clegg, who was driving, sat rigidly in the Humber. 'It's a long time since I conducted a marriage ceremony,' the mayor said, leading the way into his office. Above his head was a picture of Mussolini – prognathous jaw thrust out, eyes fixed in a stare of determination – being aggressive under a steel helmet.

'There are few marriages in Zuq these days,' the mayor went on. 'All the men have gone away. The last one was an officer from a Blackshirt battalion who married a widow from Derna. It was very elaborate. Flags. Saluting. Heel clicking. Very impressive,' he ended in a flat voice to show how little impressed he was.

They were waiting on the steps when Scarlatti drove up in his Lancia. He was sitting alongside the driver and as he saw Morton he leapt out at once. By this time, under Morton's influence he had abandoned the rigid straight-armed Roman salute for Morton's languid British-type flick of the hand. Morton glanced about him warily.

'Where's Faiani?' he asked. 'Is he coming?'

'Someone has to stay behind,' Scarlatti said. 'To look after the shop. I told him he could take the afternoon off but he said he was busy. Occupied with a signal from Rome about something.'

In the back of the car were Rosalba, her uncle and another girl, who turned out to be Teresa Gelucci. The dress from Scarlatti's store was a confection of subdued yellow that suited Rosalba's dark skin and black hair and, with the low neck, tight skirt and the posy of wilting flowers she carried, she looked remarkably pretty. Caccia decided that his mother would approve. The bridesmaid was wearing what looked like a borrowed dress many times darned, and starched and ironed until it was shiny enough to pick up the sun. Barbieri was clad in his best black suit, white shirt and black tie and looked as if he were dressed for a funeral. But there was a suppressed excitement in him, so unlike his normal depressed gloom Caccia was puzzled.

Sidling alongside, Barbieri laid his finger to his nose. 'I have petrol,' he announced quietly. 'Enough to last me for weeks if I'm careful. From the Venezia Armoured Division.' He made a spitting gesture. 'Armoured division? The British will make mincemeat of them.' The smile returned. 'One hundred and twenty litres. I had brandy. From the dump on the night of the air raid. It was good for barter.' He kissed his fingertips. 'British petrol,' he ended. 'In beautiful square silver cans.'

'Make sure they're not leaking,' Caccia advised. 'British petrol cans *always* leak.'

Barbieri smiled. 'One or two. Here and there. But the floor of the shed's covered with shavings from the furniture factory so there can be no sparks. They absorb all the noise.'

'They'd make a nice bonfire, too,' Caccia observed.

Avvocato Carloni, who'd been having a quiet talk with Rosalba, announced that he was ready and they lined up in front of him. Rosalba gave Caccia a possessive glance, then shyly lowered the lace shawl she wore over her head so that it covered her eyes. Their fingers touched and Barbieri reached across to hand over his own wedding ring for the ceremony. After they had signed the register, they headed for the church for the blessing. The end of the building had been hit by a bomb and part of the wall had fallen across the altar, but the priest had rigged up a makeshift arrangement with a square slab of marble from the top of an old-fashioned washstand on a pile of sandbags, with a flapping linen cloth spread over it and a couple of brass candlesticks – one badly bent – gleaming in the sun. Behind the 'altar' a picture of the crucifixion rested against a scarred wall, white against the deep blue of the sky.

As they reappeared in the street, Barbieri was weeping with emotion. Rosalba looked radiant with happiness and Scarlatti made a little speech, telling her she could keep the dress as a wedding present. He even took a photograph which he promised to hand over to the happy couple as soon as he could persuade the Photography Unit of the Regia Aeronautica at the airstrip to develop it.

'And now,' he said, fishing in his car and producing a bottle. 'The champagne! Perhaps the bride and groom would like to ride with me.'

They shot through the town in a cloud of dust followed by Clegg and Morton in Dampier's car.

'I reckon this is the best performance the Ratbags have ever given,' Clegg grinned.

The Bar Barbieri had been so decorated with coloured paper and ribbons it looked as if it had been made ready for a children's Christmas party. The food consisted of hors d'oeuvres of pilchards on German black bread but from somewhere Barbieri had also managed to acquire a little Parma ham and a few biscuits.

As Scarlatti was ushering his driver inside he waved to Morton. 'Bring your driver in, too,' he suggested magnanimously. 'Numbers will add to the gaiety.'

Morton could just imagine what sort of gaiety it would be if Scarlatti started asking questions of Clegg, whose Italian amounted only to the few words he'd learned for their sketches and a few he'd picked up since.

'He'd better stay with the vehicle,' he said with a grin. 'He's not very bright and given half the chance he gets drunk.'

'Thanks, pal,' Clegg said out of the corner of his mouth. 'For nothing.'

Scarlatti was clearly enjoying himself and after a few glasses of wine insisted on making a speech which he followed with a song. Barbieri produced drink as if there were no tomorrow and Teresa Gelucci began to make eyes at Morton because he was the best-looking man there and she'd heard he was a count. When he ignored her, she turned her attention to Scarlatti, who had already twice tried to pinch her behind. As the party began to grow noisy, Morton decided it was becoming relaxed enough to be dangerous and started pushing everyone out of the room. 'Work to do,' he said loudly. 'Both for us and the bridegroom.'

'But we're just waking up, count,' Scarlatti insisted.

Morton looked at his watch. He could just imagine what would happen if Erwin arrived at 64 Light Vehicle Repair Unit when there was no one there who could speak Italian.

'I have seven vehicles coming in,' he pointed out firmly. 'All have to be serviced before the move forward.'

'You are devoted to duty, count,' Scarlatti said. 'Sometimes, I think you must like the desert.' He pulled a face as he headed for his car. 'Personally, I wish I were back in Milan.' He'd had plenty to drink and, with the heat working on it, there was a catch in his voice. 'Soon *everybody* will be back in the desert. I've been ordered to prepare to set up a new dump along the coast at Sofi. The journey will be awful and doubtless that swindler Ancillotti will continue to remain in comfort in Derna.'

Morton pushed him into the car and, pushing the grateful Teresa in after him, watched it roar away. When he re-entered the bar, Rosalba and Caccia were clutching each other while Barbieri pretended to look the other way.

'You've got until dark,' Morton said bluntly. 'I expect it'll be long enough.' He looked at Rosalba. 'What about the map? Don't lose it in the celebrations.'

Clegg was waiting by the Humber, a bottle in his fist. He looked remarkably cheerful, his eyes dancing with mischief.

'Where did you get that?' Morton demanded.

'Barbieri considered it unfair,' Clegg said, 'that I should be sweating out here while you lot were in there wetting your whistles. It arrived with a lecture on what a lot of shits Italian officers are. He didn't feel it was right for me to be ignored.' He grinned. 'Come to that, old comrade and boon thing, neither did I.'

4

Dampier was sweating with nerves when Morton reappeared.

'You're late,' he accused.

'He's not come?'

'No.'

'Then I'm *not* late,' Morton said coldly.

Checking that Jones was ready, he noticed that Clegg was beaming all over his face and looked drunk. But he knew he was a complete professional and, drunk or sober, if Jones's voice failed him, he'd probably go into a song and dance routine to keep the show going. Clutching in his tiny hands the song book Scarlatti had found for them, Jones was on edge with nerves.

'I think I've got a headache coming on,' he wailed.

Morton was waiting by the tent when Erwin's car appeared. As it stopped, Erwin smiled.

'Everything is ready?' he asked.

'Everything, excellency. There've been one or two small problems but we've overcome them. There is one thing, however, for which I need the general's permission. Our singer is shy. He's never sung in public before. He wishes to remain out of sight.'

Erwin shrugged. 'So long as he's not so far away we can't hear him.'

'He'll be just over the brow of the wadi. The general will

hear perfectly. And Soldato Cleghi will accompany and play in the intervals while Soldato Iones gets his breath back.'

Erwin smiled. 'So long as we have music. Very soon the only music we'll have will be the music of the guns.'

As the car moved off down the wadi, Morton looked at Clegg and Jones. Jones gave a nervous grimace that was supposed to be a reassuring smile, his lips moving as he went for the thousandth time over the Italian words of 'Santa Lucia'.

Erwin's celebration was more of a success than they'd believed possible. At six o'clock Morton drove down the ravine with Jones and Clegg, pushed them out of the car where they couldn't be seen, then continued to where Obergefreiter Bomberg had placed a folding table on the sand. Erwin and Captain Stracka sat alongside it under their umbrella, straw hats on their heads, toying with their food in the heat. Wine glasses in their hands, they were staring at the two easels set up a few feet away and discussing their work.

'I've acquired something of the light there,' Erwin was saying critically. 'And that patch of pinkish gravel on the right brings in a dramatic touch of colour, don't you think?'

'I think, Herr General,' Stracka commented, 'that perhaps the pink should be a little deeper to offer a greater contrast.'

Erwin frowned. 'Perhaps you're right, Stracka,' he agreed. 'Perhaps the light's going. We'll come here one last time to finish it off. Tomorrow night at the same time, so that the sun's in the same position. We shall just have time before we have to leave.' He became aware of Morton standing nearby and rose to his feet. 'Please join us in a drink, tenente.'

As Bomberg poured the wine, Morton noticed that there was no chair for him. Typical of the bloody Germans, he thought. The arrogant bastards expected him to stand.

As he lifted his glass, the first strains of Clegg's piano accordion came with Jones's soaring voice:

> *'Sul mare lucia*
> *L'astro d'argento –* '

Erwin swung round and smiled. 'I can see nothing,' he said. 'Your shy Soldato Iones has chosen his spot well.'

> *'Barchetta mia*
> *Santa Lucia –* '

Jones the Song was in good voice and Erwin nodded, pleased. 'I always think the Neapolitan songs are the most melodious in the whole world,' he observed cheerfully. 'I expect you know *"Torna a Surriento"*, *tenente*?'

Morton did. Who didn't? It was the one song that every screeching tenor in the army – most of them not a Jones – who felt he could sing, always pounded out at Naafi concerts. Even the Ratbags had had to endure a few impromptu *'Tornas'* at their shows when some drunken corporal had insisted on getting up on the stage. It was obviously the same in the German army and the fact that Morton knew the song didn't stop Erwin going on to describe it and his feelings for it. By the time he'd finished, Jones had changed to a different tune.

'Are you an opera lover, *tenente*?' Erwin asked.

'All Italians are opera lovers, excellency.'

'The Führer's favourite is Wagner.'

It would be, Morton thought.

'Freude durch Arbeit, perhaps.' Erwin laughed. 'Joy through hard work. Another of Dr Goebbels's sayings. There are other German operas, of course.' He refilled his glass. *'Martha*, by Flotow, who was born in Darmstadt. Beethoven's *Fidelio*. And what about Richard Strauss, born in Munich, and Offenbach, born in Cologne?'

They discussed Beethoven for some minutes, by which time Jones had got through another two songs. Nobody had bothered to offer Morton another glass of wine or to provide him with a seat and at one point he became aware of Clegg's indignant face peering over the edge of the wadi behind

Erwin's back, clearly wondering if anybody was taking any notice of them.

In the hope of attracting some attention, they sang 'Lili Marlene' because everybody in the desert sang 'Lili Marlene'.

> *'Tutte le sere, sotto quel fanal'*
> *Presso la caserna. . . .'*

But, having discussed German and Austrian composers, Erwin had launched by this time into a lecture on art, with reference to watercolour and in particular to his own watercolours.

> *'. . .Con te, Lili Marlene,*
> *Con te, Lili Marlene.'*

As the voice stopped, Morton could imagine Jones and Clegg staring at each other, wondering why they'd bothered. By this time, he was seething inside himself and his opinion of Erwin had changed considerably for the worse. The German was still happily chattering away, half the time to Stracka, Morton standing alongside like a wet hen, and eventually he became aware that what he was listening to wasn't Italian any more but Welsh. Indignation that a Welshman should be singing his socks off without even being noticed had led Jones into a brisk defiant run through 'The Men of Harlech'.

> *'Wele goelcerth wen yn fflamio,*
> *A thafodau tân yn bloeddio,*
> *Ar ir dewrion ddod i daro,*
> *Unwaith eto'n un – '*

Erwin finally stopped talking and looked up. 'That is an Italian song, *tenente*?' he said, puzzled.

Morton swallowed. 'Dialect, excellency. From Stresa. Our dim little soldier is, I think, trying to translate it into German.'

Erwin frowned. 'I have been a German all my life,' he

said. 'But I have never heard *that* German. Tell him to sing another.'

As Erwin launched into another diatribe, Morton had a feeling that Clegg at least wouldn't need prompting. After all they'd put into their act, to see Erwin talking through it was enough to make any professional indignant and, fuelled by the wine he'd drunk, Clegg's sense of mischief would be working overtime.

He wasn't wrong. This time it was a jingle they'd picked up from the South Africans, sung in a broad *backveldt jaap* accent, also picked up from the South Africans.

'The monkey and the babejaan sat upon the grass,
And the monkey stuck its finger up the babejaan's arse.
And the babejaan said "God bless my soul!"
Take your dirty finger out of my arsehole.'

'And,' Clegg's voice ended indignantly. 'Up yours, too!'

Morton's heart stood still at what might come next, but Erwin had talked through the whole thing and it seemed to be the end of the concert; only silence followed. Erwin and Stracka were still chattering away but, as he became aware that the singing had stopped, Erwin gestured at his driver.

'The wine, Bomberg,' he said quietly.

Bomberg produced a bottle of German hock, which Erwin pushed towards Morton.

'For the singers, *tenente*. Convey my thanks to them. An excellent entertainment. And now, if you will forgive us, we must return to the business of war. We have to go into Zuq. A conference with General Bergonza and the Italian staff.' He laughed. 'Our barrier to Cairo.'

It seemed to be a gesture of dismissal. Morton clicked his heels, saluted and, clutching the bottle of wine, stalked to the Humber. The self-important bastard, he thought. Treating a bloody Italian like that! As if they were an inferior race! By the time he tossed the bottle on to the seat and climbed behind the wheel, Morton might almost have *been* an Italian.

Bomberg, who had been removing all the implements of the picnic one by one, was already placing easels and the last of the painting equipment in Erwin's Mercedes. As the Germans climbed in behind him, Morton watched the car swing round and head north towards Zuq, then he climbed into the Humber and headed towards the desert.

He was so preoccupied with his indignation he didn't notice that Erwin's Mercedes had stopped. Erwin was sitting twisted round in his seat, frowning as he stared back at the cloud of dust thrown up by the Humber.

'I think that young man should be investigated, Stracka,' he was saying slowly. 'His singer, too. I suspect they're not quite all they seem. I thought there was something a little strange when we first met them, you remember.' He paused, thinking. 'And that unit of theirs has grown incredibly swiftly, Stracka. Had you noticed?'

'I had, Herr General,' Stracka agreed. 'It puzzled me, too. But, after all, the Italians *are* re-equipping for their attack.'

'Indeed. But those songs.' Erwin was speaking half to himself. 'My English is not good but that last one contained English words, I think. And I suspect I've heard the one before. At Dunkirk, when the British prisoners were filing past us. They were singing it then. Defiantly. A whole group of them. It was very impressive. It has a strong melody – almost Germanic in strength – the Führer would approve of it. It remained in my mind a long time. I think we should look into them.'

'This is an Italian military district, Herr General.'

'It's a German war, Stracka. However, have a word with their parent unit and see if they have also noticed anything.'

Unaware that things were closing in on them, Morton picked up Clegg and Jones the Song at dusk.

Dudgeon was in Clegg's very bearing. 'He talked through the whole bloody programme!' he said in his raspy comedian's voice. 'It was worse than when the show died on us in

Wigan and they all got up and walked out. It makes an old pro like me feel like the missing piece of a jigsaw.'

They climbed into the car and sat stiffly in the rear seat, Clegg muttering to himself about ingratitude, Jones uttering shrill little cries of indignation. Then Jones giggled. 'In the Welsh, man,' he chortled. 'An' he never noticed.'

It brought Clegg round a little and Morton listened to their chatter, their delight swamping his anger, and it was only as they reached the end of the *wadi* that he became aware that a vehicle had appeared in his rear mirror. Almost unconsciously, it registered in his mind as a British three-ton Chevrolet. A Chevrolet, he thought. A Chevrolet? *Here?* Then, out of the corners of his eyes, he saw Chevrolets on either side of him. They had no windscreens, doors or cabs, and carried spare wheels, camouflage nets and sand channels. They also seemed remarkably dusty and were overfull of dirty, bearded men in shorts, shirts and sandals, bristling with guns. With alarm, he realized that the guns were all pointing at him and stopped the Humber in a hurry. Immediately, the trucks on either side stopped, too. The first truck stopped behind him and a fourth, coming up at full speed from nowhere, swung round and slammed to a stop across his front, barring his path. At once men with long matted hair appeared alongside, gesturing with their weapons.

'*Mani in alto!* Stick 'em up, you Eyetie bastards!' The speaker was a man with bleached hair and eyebrows and the three stripes of a sergeant.

Clegg glared, still a little tipsy and aggressive. 'Who're you calling an Eyetie bastard?' he demanded.

'I said, "Stick 'em up, you Eyetie – " ' The sergeant stopped dead. 'What did you say?'

'I said, "Who're you calling an Eyetie bastard?" '

'*Aren't* you an Eyetie bastard?'

'No.'

'Well, you fucking look like one. Who *are* you?'

'Come to that, who're you?'

'Who do we look like?'

'The Long Range Desert Group.'

'That's who we are.'

A young officer with a curly yellow beard, eyeballs seared by the sun, wearing a red neckerchief and a peaked hat that looked as if it had been run over by a tank, strolled up. He seemed to be loaded down with weapons but his right hand wielded nothing more dangerous than a blue horsehair fly whisk.

'What's the trouble, Tom?' he asked the sergeant. 'Why aren't these chaps being stripped? We want their uniforms – undamaged and unstained by blood – so why haven't you got on with it?'

The sergeant swung round. 'Because they're not fucking Eyeties, sir.'

The officer stared at Morton and the others. 'They're not?' He sounded as if he'd discovered they'd all got two heads.

'No, sir.'

'Then what the hell are they doing in Eyetie uniform?'

The sergeant looked at Morton. 'What the hell are you doing in Italian uniform, the officer wants to know.'

'We're doing the same as you're doing,' Morton said coolly. 'Operating behind the enemy lines.'

The officer and the sergeant stared at each other, then the officer turned to Morton. 'Who are you? SAS men? Or one of our patrols we don't know about?'

'Neither,' Morton said. 'We're the Desert Ratbags.'

'The Desert Who?'

'We're a concert party. We got cut off. We've been living in Zuq ever since, waiting to get back to our own lines. There are some of our chaps back there. One's a colonel.'

The officer frowned, then he gestured with the fly whisk. 'This is bloody nonsense!' he said. 'We didn't come here to talk to you lot. We came to pick up two or three Italian uniforms.'

'That's all right,' Clegg said. 'We've got plenty of those. German ones, too, if you want 'em.'

The officer looked at the sergeant. 'Where?'

Morton gestured in the general direction of 64 Light Vehicle Repair Unit. 'Over there. We've got enough enemy uniforms to dress the lot of you if you want 'em.'

The officer thought for a moment, then he introduced himself. 'My name's Coffin,' he said. 'Miles Coffin. Not a particularly appropriate name in wartime. After all, it's not the cough that carries you off, it's the coffin they carry you off in. This is Sergeant Grady.' He turned again to Morton. 'Did you say you could fit us *all* up with a uniform?'

'German or Italian. One or the other. Take your pick. We've got plenty of spares.'

Coffin beamed at Grady. 'Well, that's better than just three of us, Tom. We can all go now. Safety in numbers, what?'

'What are you up to, anyway?' Clegg asked.

Coffin shrugged. 'Well, we came originally to knock off the airstrip here near the Wadi Sghiara. There's a squadron of Fiats there. We can polish the lot off with a bit of luck. Then we heard about the general. We heard he was coming to Zuq. So we decided we might as well kill two birds with one stone. Well, not kill 'em. First we knock off the airstrip, then we kidnap the general.'

'Which general?'

'Which general do you think? Erwin. The man himself. Taking him prisoner would make 'em sit up a bit, wouldn't it? They wouldn't know whether they were sittin' on pos or piano stools.'

Clegg, Morton and Jones exchanged glances. 'You're too late,' Clegg said. 'He's already gone into Zuq.'

Coffin frowned. 'We heard he wasn't coming until the day after tomorrow. We heard he was due to make an inspection.'

'He never said anything to me,' Morton pointed out.

Coffin's eyes widened. 'Do you know him?'

'We've just been singing to him.'

'You've – what the Christ is this?' Lieutenant Coffin, like everyone else they met, seemed to become a little bogged down in their explanations.

'He's a painter,' Morton said. 'Watercolour.'

'I never heard that.' Coffin stared at Sergeant Grady, then back at Morton. 'You're not having us on, are you?'

Morton shook his head. 'I've just been watching him,' he said. 'At the end of the wadi there. He was splashing the stuff all over the shop. You could pick him up easily. He said he'd be back around this time tomorrow to finish his picture.'

5

With the arrival of a British officer who hadn't a bad back and seemed to know what he was doing, it seemed to Morton to be time to hand over command.

Within half an hour, the Long Range Desert Group had met Dampier and Rafferty, and the planned kidnap had been brought forward to the following night, particularly in view of the half-map which Dampier produced.

'The girl will bring the other half tonight,' he said.

'Which girl?' Coffin asked.

'The girl Caccia married.'

'Who's Caccia?'

'One of our people. He has an Italian name, but he comes from London. He got married this afternoon.'

The glazed look returned to Coffin's eyes and Rafferty explained quickly, starting at the beginning and taking everything in its proper order.

'Christ,' Coffin said when he'd finished. 'You've been having quite a time, haven't you?'

'You could say that, sir,' Rafferty agreed.

'And this girl's going to be taken through our lines with the map?'

'When we get the other half. We promised she'd go with us.'

'Can't you just leave her?'

'She could get shot if anybody finds out,' Morton explained.

Coffin didn't seem unduly disturbed by the possibility. 'How're you going to get this map to our people?' he asked.

'The Italians are going to open the minefield the other side of Sofi. We thought we'd try to get through with them.'

'Sounds a bit dicey. Be a bit late, too. Why don't we radio the details? We've got a couple of trucks out in the blue waiting for us.' Coffin gestured towards the desert. 'Down there. One's a radio truck – with a No. 11 high-powered set. We often signal a distance of several hundred miles. Once somebody managed fourteen hundred. No plain language, of course. It'd save a lot of trouble. We could have all the grid references in their hands within an hour or two. They expect us to come up every evening and they're listening out for us. We could send two of our vehicles off with it – we always move in twos – and have them back in the morning ready to pick up our little German friend, the general, when he appears.'

Two of the LRDG Chevrolets had just departed southwards when a Lancia truck appeared over the rise. Just ahead of it was Faiani's little Fiat.

It was Morton who spotted them first. 'You know,' he said thoughtfully, 'this looks to me remarkably like trouble.'

Faiani was smiling grimly as he clapped on the brakes of the Fiat. The little car slid sideways in a spectacular stop, throwing sand, dust and small stones on to Morton's boots. The truck drew to a more sedate halt just behind and, as the tailgate slammed down, half a dozen men with rifles jumped out.

'Faiani,' Morton said, moving forward. 'To what do we owe this splendid visit?'

'To me,' Faiani snapped. 'And to General Erwin! He suspected you of being something other than what you claim to be, and what he suspected confirmed not only what Sergeant Schwartzheiss suspected but what I myself suspected from the minute you arrived.' His eyes swept over the group of men who formed 64 Light Vehicle Repair Unit.

'First of all, we'll have your hands up. All of you. Then, please, we'll have everybody in a line.'

As he stood them in line, their hands on their heads, watched intently by his half-dozen men, Faiani's glance fell on Clutterbuck. 'So,' he said. 'It isn't often one takes the same prisoner twice.'

'Arseholes to you, mate,' Clutterbuck returned delicately.

Faiani was staring with glittering eyes now at Morton. 'You were not so clever as you thought, my friend.'

He was in a cheerful mood. Having drawn a blank with the Barda family's home, it had suddenly occurred to him that perhaps he might find out more about Barda himself. The police had supplied the information that, like most other Italians, Count Barda had been swept into the army with his class. After that it had been easy and a signal to the War Department in Rome had brought him his answer.

'I guessed there was something fishy about you the moment I saw you,' he said triumphantly. 'I decided you were deserters, living off the army and doing nothing towards victory.'

Morton's eyebrows lifted sardonically. 'I'd heard you have them, too,' he said.

Faiani frowned. 'Don't be too amused, my friend. I then suspected you might be more. I watched you and I noticed that, while you could pass as Italian, not all of your men could. So I took the trouble to check with Rome. You are not Count Barda. Count Barda is a prisoner of war in Greece. He was captured near the Italian border at Koritsa last November.'

'Oh, hard luck!'

'I think you're being sarcastic.' Faiani was marching up and down now, his hands clasped behind his back. 'I even have your name,' he said. 'It is Morton. Lancelot Hugh Morton.'

For the first time, Morton looked surprised. 'You're cleverer than you look,' he commented.

Faiani smiled. 'I was once a policeman. I found out that

Count Barda had an English companion who was constantly being investigated by the police. You are that companion. You are in trouble, my friend. You realize you could all be shot as spies.'

'I doubt it,' Morton said. 'Not this time. And it's you who's in trouble, old son. Right up to your eyebrows.'

'Trouble?' Faiani glared. 'What sort of trouble?'

It was Morton's turn to smile. 'You were good. Damn good. But you were unlucky enough to arrive just when we were having visitors. I think you'd better shove your hands up.'

'That's it!' Sergeant Grady's iron voice rang out. '*Mani in alto*, you bastards. Up with them bleedin' 'ands.'

'And don't turn round,' Morton added. 'Just throw your weapons down and shove your hands on your heads, there's good chaps. Half the British army's at your backs ready to blow your heads off if you move.'

As the rifles clattered down and the hands lifted slowly, Morton stepped forward and removed Faiani's pistol.

'Terribly sorry,' he apologized. 'You deserve better. Especially as you seem to be the only one to have caught on from the beginning. You can turn round now.'

Faiani turned slowly to find himself facing Sergeant Grady and half a dozen men armed with sub-machine guns. Coffin was leaning elegantly on the wing of one of the trucks. It was then that Faiani noticed for the first time that there were two British Chevrolets parked among the Lancias of 64 Light Vehicle Repair Unit.

'You said half the British army,' he said bitterly.

Coffin strolled forward, flapping at the flies with his blue horsehair whisk. Stopping in front of Faiani, he pointed with the whisk. 'Know him?' he asked.

'Oh, yes,' Morton said. 'He's worried us a lot. He's deputy to Scarlatti, the chap who runs the dump here.'

'What about Scarlatti?'

'More trusting.'

'Scarlatti is a stupid fool,' Faiani snapped.

Morton shrugged and looked at Coffin. 'What do we do with 'em?' he asked.

'Don't trouble your heads about them,' Coffin said. 'They'll not escape.'

'Treat 'em carefully,' Rafferty put in. 'Faiani came from the sharp end and stopped a piece of our shrapnel last December.'

'No bother,' Coffin agreed. 'Decent war out here. Don't believe in violence to a chap who's done his stuff. We'll leave a guard and the rest of us will come with you. *Then* we'll knock off the airfield.'

'In the meantime,' Morton commented, glancing at his watch, 'we'd better pick up Caccia. We don't want him making a pig of himself.'

There was a lot of activity in Zuq when Morton and Clegg arrived in Dampier's Humber. Lines of vehicles were already moving down the hill towards the desert, followed by groups of the small Italian tanks. Soldiers were dragging equipment from houses and dumping it in lorries and lines of men were carrying shells, yellow Italian ammunition cases and German jerricans of petrol from a warehouse. Coffin, Grady and a group of their men who had accompanied them studied it from one of 64 Light Vehicle Repair Unit's borrowed Lancias. They had washed and were all wearing Italian caps; even their beards didn't look out of place because the Italians went in a lot for beards.

'Very interestin',' Coffin observed quietly. 'We could knock that off as well as we're leaving.'

They drew to a stop with faint squeaks from the brakes as darkness came. There was a brief discussion with Coffin, then they pushed through the streets towards the harbour. Here the LRDG men left them.

'You carry on,' Coffin said cheerfully. 'We'll be watching and, if you're in trouble, we'll be there. Just get that map, that's all.'

The air-raid siren had gone and the nightly bombing of

226

the Italian airfields had already started, and they could see the flashes against the horizon. The sky seemed full of aircraft but for a change none of them seemed to be near Zuq.

Barbieri was waiting inside the bar, all smiles. 'Party-rally bombing,' he said, pointing upwards. 'They sail over in lines like a Nazi get-together.' He gestured to the Italian army trucks moving beyond the trees on the road out of town. 'They are all going. Soon they'll be in Cairo. Perhaps not, of course. But at least they'll be away from Zuq. They say Mussolini's thinking of having a white horse brought from Italy so he can ride through Cairo at the head of his army. Perhaps someone will shoot him. He'd made a good target.'

The Italian vehicles were swinging eastwards near the harbour, heading along the coast road, the noise of their engines loud. Morton studied them for a moment, then he pointed to the stairs.

'Time's up,' he said. 'Fetch 'em down.'

Barbieri rolled his eyes. 'They've had so little time together, *Signore*. Give them a little longer.'

Morton didn't argue. He ran up the red-tiled staircase and started banging on the only door he could see. 'Morton here. Out you come.'

'Already?' It was Caccia's voice. 'We've hardly started.'

'You've had long enough to last you till the war's over.'

The door opened and Caccia appeared, holding a towel round him. Beyond him, Morton could see Rosalba staring indignantly at him over the top of a sheet.

'The missis, too,' Morton said. 'I've come for the map. We fulfilled our part of the bargain. And look slippy. Things are moving.'

Rosalba slid from the bed and Morton had a tantalizing glimpse of a great deal of bare flesh. When she appeared at the door, she was wearing a cotton dressing gown tied at the waist. It was open for a long way down the front and didn't conceal much. She thrust the second half of the map at Morton.

'There,' she said. 'Now leave us alone.'

'We're going,' Morton said. 'All of us.'

'Now?' Her eyes widened. '*Mamma mia!* I haven't packed.'

'You have five minutes.'

As Morton appeared downstairs again, Barbieri thrust a glass into his hand. 'A toast,' he said. 'To the young couple. And perhaps a cigar. German cigars. Very good ones.'

He handed cigars round and Morton and Clegg lit up, drinking with Barbieri until Caccia and the girl appeared, both a little flushed.

'The car's outside,' Morton said.

The girl dropped the small leather bag she carried containing her belongings. Sticking out of one corner was the yellow dress Scarlatti had obtained for her. She clutched at Barbieri.

'I'll send for you,' she said. 'Everything will be all right. In England everything's always all right. We shall be rich.'

The all-clear was sounding as Morton pushed them towards the door and stuffed Rosalba into the back of the car.

'No standing on the platform,' she chirruped. 'Pass down the bus.'

As he turned to give Caccia a push, Barbieri indicated the shed where he kept his stores. He gestured conspiratorially.

'*Un momento*,' he pleaded. 'A bottle for them to take with them.'

There was a strong smell of petrol as the door swung open and they could see stacked square silver cans among the straw and shavings.

'What's he got in there?' Morton asked. 'It looks like petrol.'

'It *is* petrol,' Caccia said. 'For Christ's sake, don't go near it with that cigar! It's British petrol and, judging by the smell, the cans are leaking as usual.'

As they turned away, they became aware of Schwartzheiss, the German sergeant, standing in the shadows. He'd obviously been watching them for some time.

'So,' he said, grinning. 'What have we here?'

'They've just got married, sergeant,' Morton explained in German.

'And now they're going where?'

Morton shrugged. 'To the bridal bed.'

Schwartzheiss stepped forward. 'They've already been in the bridal bed,' he said cheerfully. 'I was standing beneath the window listening. It was most entertaining. Who *are* you?'

'Mortoni, Ugo. Conte di Barda. Tenente, 34th Engineers. In command of 64 Light Vehicle Repair Unit.'

Schwartzheiss smiled. 'I dare bet you're not,' he said. 'Faiani doesn't think you are either.'

Morton's heart began to thump. Clegg was watching him, wondering what had gone wrong, and Rosalba's face appeared from the back of the Humber.

'Your car,' Schwartzheiss went on. 'An English Humber, no? And' – his smile widened – 'according to my instructions, army vehicles are not to be used for the transportation of civilians.'

Morton managed a shrug. 'It happens,' he said.

'Not in the German army. Of course, I know that the Italian army is different. It provides lorries to transport its whores. Perhaps this lady is one, *hein*?'

It was a mistake. Rosalba understood German and her screech of rage swung their heads round.

'*Porca miseria!*' she screamed. 'I'm a good girl!'

She scrambled from the car and stood in front of Schwartzheiss, shaking her fist under his nose. 'We were properly married! I have the documents! The mayor himself, Signor Carloni, performed the ceremony! And then the priest, Father Anselmo, who's with the army, married us in the eyes of God! He's my husband!'

Schwartzheiss seemed to be laughing to himself. 'I think you're lying,' he said mildly. 'I think he's not even Italian.'

'He's my cousin! I have proof! In the house is a picture of him with me, taken when we were children!'

'It's the picture of my cousin Ansaldo,' she murmured to Caccia as she headed for the bar. 'But he's so stupid he'll never know the difference.'

By this time several Italian soldiers were watching with interest and amusement, and it was clear that with every second they stood there arguing it was going to be more difficult to get away. Barbieri, who had reappeared cheerfully from the shed to slam a bottle of brandy into Clegg's hand, had taken in the scene at a glance and was clutching his fat cheeks in horror, his eyes as huge as saucers.

His mind moving swiftly, Morton was wondering where the LRDG men were. 'If you're in trouble,' they'd said, 'we'll be there.' They ought to be here *now*, he thought, like the man on the white horse, with the reprieve tucked into his gauntlet. But there was no sign of them, and bitterly he assumed the bastards were looking for something to blow up. As he stared about him, his eyes moving desperately, Clegg, big, square, long-jawed, looking like an amiable drayhorse, was standing near Schwartzheiss, holding the bottle of brandy and shrewdly assessing the histrionic possibilities of the situation.

'I think you'd better come with me,' Schwartzheiss said cheerfully. 'All of you.'

Clegg watched carefully. Most of the Italian and German that had been spoken had passed over his head but it had dawned on him from Schwartzheiss's manner and the expression of horror on Barbieri's face that what was happening looked, unless it was stopped, as if it were about to develop into a right old upsadaisy. He was still a little tipsy and, as always when he'd had a few, was ready for anything. As Schwartzheiss turned to summon help, he took a good puff at his cigar so that the end was glowing red, then, taking it from his mouth, calmly tossed it into the open door of the store shed. Schwartzheiss was just pointing at the

Italian soldiers to demand their assistance when someone shouted.

'Fire!' The cry came from in the crowd. '*Il capannone è in fiamme!*'

The flare of the flame in the darkness lit the faces of the gathering crowd as they all swung from Schwartzheiss towards the blaze.

'*Santa Maria, madre di Dio!*' Barbieri moaned. 'The petrol!'

Even as he spoke, the shed disappeared. There was a tremendous whoof, the roof seemed to lift into the air, and blazing petrol shot in all directions. As they picked themselves up, Italian *carabinieri* appeared from nowhere, shrieking with fury.

'Put that fire out,' they began to yell. 'The British bombers will come, and the army's on the move!'

Someone turned to the standpipe just down the street and buckets appeared. Civilians and Italian soldiers formed a line, all shouting instructions at once. Rosalba was standing in the shadows among the trees near the bar, screeching blue murder and, red in the face with fury, Schwartzheiss was shouting orders at anyone who was near enough to hear. But the petrol had gone up in one great sheet of flame and no one took the slightest notice of him in the panic.

There was a good blaze going now from the remains of the shed. More buckets appeared and they seemed to be getting the flames under control when Clegg stepped into the line and did his Will Hay fireman act. Switching hands, he sent the empty buckets back to the fire and the full ones back to the standpipe. As they were passing them automatically, it was some time before anybody noticed. Then a yell went up from the fire.

'*È vacue! Le secchie sono vacue!* The buckets are empty!'

'*È piene! Le secchie sono già piene.*' Almost as if in chorus, another wail went up from the standpipe. 'The buckets are already full!'

The fire brigade had arrived by this time, the ancient vehicle rattling noisily into the street, manned by firemen in shining brass helmets.

'*Aprire la strada! Aprire la strada!* Clear the way!'

The hose was hitched up and run out but the leaks still hadn't been repaired and water shot into the air like miniature fountains. The shouting increased to hysteria. Then, in the middle of it all, someone yelled that he could hear the RAF coming back.

Almost immediately the air-raid siren sounded again and there was the crash of an explosion nearby. The crowd scattered like cockroaches before a light, the firemen close behind so that the abandoned hoses, still leaking like colanders, whipped backwards and forwards across the ground like panic-stricken snakes. Schwartzheiss seemed to divine that the performance had been put on for his benefit and now, as the flames roared up again, he got a good look for the first time at Caccia, who had been carefully keeping out of the way.

'You!' he roared. '*Mein lieber Gott!* I've seen you before!'

He was just dragging his pistol from its holster on his belt when Clegg hit him over the head with the brandy bottle.

As the German collapsed, Clegg seized him by the seat of his trousers and the neck of his jacket and, with a muscle-cracking swing of his powerful arms, tossed him into the back of the car. 'After you, Cecil,' he said.

'Get in, Wop!' Realizing that Clegg had saved the situation, Morton shoved Caccia aboard.

'The petrol!' Barbieri wailed. 'They'll shoot me for having petrol!'

Without arguing, Clegg pushed him into the car, too, and, treading on his heels, scrambled into the driver's seat. With a scrape of gears, he let in the clutch and the vehicle jerked and began to lurch down the street.

Morton gave him a terrified look but Clegg was actually laughing, a deep-throated chuckle coming from his throat.

On the edge of the town, they recognized the LRDG's borrowed Lancia at the side of the road, and Morton was just about to demand a little help when he realized it was near the warehouse where they'd seen lorries being loaded with ammunition and petrol and changed his mind. As they passed at full speed, Caccia yelling through the din in infuriated incoherence from the rear seat, Coffin and Sergeant Grady appeared from the doorway and started running for their lorry. As they scrambled aboard, they recognized the Humber.

'Keep going, mate!' Grady yelled. 'It's going up any second!'

As the ammunition store went up, it seemed to give the Humber a shove from behind and they felt the heat as the sear of flame shot skywards. Outside the town, they halted. Half the Italian army seemed to have come to a stop, too. The columns moving eastwards had all ground to a standstill, the crews of tanks and lorries staring back at the flames and whirring tracer rising from the direction of Zuq. Searchlights were probing the sky but the flames had attracted the RAF and they could see the flares and feel the thuds in the bones of the earth as the bombs screamed down.

Clegg was crowing with delight, and it was some time before they became aware of Barbieri's moans and Caccia's strangled shouts of fury. As they swung round, they saw his face was stricken.

'What the hell's up with you?' Clegg asked.

Caccia turned on them wildly. 'You stupid daft silly sod!' he stormed. 'You've left Rosalba behind!'

6

There was no going back into town, Rosalba or no Rosalba. Too many people had seen them and too much had happened. Besides, all Italian traffic was moving south and east now and the Italian military police would be watching for deserters and stopping anything going in the wrong direction. They didn't even dare stay near the wadi.

'You can always come back when we've won the war,' Clegg said.

Caccia exploded. 'In a thousand bloody years' time,' he snarled.

'Is she that important?' It hadn't occurred to Clegg that she was.

'I married her,' Caccia yelled. 'That's important!'

Soon after daylight the Lancias they'd loaned to the LRDG arrived and drew to a stop alongside their own vehicles. The men in them, still dressed in German and Italian uniforms, had handed over Faiani and his men to one of their patrols and were now bubbling with excitement because they had since raided the airfield and claimed to have destroyed several Italian aircraft on the ground, together with a few of the lorries parked outside the fort.

'The stupid bastards never learn,' Sergeant Grady said. 'The buggers weren't even guarded. Because they were fifteen miles behind their lines they thought they were safe. What's fifteen miles on wheels with us lot about?'

They had had two men slightly wounded but the raid seemed to have been a success. They had destroyed nine aircraft, several lorries and a petrol and ammunition store, and were only waiting to cap the feat with the kidnapping.

They took over Schwartzheiss but didn't stay long to ask questions. It wasn't their policy to remain in one place for long, but as they clambered into their vehicles Coffin studied the two halves of the map Rosalba had marked. 'Jesus,' he said, awed. 'She's got the lot!'

As they peered over his shoulder, he jabbed a finger at the marked arrows on the squared sheet. 'Right along the inter-corps line, right between the Bologna Division and the Buckhardt Brigade. Seventh Armoured's just to the south. If we move 'em up a bit, they'll run smack into 'em. And that,' he ended with satisfaction, 'ought to stop the bastards laughing in church.'

He folded the sheet and stuffed it into his map case. 'When we put this through, the whole of the Eighth Army'll be waiting for the poor sods,' he said with murderous cheerfulness. 'It'll be a massacre.' He climbed into the passenger seat of his Chevrolet and nudged the driver. 'Okay, George. Take her away and pile on the coal a bit. We're in a hurry.' He waved – to Morton, Dampier noticed bitterly, not to him. 'We'll be back here at four thirty to pick up your painter pal.'

The Italian units in and around Zuq were vanishing into the folds of the desert now. But the RAF was on the move, too, and there seemed to be aircraft over them all the time. Fortunately, the attacks were chiefly directed at the bigger groups of vehicles and none of them bothered with the few belonging to 64 Light Vehicle Repair Unit.

Then, suddenly, the desert became silent. They all knew what it meant. The Italians were poised for their move forward. The minefield had been opened and their tanks were waiting. Behind them the infantry was ready, with all the support columns eager to follow them.

Clutterbuck had brushed Dampier's uniform and Dampier was dressed as a British colonel again. His lumbago had improved a little, thought it still troubled him; but, if there were to be any fighting, he was determined to be in it dressed as a British officer not as a bloody bottle-washer and errand runner in the Italian army, and had insisted on his proper seat in the Humber next to the driver. They were all anxious to revert to their proper identities, in fact, all save Caccia who sat on his own, still wearing the Italian sergeant's jacket, his face stony and expressionless.

'I think he must have thought more of her than we realized,' Clegg murmured sympathetically.

As they wondered what to do, Dampier became aware of the Australian, Fee, standing beside him.

'What about my cobbers?' he was demanding. 'There are over two hundred of 'em out there outside Sofi, waiting to be shipped to Italy. Aussie isn't a heavily populated country and two hundred men will be missed.'

'What had you in mind?' Dampier asked politely.

'Rescuin' 'em.'

'On your own?'

'No. With you lot.'

'Including you, there are eleven of us,' Dampier pointed out patiently. 'Eleven, that's all. And that includes Caccia, who isn't feeling much like a hero at this moment; Micklethwaite, who's a civilian; three other men belonging to a concert party, who aren't trained to fight; Signor Barbieri, who's a bar owner and belongs to the other side, anyway; Corporal Clinch, Clutterbuck, myself and Mr Rafferty. Out of that lot, only you, me and Mr Rafferty appear to be trained fighting men, and Mr Rafferty and I have been relegated to picking the nits out of army equipment because we're considered too old to go into battle.'

'Fair dinkum?' Fee seemed surprised. 'Can't nothing be done?'

Dampier frowned. Fee seemed to fit in very well with the rest of his little group and was as chary at calling him 'sir' as everybody else. He was beginning to think, in fact, that, apart from Rafferty, the only one who showed him any respect was the man he'd arrested, Clutterbuck.

'I have to admit,' he said, 'that I've been bending my mind to the possibility. I joined the army to fight the Germans and I don't consider picking up fiddlers and deserters a soldier's job. We shall do our best to release your friends. Would you be prepared to go back into that camp?'

Fee's face fell. 'Jesus, I only just got out.'

'It might make all the difference to your friends. We need to have them organized, not just swanning off in every direction imaginable. If we stick together, we ought to be able to expect the Eighth Army to be looking out for us. Of course, it may not work, and we're pinning our faith chiefly in the fact that the gentlemen of the Long Range Desert Group have passed on the details of that map of ours to British headquarters so that the Italians will be defeated and the British army will use the opportunity to follow up the defeat. It seems to depend on you.'

'What do I have to do?'

'Get back into the compound, get hold of everybody who has authority such as NCOs and warrant officers, and inform them of what we intend to do. The Italians will be busy, I expect, but we've got to get to that compound before they move those friends of yours away, as they undoubtedly will when they start to retreat. But they'll also be rather busy with their battle so there shouldn't be many of them running the place and, with the aid of the LRDG, we ought to be able to overwhelm them. Understood?'

'Understood.'

'Your people must do as they're told.' Knowing the Australians, Dampier didn't have much hope that they would, but it was worth a try. 'They're to form up in an organized group, so we can handle them, not scatter all over the desert. Think you can make them understand that?'

'Yeah. I reckon I can.'

'How will you get in?'

'Same way I got out. Dig a hole under the wire.'

'I think there's no need for that,' Rafferty put in quietly. 'We can supply you with a pair of wire-cutters. By permission of Major Scarlatti. Clutterbuck pinched 'em. They were our first proud acquisition.'

The LRDG's vehicles reappeared in the middle of the afternoon. Coffin's face was full of smiles.

'The message's gone through,' he announced. 'They'll act on it, have no fear. They've learned to rely on our lot. Now for our German friend. We'll be near the end of the wadi. Think he'll come?'

'I'm sure he will,' Morton said. 'He's enough of an artist to insist on finishing his picture.'

When Dampier mentioned the freeing of the prisoners, Coffin was all in favour. 'Oh, Christ, yes,' he said. 'We'll help with that. Two hundred Aussies are always worth rescuing. They'll fight anything – even their own side – and they'll be so bloody mad at the Italians for capturing them you'll only have to shove rifles in their hands and they'll go through 'em like a knife through butter all the way to Tripoli.'

They surveyed the wadi carefully and Coffin chose a point where he could park his vehicles without them being seen, but where he could see the lip of the desert from where Morton was to give the signal that Erwin had arrived.

When Erwin appeared, they saw he was in a single car and with only Stracka to accompany him. There were no luxuries this time, no sign of the hamper or wine, just the easels sticking out among the equipment stuffed into the rear seat. As the car moved down the wadi, Morton gestured to Clegg. 'This we must see,' he said.

Moving further down the wadi, they saw Erwin's car reach the open end. Then, as the valley widened, the Mercedes put on speed and began to head for the patch of pink gravel. As it did so, two Chevrolets, hidden until that moment by the ridge, came into view, one on either side. Putting on speed, they appeared alongside the Mercedes, and Morton and Clegg saw Erwin's head turn quickly to right and left. Then another Chevrolet appeared and, a second later, a fourth shot ahead of the whole group and swung in front of the German car, exactly as it had when it had stopped the Ratbags. The Mercedes slid to a halt and they saw Erwin rise to his feet in the rear seat. Stracka rose, too, then they saw them slowly lift their hands above their heads.

By the time Morton and Clegg reached them, the Germans had climbed out of the car and were standing together, their hands on their heads, covered by a plethora of guns. Coffin was just scrambling from his truck and walking back to join Grady.

Erwin saw Morton and frowned. 'You are in on this?' he said.

Morton smiled cheerfully. 'Oh, yes,' he agreed. 'I'm on their side.'

Coffin had stopped in front of Erwin now. He looked puzzled. 'Who's this?' he demanded.

Clegg smiled proudly. 'Erwin.'

'No, it isn't. He's taller than Erwin.'

'*That's* Erwin,' Morton insisted. 'Ask him.'

'It isn't bloody Erwin!' Coffin snapped.

'It's the only Erwin I know.'

'Well, it's not *our* Erwin.'

'Which bloody Erwin were you expecting?'

'*Uncle* Erwin. Rommel. The commander in chief of the bloody Afrika Korps. The big boy. We've been fighting the bastard ever since March.'

'*We* haven't,' Morton said. 'We've been singing to him. And you didn't say "Rommel". You said "Erwin."'

Coffin glared. 'Everybody calls him Erwin. Or Uncle Erwin. Or Harry Rommel.'

'We didn't.'

'You must have been in bloody purdah!'

'It's a bit like that in Cairo.'

'And who the Christ is this?'

'General Erwin. General Max Erwin. You said you

wanted Erwin. I said I knew where Erwin was. If you'd said Rommel we might have got somewhere.'

Coffin seemed a little uncertain what to do next. 'Well,' he said, looking at the Germans, 'this feller's not a very big fish.'

'Thank you,' Erwin said coldly. 'I am flattered.'

'If he's not a very big fish,' Clegg asked, 'why not throw him back?'

Coffin gave him a sour look. 'I suppose,' he said, 'that he'll have to do. After all, we didn't come out here *just* to get Rommel. We just happened to be around here after the airfield when we heard he was coming to Zuq so we thought we'd have a go. We might as well bugger off with him and his pal now. After all, he *is* a general, and that isn't bad. We'll get rid of him and come back to help you lot with those Australian prisoners of yours.' He gave Morton a sharp glance. 'I suppose they *are* Australians, aren't they, not Austrians or something?' He looked at Grady and shrugged. 'Oh, well,' he said, 'I suppose you could call it a decent day's work.'

All the same, as he looked at Erwin, he didn't feel too sure. With the whole Italian army to choose from, they'd swooped on a lot of dressed-up actors and now they'd got the wrong bloody general.

'Perhaps,' he said thoughtfully, 'we'd do better if we went at it a bit more slowly.'

7

During the evening, to the sound of Italian bugles, they moved further east. All round them over the chirp of the crickets they could hear the quiet voices of men sitting on the ground, their rifles propped on ammunition boxes as they waited to go into battle. Then the engines started up with explosive barks and a few vehicles moved past, men huddled in the back, blank-faced, busy with their thoughts, clutching their weapons, the dust cloud they kicked up tinted pink by the setting sun. As the light vanished, in the growing darkness it was just possible to see stubby Italian helmets with their spherical grenade insignia, and a sergeant with a carbide torch directing the traffic.

As the men of 64 Light Vehicle Repair Unit waited in their lorries, the wind got up to blow the sand about their legs in gritty swathes. The bombing was still going on in the west but a few aircraft had begun to appear overhead now, heading in a north–south direction, their motors swamping the rumble of the moving tanks. Immediately, searchlights behind the British lines began to probe the sky. The aircraft noises grew louder, then a Very light arc-ed up from the desert and they heard the growling of tank engines as the slow Italian M13s began to edge forward.

Grunting at the pain in his back, Dampier climbed from his seat and stood alongside Erwin's staff car staring eastwards. Morton, Coffin and Rafferty joined him.

'I think it's about time we moved up,' Coffin said.

They climbed into their vehicles and started to edge slowly

ahead, conscious of a whole alien army moving with them. For another quarter of an hour they moved forward, their eyes flickering from right to left, conscious of half-hidden shapes in the darkness.

'The Eyeties should be entering the gap in the minefield soon,' Rafferty said.

As they approached Sofi, the Italian troops who had occupied it were also moving eastwards, joining the rest of the army. Some of them were bleating like sheep. They had long known that their generals, often careerist and riddled with jealousies and personal antipathies, were good only for emotional demands for the defence of Italian territory and, with their limited mobility, weak armament and little striking power, they had few illusions. Something was always lacking, food, vehicles, or ammunition, and they had a defensive mentality because they knew the Duce's war machine didn't work, and there were even stories of officers leaping from trenches to lead advances only to find their men had stayed where they were, clapping their hands to applaud their courage.

'Poor devils,' Dampier said with all the compassion of a conscientious officer for his men. 'Even their lorries will break down. Clutterbuck must have peed in half the petrol tanks in Libya.'

Just outside the town they saw lights and realized they had reached the prisoner-of-war compound. Over the noise of engines they could hear angry voices.

'Right, Fee,' Dampier said. Since Fee didn't address him by his rank, he saw no reason to use Fee's. 'Off you go. Will your chaps do as they're told?'

'They might not,' Fee admitted bluntly. 'Aussies only do what suits 'em.'

'Well, you'd better convince 'em,' Dampier said shortly. 'How do you propose to let us know you're in?'

Fee gestured. 'You can hear 'em arguin',' he said. 'That's Aussie all over. I'll get 'em singin'. When you hear

"Waltzing Matilda" you'll know I've put the word about and they're ready.'

He started to walk forward and within seconds had vanished from sight. The others settled down to wait again. Twenty minutes passed.

'How far do you reckon we are from the British outposts?' Dampier said.

Coffin rubbed his nose. 'Fifteen miles, I reckon.'

'It's a long way.'

'Not on wheels. It's not even far to walk if you're willing.'

Another half-hour passed, then they caught the sound of male voices singing.

'Waltzing Matilda, Waltzing Matilda,
Who'll come a-waltzing, Matilda, with me – '

'That's us,' Rafferty said.

As they turned to the lorries, there was a colossal bang that made them jump and the ground seemed to vibrate under their feet like the skin of a kettledrum. Darts of red tracer shot through the air in arabesques with luminous yellow slots whirring overhead like beads on a rod, and suddenly the whole eastern horizon was lit up with searchlights that caught the flanks of the rolling clouds of dust. The swish and crash and the trumpeting of guns filled the air with sudden demonic sounds. Their hearts began to thump.

'It looks to me,' Coffin said dryly, 'as though the Italians have been caught bang in the middle of the minefield and that our lot have turned the tables on 'em by starting first.'

Clambering into the vehicles, they edged forward again until they were in sight of the barbed-wire compound. The sudden crash of the guns when none had been expected had brought the Italians out of the guardhouse to see what was happening and they caught glimpses of stubby helmets silhouetted against the distant flashes.

'Let's go,' Coffin said.

The four LRDG trucks hurtled off, followed at a discreet

distance by the vehicles of 64 Light Vehicle Repair Unit. Then, just ahead, they saw fresh lines of tracer and, against the flashes of the explosions in the distance, Italian soldiers running for their lives. As they moved forward, men hurtled past them, heading westwards.

'*Ocio che te copo!*' one of them yelled. '*Guardatevi!*'

'What's he say?' Dampier demanded.

'He says, in effect,' Morton explained calmly, ' "Woe betide you. Look out." I think the LRDGs must have arrived.'

More men ran past them, shouting, then they found themselves hard up against the compound. Inside, they could see men scuttling in every direction and tents lurching and falling flat. The terrified Italian guards, startled by an attack from the wrong side, were already being chased out of their quarters. Fee's wire cutters had obviously done their work and the Australians were in the process of rescuing themselves. The last of the Italians had taken refuge in the guardhouse near the gate but a long burst from one of Coffin's heavy machine-guns sent splinters flying and there were screams from inside. Bullets twanged on wire and the Australians flung themselves flat. Several of the Italians made a dash for safety but a machine-gun brought them down, then a grenade was tossed into the wrecked hut. There was a crash and a flash and the roof lifted. When they next looked, the hut was a wreck, with splintered sides and a shattered roof. A solitary Italian staggered out, bleeding, his hands in the air.

'*Mamma!*' he moaned. '*Aiuto!* Help me, please! I am hurt!'

The prisoners themselves were kicking the surviving Italians into a group and snatching at their weapons. Then Coffin appeared in an Italian staff car, roaring round in a wild dust-laden turn to come to a stop near Dampier. Fee was with him in the front seat.

'Get 'em formed up,' he was yelling.

The Australians were running towards them. Among

244

them was the tall lantern-jawed corporal who had recognized Clegg in Sofi. Grinning all over his face, he clutched Clegg to him.

'Good on yer, cobber,' he grinned. 'I never expected to see you again. Was it you who got us out?'

Clegg saw no reason to suggest it was anyone else and the Australian hugged him and clapped him on the back.

'Any time you're in Sydney, mate,' he said, 'just ask for Ted McBean and the beer's on me.'

They were without officers but had NCOs and, among the delirious shouts at gaining their freedom, there were harsher yells. Fee had got his story across well and the Australians reacted quickly and efficiently. In no time they were in a column of threes, with a group of terrified Italian prisoners in a bunch in the middle of them. An Italian corporal spoke to Morton.

'they told us the Australians never took prisoners,' he said nervously in English. 'What will they do to us?'

'Probably eat you,' Morton said cheerfully. 'But have no fear, they have good table manners.'

With the LRDG vehicles ahead and on the flanks, and Dampier with the staff car and the vehicles of 64 Light Vehicle Repair Unit bringing up the rear, they prepared to move off. The din of the battle that had started to the east had grown louder with distant flashes and flickers and low booming thuds. Few of the German and Italian guns seemed to be answering the deluge of British shells, but then rockets started to curve up into the sky and the Italian barrage finally started. First one battery then another came into action until a nearer pounding added to the general racket.

The Australians were excited and noisy but Fee's voice rose above the din. 'All right, you bloody Aussie bastards! Let's go! By the Christ, quick march!'

It was light enough in the flashes of the explosions to see what was happening. With the terrified Italians, wiping away the blood and the tears, still in the middle, surrounded by

245

tall vengeful Australians, the column of men began to move eastwards. They were heading across ground as furrowed by wheels as a ploughed field as daylight came, a thin grey daylight that seemed to have been strained by the dust clouds that hung over the desert floor. A few vehicles were moving backwards now towards the west, mostly ambulances and lorries full of injured men. Then in the distance they saw specks which, with the aid of the X12s, Rafferty was able to identify as an Italian tank squadron rattling up from the south.

Fee looked at Dampier. 'Now what the Christ do we do?' he demanded.

Dampier looked disconcerted for a moment, then an idea occurred to him. 'Order 'em to about turn,' he said.

'*About turn?* Jesus, I can see 'em doin' it! They'll be marchin' the wrong way.'

'You have no weapons, so they'll assume that you're still prisoners and that those of us with Italian uniforms are guards. If you don't, that lot over there will want to know what you're up to. If you appear to be heading towards captivity, they won't worry.'

'Like the husband who caught the milkman in the sheila's bedroom?' Fee said. 'Because he walked out backwards he thought he was just arriving. Okay, we'll give it a go. We can always turn 'em round again when they've gone.'

He turned to the anxious files of men. 'Okay, you lot. About – turn!'

There were yells of disgust but he shouted them down and explained. 'So, for once, you stupid bloody Aussie bastards, do as you're told!'

As those who had them hurriedly changed into Italian tunics and caps, the column about turned, strong Australian hands swinging the Italian prisoners round with them. As the tanks approached, the Australians glared aggressively. Struggling to fasten the buttons of his Italian tunic, Clegg groaned.

'Jesus,' he said. 'As actors they'd make good dustmen.'

Fee caught on at once and began to shout. 'You're bloody prisoners, you stupid Aussie sods,' he roared. 'Don't look so bleedin' hostile!'

For a moment they stared at him, then they also began to catch on. There was a lot of nudging and the long Australian stride dwindled to a tired shuffle. Heads went down and shoulders hunched dejectedly.

'Gawd,' Fee said disgustedly. 'There's no need to *over-act*.'

They got it right in the end and finally began to look like a column of prisoners. Intent on their task, the Italian tanks rolled by, kicking up clouds of dust, and Morton stood up in the Humber and saluted as they passed.

'*Prigionieri!*' he shouted. 'Ordered to Zuq for Italy! How goes it?'

The Italian officer shouted back and Morton translated for Dampier.

'He says they were caught with their trousers down,' he explained. 'They were just entering the minefield when our shells fell on them. At first they thought it was just a rearguard action, but he says he thinks now it's developing into a full-out counter-attack while they're off-balance.'

Delighted with the success of the deception, as the Italian tanks moved on the Australians shuffled to a stop and there were satisfied grins.

'All right,' Fee yelled. 'Other way again! Column – about turn!'

As the Italian tanks disappeared into the distance, the Australians about-turned once more, still dragging the bewildered Italians with them, and heads came up as they began to move eastwards again. Two Messerschmitts appeared on the western horizon and, once again, the column turned to face the west. The Messerschmitts passed low over their heads but made no attempt to interfere with them. As they lifted into the sky, a squadron of Hurricanes howled down out of the blue. Guns clattered and one of the Messerschmitts swept upwards in a screaming zoom, then fell off sideways at the top and sideslipped into the desert about a mile away.

As the column of black smoke lifted into the air, the Australians began to cheer but the shouting was silenced as another group of Italian vehicles appeared in the distance from the west. This time they didn't need any explanations. They about turned, heads down, shoulders hunched, a few of them even entering into the spirit of the thing enough to throw sour catcalls as the lorries passed, vanishing eastwards into the dust and smoke without their crews looking twice in their direction. By this time it was becoming a game, and in great good humour the Australians about turned again to face eastwards with a great show of lifting their knees, swinging their arms and stamping their feet as if on parade.

The horizon was full of smoke and dust. They had no idea what was happening but it seemed now that the battle was bigger than they'd expected. It had spread southwards, too, and occasionally they caught glimpses of vehicles heading in that direction. The foglike cloud of dust spread across the whole desert and, though the sky above them was clear, aircraft passing overhead disappeared almost at once as they headed into the rolling coils of smoke.

'There's just one thing.' Fee was suddenly looking worried. 'Suppose some half-baked Pom pilot in a Hurricane comes along and sees us marching west, won't he think we're Italians and shoot us up?'

It was something that hadn't occurred to Dampier. But he produced an answer quickly enough. 'Have you still got that flag of yours?' he asked.

'Fair dinkum, I have. No bloody Eyetie's havin' that.'

'A splendid sentiment, sergeant major. If anybody on our side starts being awkward, let's just make sure it's well and truly visible.'

The sun appeared, bursting over the horizon like a flash of fire, and almost at once it began to blister their breath. The battle seemed to have changed direction now and, by a trick of the wind, they could hear the grind and clatter of armoured vehicles moving into action. The column of Australians had gone some distance eastwards now, but as they drew nearer the cloud of smoke they exchanged glances, beginning to wonder what they were heading into. Stray shells made a mewing, squealing chorus overhead and small-calibre missiles whizzed and whined past. Then, unexpectedly, an object appeared out of the murk ahead to curve downwards, strike the earth, and leap upwards, end over end, until it finally plopped into the sand at the end of its trajectory.

'Tank shell,' Coffin said laconically. 'Solid shot. If you ask me, I reckon we're getting too near this bloody battle for safety!'

Even as they halted, they saw a swarm of British aircraft bursting out of the cloud of smoke and dust. One of them, clearly imagining the column to be Italian since it was on the Italian side of the line, headed towards them. Immediately, Fee's flag was produced and waved. But they hadn't allowed for the height of the aircraft and the difficulty of seeing details at speed, and the Hurricane opened fire. Fortunately, the shooting went wide and the men in the column began to yell.

'You stupid Pom bastard!' McBean roared. 'Can't you see we're Aussies?'

During the afternoon they came across an Italian column which had been caught by the RAF, a string of lorries deserted by their crews and smoking in the sun. One of them was a water tanker, which was a gift from heaven, and they also found coffee and tins of captured British bully beef that slid out of the tins like grease.

As they brewed up, they were fired on again and had to scatter. The middle of a battle was clearly not a good place for a column of unarmed prisoners to be and, as they re-gathered, Dampier reluctantly came to the conclusion that until the battle had sorted itself out it might be best to head back towards Zuq and get the LRDGs to signal the navy to lift them off. There was a howl of 'Not bloody likely' when the idea was put to the Australians and a great deal of muttering as they discussed it, but in the end everybody saw the sense of the plan.

It was evening before they gained sight of the round dome of the mosque at Zuq. In the east they could still hear the roar of the battle and see the groups of Italian vehicles heading towards it.

They finally brewed up again in the dusk and lay down in the desert where they stood, crowding together in the wind to get what warmth they could from each other. Flat and lifeless during the day, in the late evening the desert was throwing dark shadows and the low sun was making a miracle of the yellow dunes. As the light vanished hundreds of thousands of stars appeared.

'Beautiful.' Dampier was trying to climb stiffly to his feet. 'But cold, Mr Rafferty. Damn cold.'

When they rose at dawn the stars had all gone but there was something sharp, exhilarating and encouraging about the smell in the air. It was fresh and clean and tantalizingly different from what they knew it would be when the sun came out to drain them of energy.

The wind had died and when the sun did arrive there was no relief. Those men showing signs of distress were pushed aboard the vehicles and they began to edge closer to Zuq. As they did so, an Italian ambulance column came roaring past, heading for the town. Behind came another vehicle, limping badly.

'The whole British empire fell on us,' the driver said as he came alongside. 'They're still hammering it out. So far we're holding them but they're chewing up the armour like a mincing machine.'

As they headed into town, it was decided to commandeer the warehouse where 64 Light Vehicle Repair Unit had first been thought of.

'We can put everybody inside and post guards outside in Italian uniform,' Rafferty suggested. 'It'll look like a temporary POW compound.'

'There's just one point,' Dampier said. 'What do we do about food?'

Morton smiled. 'Scarlatti's dump's still here,' he said. 'And there's always Clutterbuck.'

8

Zuq seemed strangely empty as they drove in. As usual the civilians had taken their cars and lorries and donkeys and camels and headed into the desert to camp out among the dunes until the fighting they were expecting had finished and they could return. Several Arabs stood by the side of the road as they arrived, but there were few soldiers.

The Italian uniforms they had acquired were prominent as they established themselves in the ruined warehouse once more. Clegg, Jones and Rafferty, clad in the tunics of Italian privates, appeared at the doorway as guards, with Morton strutting up and down behind as their officer. Coffin's men, their vehicles hidden round the back of the warehouse, preferred to prowl round the town but one or two of the Australians, entering into the spirit of the thing and wearing the tunics of their late custodians, added to the appearance of a well-guarded column of prisoners.

They had barely established themselves when Barbieri vanished. He returned later in his car with Rosalba, who look as though she didn't know whether to be frightened or furious. She had locked the Bar Barbieri and spent the three days while Caccia and Barbieri had been away with Teresa Gelucci, whose father had persisted in trying all the time to get her in a corner away from the light. She was overjoyed to have Caccia back, but nevertheless, as soon as she saw him, she went for him with both hands swinging.

'So!' she yelled. 'After two hours of marriage and the

grandissima fornicazione, it has succeeded that you didn't want me!'

'It's not true,' Caccia yelled back. 'They shoved me in a car and drove off!'

'But you didn't fight back, *eh, soldato?* You wooed me – ravished me as if I were a whore – but you didn't fight to the death to rescue your Rosalba.'

Watched by grinning Australians offering encouragement, Caccia managed – not without difficulty – to convince her of his good intentions and she finally burst into tears.

'You are not crossed with me? I thought wrong things about you because I awaited too long.'

Then she saw Morton and promptly went for him instead. '*Porca miseria!*' she stormed. 'You do a wrongness! You take away my husband! You leave me to be shot by the Germans!'

'Oh, you little beaut'.' McBean grinned. 'Give it to him, girl!'

Though Barbieri went back to his bar, claiming that he was hoping for a few customers when the British army arrived, Rosalba was clearly determined not to permit Caccia out of her sight again. Still muttering in flashes of angry fire, she allowed herself to accept a pair of khaki drill trousers and a blouse from the Ratbags' property basket.

Taking a lorry, with Clutterbuck, Caccia and Clegg, Morton headed for the dump. Scarlatti looked nervous and hardly listened as he explained that they'd been taken off repairs and told to feed two hundred-odd prisoners of war.

'It isn't my job to feed prisoners!' There was a mounting hysterical note in Scarlatti's voice. 'Faiani's disappeared and I've been warned that there's a possibility of defeat and that my job will be to destroy the dump.'

'It's *my* job,' Morton said coldly, 'to keep the prisoners under control until we can get them away to Europe. If they starve and I'm asked why, I shall tell them that Major Scarlatti, of No. 7 Base Stores and Resupply Depot, refused to provide rations. There'll be enquiries by the Red Cross at international level.'

Scarlatti threw up his hands and gave in. A shed was opened and cases of rations were handed out. The food they contained was spartan enough but nobody complained.

'It's only for a few days,' Dampier pointed out loudly.

McBean looked at Clegg. 'Who *is* that bloody Pom?' he asked. 'Wearin' an Eyetie private's uniform and always tellin' us what to do.'

They tore down a few doors to make fires and as it grew dark they noticed that the noise to the east seemed nearer. The following morning a whole string of ambulances appeared in the streets, heading for the hospital. Scarlatti gave Morton the news.

'Our army suffers terribly,' he said, tears in his eyes. 'An attempt at a counter-attack ended in complete failure and the Germans have refused to help. The British armoured divisions still keep coming and they say the desert's full of burning vehicles.'

As the battle continued to rage, there were mutinous sounds from the Australians, but then they heard that the Italian army was beginning to crack.

Scarlatti was in a panic. 'They're going to make a stand here in Zuq!' he told Morton. 'The Ariete Division's been pulled out of the line and they're heading for Zuq to throw a defence round the town!'

When Morton passed on the news to Dampier, the old warhorse started smelling battle. 'They've got to take it off us first,' he said. 'Possession's nine points of the law and it seems to be – er – up for grabs.'

'We're not exactly over-supplied with weapons,' Morton pointed out.

'I can get you summat,' Clutterbuck said. 'I've still got me pass into the dump and there are 'undreds of British rifles in there what was captured at Mechili. They're due to go to Derna. I've seed 'em.'

To Dampier's ironbound honest military soul, it went

hard to steal arms – even from an Italian dump. 'There are over two hundred of us,' he pointed out.

'Well, two hundred's a bit of a tall order,' Clutterbuck admitted. 'But I ought to be able to get a few.'

Dampier raised no objections. 'Sergeant Clegg,' he said. 'Fit him out with an Italian uniform.'

When Clutterbuck returned with the lorry after dark, he was grinning all over his face.

'Only twenty-five,' he apologized. 'But about five thousand rounds of ammunition and a Bren. I couldn't make it no more.'

'Never mind. Never mind. We already have a few.' After so long in the wilderness, Dampier was excited to be back into his own as commanding officer of an armed unit. 'How did you do it?'

Clutterbuck touched his nose. 'That's a trade secret, innit.'

That night Italian Lancia trucks prowled round the town. The Italians, still unaware of the Australians' presence and startled to find themselves looking down the muzzles of rifles held by gaunt-looking Antipodeans, could see no other option but quietly to put down what they were doing and march off into captivity. They were thin on the ground now because most of the Italian units had been moved east into the desert and those who were left were largely lines of communications troops. One after the other they were snatched up in shadowed corners and their weapons taken. Doors were flung open and ferocious Australian faces appeared, and the number of prisoners taken at Sofi gradually grew larger and the stock of weapons increased.

The next day had hardly begun when they added two 47 mm guns, two machine-guns and more rifles, and, guided by the enthusiastic Dampier, Rafferty and the Australian NCOs, they were taking up positions in the trees and buildings on either side of the main road running into the town from the south. Dampier might have been pompous, lacking in humour and a bit of a bore, but he knew his job as a soldier. And this was the opportunity he'd been waiting for ever since 1939. Standing in the middle of the road, he directed small groups of men into drainage ditches or to the rooms and flat roofs of the empty houses. It seemed a perfect place for an ambush.

Late in the afternoon, Coffin, who'd been reconnoitring to the south, appeared at full speed in Erwin's Mercedes, trailing an enormous cloud of yellow dust.

'They're on the way!' he yelled.

'Who are?' Dampier yelled back.

'Looks like a Blackshirt battalion.'

'Which way are they coming?'

'Right up your nose,' Coffin said cheerfully. 'They should be here in a quarter of an hour.'

The approaching cloud of dust was spotted within five minutes. Gradually it took the shape of a column of vehicles, mostly open trucks crowded with men, interspersed here and there with light armoured vehicles and led by two motorcyclists and a staff car containing a group of officers. Through the X12s they looked dusty and bedraggled and Morton identified them with ease.

'They're not Blackshirts,' he crowed. 'They're the good old Longhi Hares. They won't give us much trouble.'

The Italians weren't expecting any opposition. Zuq had been Italian when they'd left and, since it was behind them, they were expecting it to be Italian when they returned. The Australians waited in a vengeful mood.

'Wait till you see the whites of their eyes,' Fee ordered. 'Nobody fires until the word's given.'

When Dampier gave the word the blast that hit the leading vehicles created chaos at once. The two motorcyclists veered from the road and disappeared into the drainage ditches on either side. The staff car followed, to end up nose-down, its rear wheels spinning, a cloud of steam rising from the engine. The lorries behind it swung aside and stopped dead. An armoured car endeavoured to bring its gun to bear but one of the Australians who had been practising with the 47 mms hit it with his first shot and it burst into flames.

Clegg watched the slaughter, shocked. Up to that moment, he hadn't seen much of the war because he'd left England before the blitz had started. In Cairo he hadn't been involved with the desert fighting at all and their adventure behind the Italian lines had been almost a joke. Even the killing at the prisoner-of-war camp at Sofi had been in the dark. This was something new and in the full glare of the sun.

A machine-gun opened up and, his head down, trying to shoot without getting hit himself – something he hadn't completely worked out how to do – Clegg heard a cry behind him and saw someone reeling away. But there were more bodies in the road now and the Australians further down the hill began to pour in a withering fire from behind the Italian column. Their bullets started to whistle over his head.

'Comrades and bosom friends,' he gasped. 'I reckon the Italians are going to win this battle! They'll still be around after we've all shot each other!'

For a while it seemed he might even be right because the Italians were beginning to take cover under the lorries and fire back. Then a white flag appeared on the end of a pole with such alacrity it seemed almost as if the Italians had had it ready, and the firing died down a little. They were just about to stand up when it started again with renewed vigour and it was then that Clegg saw a Union Jack being waved from the drainage ditch by the side of the road. It was held by Micklethwaite and he looked frightened to death.

'What's he doing there?' Clinch said. 'The silly bugger'll get his head blown off.'

The sight of the terrified Micklethwaite almost among the Italians did something to Clegg. Micklethwaite had looked bewildered most of the time he'd been with them and a lot of the time scared stiff, but at that moment he seemed totally lost and, with the ditch behind him crumbling under the fusillade, without thinking Clegg jumped up and started to run. Spurts of dust leapt up from the ground round his feet but he seemed to bear a charmed life. An Italian sergeant rose up in front of him, apparently from nowhere, and Clegg swung the rifle in his hands almost without noticing he held it. As the sergeant spun away, an officer appeared, holding a revolver, but Clegg's weight sent him with a yell after the sergeant, then he was diving for the ditch and, gathering the petrified Micklethwaite in his arms, he carried him with him until they crashed to the bottom.

Winded, Clegg looked up. Bullets were clipping the dried yellow grass along the lip of the ditch. Micklethwaite's face appeared from somewhere beneath his right elbow.

'You all right?' Clegg asked.

Flattened by Clegg's fifteen stone, Micklethwaite was unable to do any more than nod speechlessly.

Clegg gave him a shaky grin, as usual unable to resist a joke. 'Dead,' he said. 'And never called me mother.'

Somehow the dash he'd made had shaken the Italians and, as they hesitated, Sergeant Grady and one of the LRDGs ran along the column and began to toss grenades under the vehicles. Two of them went up in flames at once and there were screams. Then the white flag reappeared. More followed and Italians began to jump from the trucks, their hands in the air, shouting for mercy.

'*Sono prigionieri! Ci arrendiamo! Tedeschi no boni! Evviva Inghilterra!*'

The Australians appeared warily from behind their walls and trees and out of the ditches and began to stalk forward. They were gaunt, their faces ugly with dislike. As they reached Micklethwaite, Fee snatched the flag off him. 'Bloody sauce,' he said. 'Pinchin' my flag.'

Rafferty appeared and pulled Micklethwaite to his feet. Clegg looked up to see Morton staring down at him.

'You okay?'

'Cured and ready to be killed again, old mate.'

'I think you stopped the battle,' Morton said. 'They'd never seen anything as big as you before. They probably thought it was King Kong.' He turned to the newspaperman. 'What in God's name were you doing there?'

'I was trying to reach the Australians,' Micklethwaite explained. 'I thought the flag would stop me being shot.'

'They'd shoot all the harder with that in your hand.'

'I wasn't thinking of the Italians. I was thinking of you lot.'

Rafferty's eyes were dancing with merriment. 'You had 'em surrounded, boy,' he said.

They began to laugh, a little hysterically now that it was all over, because Micklethwaite was the last person in the world from whom they'd expected anything brave or unusual. Staring at the Italians, Dampier listened proudly as Rafferty reported. He was wearing his British uniform and cap again, his 1914-18 medal ribbons bright on his chest and a glow in his eye as if he'd thoroughly enjoyed himself.

One of the prisoners, a Libyan conscript, approached. 'Why don't they let me go?' he asked Morton. 'I'm not Italian.'

'What's he say?' Dampier asked.

'He says he doesn't like it here.'

'Tell him neither do we.'

Morton did so and the Libyan looked at him with puzzled eyes. 'Then why don't we all go home?' he asked.

To Clegg it seemed a splendid idea.

9

By late evening they knew there would be no more resistance. The Arabs, inevitably the first to return, scented loot and came out of their shanties on the edge of the town and started going through any empty buildings they could find. Shops, offices and homes were broken open and their furniture and other contents strewn across the road. The Arabs had never had much love for the Italians who had stolen their land and were anxious to pay off old scores. Outside the house that Brigadier Marziale had occupied, a house that was gracious in the Spanish style with a cobbled courtyard and palms, lay everything it had contained, food, clothing, pictures, crockery, even doors and windows.

A few mules and an occasional dog sniffed about in search of food and water and a few of the Australians, farmers by instinct, were rounding them up and taking them to compounds to be fed. Arabs, on donkeys, on camels, even on bicycles, impeded by the loot they were carrying, were heading for the anonymity of the desert. As they went, shattered Italian units began to arrive, the soldiers gathering in groups, offering no resistance. The Germans, they said bitterly, were retiring westwards with all their vehicles and, sick of Mussolini's boasts, sick of his *guerra di povera* – the war of the poor people – they had had enough. There were so many anxious to surrender, nobody bothered to round them up, leaving them alone with their misery, disillusioned men with gaunt, unshaven faces throwing away their equipment, clothing and weapons as they came.

They limped in, clutching cardboard suitcases, the toes cut from their dreadful boots, the rotten thread broken in the seams of their uniforms, to gather in little knots, shouting to each other – 'Bruno!' 'Antonio!' '*Acqua, per favore, acqua!*' – and offering swigs of wine in exchange for cigarettes.

One group had started a fire by the roadside and were bringing out from the houses the obligatory pictures of Mussolini as fuel, but mostly they huddled together with hunched shoulders and stony faces. Among them was Scarlatti, brought in with his staff by Morton himself. He had been making a half-hearted attempt to destroy his dump but had obviously been hoping that a lack of success might put him in a better light with any British captors he might have to face. Guiltily aware of the fiddling he'd done, he assumed at first that Morton was part of the Italian field police and had been spying on him all along, and was convinced he was about to be shot. When he learned the truth, his large sad eyes gave Morton a reproachful look as he handed over his sword and the photograph of Caccia's wedding.

'It is like Caporetto,' he said. 'Except that the events are greater and the men are smaller.'

The airfield buildings were intact, even if the aircraft were not. The Italian pilots had lived in comfort with dressing tables, all equipped with wing mirrors and scent sprays, but the baths, like most Italian baths, didn't work and Arab looters had got in and electric lighting, heating and water fittings had all been smashed.

The following morning, with the fighting over, the civilian population streamed back into Zuq in a strung-out caravan; and Avvocato Carloni, the mayor, arrived with the Roman Catholic priest and three police officers, anxious to surrender the town, every military establishment, the Italian, Arab and Greek population, and anything the captors chose to regard as theirs. Those parts of the Italian army that hadn't fled were prisoners so they hadn't much choice. With them came the local Arab chief, smiling broadly and anxious to do his bit, with tribal banners flying and drums beating, trailing behind him a sheepish crowd of Italian *carabinieri*.

Leaning heavily on a silver-topped walking stick Clutterbuck had found for him in one of the looted houses, Dampier accepted the surrender with an old-world courtesy. He wasted no sympathy but he was not harsh, and it occurred to Clegg that out of them all only he could have done it properly. As he stepped back, there was a flutter of clapping from a small crowd that had gathered and he issued orders that were to last until the British army came up and appointed someone in his place. Morton translated his speech as he reappointed the mayor and all the civil officers, ordered them to make sure the shops and businesses were reopened and instructed the civil guard to act with British troops.

Micklethwaite, who had found a German camera in one of the houses, tried to set the surrender down on film for posterity and as proof of the story he hoped to write, only to discover when it was half finished that the camera had a broken shutter. By the time he'd found another one it was over and people were saluting all the British and Australians they saw, no matter what their rank. A shopkeeper took down his shutters and, as others followed suit, the town was in motion again.

As Dampier set up his headquarters in the Palazzo Municipale, on the table was a form filled with the message that Brigadier Marziale had sent to Rome before bolting for Derna: *Duce, we are in extremis. Long live Italy. Long live the King Emperor. Long live the Duce. Rome, I embrace you.*

As Morton translated, Dampier sniffed. 'You don't win wars on such stuff as that,' he said.

The first of the pursuing British arrived the following

morning. Clegg was standing with Morton as the first tank roared up the street, its exhaust echoing hollowly against the white walls. As it approached, it stopped and the hatch opened, and the head and shoulders of a lieutenant who looked about sixteen popped up.

'All right, you lot,' he said. '*Mani in alto!*'

Clegg looked at Morton and laughed. Captured by their own bloody side after all they'd been through!

'With respect, sir,' he said cheerfully. 'Get stuffed.'

The officer looked puzzled. 'Who *are* you lot?'

'British soldiers. We captured the town for you. You can have it now. We don't want it any more.'

During the day, more units arrived, their trucks full of looted wine, chocolate and tins of fruit from Italian officers' messes, a lot of it captured from their own army not very long before. They even had china plates and silver cutlery, many had new watches, binoculars, automatics and cameras, and half of them flew captured flags from their aerials. Aware of his official position, Dampier made an attempt to persuade them to hand everything over but, still aggressive and cocksure after their victory, their response was such that he wisely decided to forget it.

With the town safe, however, he insisted on gathering all of 64 Light Vehicle Repair Unit together and making them a little speech. It was faintly pompous, like most of his utterances, but he surprised them all by saying how much he appreciated what they'd done.

'Splendid chaps,' he said, trying to avoid looking at Clutterbuck and Jones the Song as he spoke. 'All of you. Now I suggest that you go and celebrate – if you can find anywhere open and they've got anything to drink.'

Feeling a tremendous warrior and mentally retracting a lot of the things he'd thought about Dampier over the past days, Clegg headed for the Bar Barbieri. Barbieri seemed suddenly to be doing very well and the bar, full of Australians, for once seemed well stocked.

'From the Italian officers' messes,' Barbieri announced. 'Il Signore Clutterbuck. What a man that is!'

Caccia was helping behind the bar, and Rosalba, radiant in the yellow dress in which she'd been married, was darting about between the tables, dodging the grabbing hands of the grinning Australians.

McBean was there, surrounded by bottles, and he shouted across to Clegg. 'Come and sit down, mate,' he yelled. 'The booze's on me.'

Clegg took it all in. This was more his cup of tea than fighting, he decided. He put a coin in the music box and to his surprise the music that came out was Gene Autry singing 'South of the Border'. It made him feel at home.

He smiled. He'd had enough of war and wanted to get back to acting the goat on a stage, to making people laugh, telling them the old jokes – 'What did the brassière say to the hat? You go on ahead, I'll give the other two a lift' – singing the old comic songs he'd got away with for years – 'Nobody loves a fairy when she's forty'. As he came out, he saw Dampier walking with Rafferty just ahead, both of them smart and starched as a British colonel and his warrant officer should be. Still suffering a little from his lumbago, Dampier was limping badly. His age and the limp made Clegg suddenly feel a strange affection towards him. The army was a funny institution, he thought. It roused a strange comradely warmth in the breasts of men like himself who had no martial feelings whatsoever and these two men in front were pretty much the reason why. Both of them unswervingly honest and well aware of their duties – Rafferty with his small poacher's features and blue, scraped chin and his immense knowledge of army procedure; Dampier, eager, a little pompous, starchy as hell at first but full of courage and a sharp sense of duty.

He was just reflecting on the thought when he heard the sound of an aeroplane engine and turned to see where it was coming from. Howling over the rooftops, bright against the blue sky, the rondels on its fuselage clear with the letter

K near the tail, was a Hurricane. He was just about to wave to it when he saw flashes coming from the wings and heard the rattle of guns.

'You daft silly sod!' he screamed. 'Zuq's ours!'

Rafferty had dived for shelter but, in a split second of shock, Clegg saw Dampier, trying awkwardly to run, flung aside, his khaki cap tossed into the air and blood on his face, then something kicked his foot from under him and he fell against the wall. As he hit his head, he passed out.

When he came round, Morton was leaning over him. 'You all right?'

'I think so.' Clegg looked down at his foot, expecting to see it torn open, but the bullet had only ripped the heel from his boot and done him no harm. 'Did anybody get hurt?' he asked. 'I saw the Old Man – '

'When I arrived,' Morton said, 'Rafferty was pushing him into the back of a lorry to take him to the hospital. He looked as if he'd been shot through the head.'

'Oh, Christ!' Clegg was shocked at the idiocy of war. 'Poor old sod! And at his age, too!' He was silent for a moment. 'Well,' he ended, 'he always wanted to be in the fighting. Pity he had to be killed by it, though.'

Epilogue

That wasn't the end, of course. Stories go on long after the last full stop.

After the war, like a few others, Clegg went into the theatre in a big way with a whole string of sketches he'd developed in the desert, among them the ludicrous one about a German tourist trying to buy ice cream from an Italian who spoke no German, and the famous Will Hay type act of a half-baked fireman getting into a bucket chain at a fire at the village inn so that the full buckets went back to the tap and the empty ones to the fire. Then, after years of appearing in music hall, he surprised everyone by going legitimate and starring in a whole string of excellent British films before appearing in a repeat of *My Fair Lady*. When he announced his retirement, he gave interviews to the press, and for the first time the full story of what had happened in and around Zuq appeared in the theatrical magazine *Beginners, Please!* It was in good theatrical journalese and contained a lot of Clegg's patter but it was all there just the same.

'That was a real bit of Elgar's "Land of H and G",' Clegg was reported to have said. 'I captured Zuq and won the Battle of Alamein. Everybody thought it was Montgomery but it wasn't. It was me.'

He then explained what had happened to the others. Morton, it seemed, was commissioned in the field, which is always a good way to be commissioned, and since by that time he'd decided he quite liked being an officer, he stayed in the army and, with his degree, his languages and his background, eventually became a major general. 'He comes to see me when I'm appearing in the West End,' Clegg pointed out. 'Sometimes, to please me, in uniform. My agent always demands higher fees on the spot.'

Jones the Song went back to Wales, opened a shop and ended up conducting the local choir. Caccia took over a thriving business in Soho and he and Rosalba now have eight children and a lot of grandchildren. 'They've put on a bit of weight since those days,' Clegg said.

Rafferty retired and did very well with a spare-parts service for garages. Clinch opened a radio business, while Clutterbuck went into the secondhand car game. Micklethwaite came off worst. He had the biggest story ever and he wasn't allowed to write it because the army refused to let him give their victory at Zuq to a mixed group of actors, singers, storebashers, deserters, prisoners-of-war and what-have-you. Even when he finally did write it, nobody believed it.

'He wasn't blessed with a lot of luck,' Clegg added.

Then, 'What about Dampier?' he was asked. 'Did you bury him out there?'

Clegg's reaction was unexpected. 'God bless you, no! He didn't die. The bullet only scraped his scalp and did no more than raise a groove like a tram track across the top of his head. When we went to the hospital to pay our last respects, he was sitting up in bed trying to get his mitts on an Italian nurse. He ended up a brigadier with a DSO and lord lieutenant of his county.'

There was also just a little bit more that didn't appear in *Beginners, Please!* but was fact, nevertheless.

'We had a reunion a few years back,' Clegg said, 'and he made a speech. Everybody turned up. Coffin and Grady and Fee, who was over on a visit from Australia. Even Scarlatti. Even Schwartzheiss and Erwin from Germany. Schwartzheiss was making a lot of money as a building contractor by then – experience, I suppose you'd call it –

and Erwin owned an art gallery in Wiesbaden and was picking up a fortune from American tourists. He wasn't a bad chap. His only fault was that he talked too much. The only one who couldn't make it was Clutterbuck.'

'Why didn't he come?'

Clegg gave a vast shout of laughter. 'Why do you think?' he said. 'He got involved in a racket at London airport and got mixed up in the Great Train Robbery. He was in jail.'

BESTSELLING FICTION FROM ARROW

All these books are available from your bookshop or news-agent or you can order them direct. Just tick the titles you want and complete the form below.

☐	THE COMPANY OF SAINTS	Evelyn Anthony	£1.95
☐	HESTER DARK	Emma Blair	£1.95
☐	1985	Anthony Burgess	£1.75
☐	2001: A SPACE ODYSSEY	Arthur C. Clarke	£1.75
☐	NILE	Laurie Devine	£2.75
☐	THE BILLION DOLLAR KILLING	Paul Erdman	£1.75
☐	THE YEAR OF THE FRENCH	Thomas Flanagan	£2.50
☐	LISA LOGAN	Marie Joseph	£1.95
☐	SCORPION	Andrew Kaplan	£2.50
☐	SUCCESS TO THE BRAVE	Alexander Kent	£1.95
☐	STRUMPET CITY	James Plunkett	£2.95
☐	FAMILY CHORUS	Claire Rayner	£2.50
☐	BADGE OF GLORY	Douglas Reeman	£1.95
☐	THE KILLING DOLL	Ruth Rendell	£1.95
☐	SCENT OF FEAR	Margaret Yorke	£1.75

Postage _____

Total _____

ARROW BOOKS, BOOKSERVICE BY POST, PO BOX 29, DOUGLAS, ISLE OF MAN, BRITISH ISLES

Please enclose a cheque or postal order made out to Arrow Books Limited for the amount due including 15p per book for postage and packing both for orders within the UK and for overseas orders.

Please print clearly

NAME...

ADDRESS..

....

Whilst every effort is made to keep prices down and to keep popular books in print, Arrow Books cannot guarantee that prices will be the same as those advertised here or that the books will be available.